A voice from the past . . .

Jocelyn sank against him, comforted by the strength of his arms about her, the heat that he so generously offered.

Then her brain began to function again. She sniffed, absorbing the scent of his linen. Even in the rain she recognized that fragrance. How could she ever forget it? It had been unique, a part of only one man she had ever met. That he was also a man she had striven to forget made it now doubly potent.

"Sit still," he commanded.

That voice—she would know it anywhere, even after five years. It was rough, as rough as he, and it had a richness in it that sent tingles to her toes when she heard him speak. Yet she obeyed him . . . this time.

The Dangerous Baron Leigh

Emily Hendrickson

A SIGNET BOOK

SIGNET
Published by New American Library, a division of
Penguin Putnam Inc., 375 Hudson Street,
New York, New York 10014, U.S.A.
Penguin Books Ltd, 27 Wrights Lane,
London W8 5TZ, England
Penguin Books Australia Ltd,
Ringwood, Victoria, Australia
Penguin Books Canada Ltd, 10 Alcorn Avenue,
Toronto, Ontario, Canada M4V 3B2
Penguin Books (N.Z.) Ltd, 182–190 Wairau Road,
Auckland 10, New Zealand

Penguin Books Ltd, Registered Offices:
Harmondsworth, Middlesex, England

First published by Signet, an imprint of New American Library, a division of
Penguin Putnam Inc.

First Printing, January 2000
10   9   8   7   6   5   4   3   2   1

Chapter One

The scene seemed unreal, as though she existed in a nether-world—no end, no beginning, no form, no reality. She had never seen such unending or blinding rain. For hours she had listened to rain drum on the roof of the coach, the splash of the wheels in the deep puddles, as they jounced and bounced on the road. How dreadfully dull—and how very like her life at the moment. Perhaps she might find a bit of excitement with her cousin.

What had at first seemed to be a light rain had begun that morning as they had set out from the excellent inn where they had spent a comfortable night. Would that they had stayed beneath that pleasant roof rather than venture forth in such a deluge.

Another look out of the window revealed that if anything the rain was harder. A curtain of water fell beyond her window, so impenetrable it seemed almost solid. She could see nothing of the Derbyshire terrain, scenery she had been promised was most breathtaking.

"I wonder," Lady Jocelyn said to her quiet maid, "should we build an ark?"

The maid gave her a look of long suffering and a wan smile. "Aye, it would seem most practical. I shall be thankful when we reach our destination. If we reach it," she added gloomily.

"Poor Mercy, to be so put upon." Lady Jocelyn smiled, albeit a trifle concerned. "We are almost there, I should think. I vow I have never seen such weather." Her comment was punctuated with the drop of a wheel, followed by a rear one, into a pothole of some dimension, tilting the carriage at a dangerous angle.

"Nor such a road, my lady," responded the increasingly ashen maid.

"We cannot make much speed at all at this rate, although it would seem to me that we must be near the castle by now," Jocelyn fumed. As sorry as she was to be leaving her brother's house, she could not wait to assume a place in her cousin's home. It was to be a temporary abode, offering Jocelyn a chance to plan for her future—as though she had not mulled over this bleak prospect for hours and days. Her smile grew even more joyless when she considered how ironic it all was. Her engagement had been terminated by the death of her fiancé: she was presumed desolate and unapproachable as a result. If they only knew.

The rude jolting of the carriage grew worse, as if possible, and Jocelyn wondered how long the carriage could withstand such punishment.

Mercy sneezed, daintily as she did all things—not that her delicacy prevented volume.

"Do not say you have caught a cold!" Jocelyn said with sympathy. Mercy's colds were legendary, with streaming nose and sneezes to wake the dead.

"I fear that may be so, my lady." This cautious statement was followed by another sneeze of ear-shattering proportion that drowned out even the sound of the rain and the road.

That was all that was needed to make the trip a total disaster. Poor Mercy could not help that she was so afflicted, but it would make life awkward for a week or so while they settled in at Castle Valletort. Her cousin Lora had married extremely well; however, Jocelyn wondered just how comfortable that castle perched on a Derbyshire hill would be. Adrian Valletort might be a handsome creature; it did not necessarily follow that he was practical as well.

"It is a great pity that the baby chose such an inclement season in which to be born," Mercy ventured to offer in the following silence.

"True," Jocelyn absently agreed. "But then, babies are ever independent of wishes in that regards, I believe."

And what would she, Lady Jocelyn Robards, daughter of the Marquis of Torrington and spinster *par excellence*, know of that? She was obviously destined to remain unwed, for at the age of three and twenty she had refused all offers for her hand following Simon's death. Thus had grown the myth that she mourned Simon Oliver, younger son of the Marquis of Gifford, to the point where she could bear no other. Fools. Or was she the fool? Wanting romance and love? Her heart to be engaged and not merely a ring on her finger and a cold marriage lacking in passion?

"Do you recall Lord Izard, Mercy?" Jocelyn asked, her thoughts turning to the men who had sought her hand.

"Indeed, ma'am," the maid replied with a sniff. She searched for another handkerchief while Jocelyn continued.

"Yes, he of the fleet of foot who would have removed me from my lonely bed so I might share him with a dozen other women. He ran quickly enough when I informed him I had no wish to share his affections merely for the sake of his name and roof. What a blessing it is that I have a comfortable competence. I need no man to provide me shelter or pay my bills."

"Perhaps . . ." the maid began, then sneezed.

"Perhaps that is my trouble?" Jocelyn concluded for her. "True, were I in dire straits I might grasp at any offer so to have a roof over my head. My brother has been more than generous in his arrangements for me."

"He said you might remain at your home, my lady," Mercy reminded.

"Not with the newly married couple. I do not approve of relatives intruding upon a pair trying to adjust to a life together. *I* would not countenance such behavior, you may be sure," Jocelyn said with a snap.

"How . . . ?" Mercy began only to be taken with another of her magnificent sneezes.

"How would I prevent such a thing?" Jocelyn wrinkled her brow, then gave her maid a sly smile. "Toads in the bed, cold coffee and lumpy porridge at breakfast, lack of a nice fire in the bedroom—there are a great many ways to rid one of unwanted guests."

What Mercy might have had to say to this heresy was never to be known, for at that moment the fine traveling coach came to an abrupt halt. Within minutes the door flew open to reveal the coachman, water streaming in cascades from his many-caped coat, the turned-down brim of his hat doing little to protect his face from a wetting.

"What is it?" Jocelyn demanded, pulling her warm pelisse more closely about her. The wind gusted around the door, hitting Mercy where she huddled in the opposite corner.

"We must lighten the load some to make it up this hill, my lady. The men will all walk. Your maid must get out as well. It's to be hoped you can remain inside," he concluded dubiously.

"Mercy is ill. I'll not think of her leaving the protection, such as it is, of the coach. I shall come instead," Jocelyn said with a forced bravado. She didn't mind getting wet so much as the cold. That, and arriving at Castle Valletort looking like a drowned rat.

The driver was clearly upset at this idea, but assisted Jocelyn as she left the coach, tsking at the very thought of her ladyship doing such a thing. Mercy sat timidly making ineffectual noises of demurral, which Jocelyn rightly ignored.

"I am not made of such delicate stuff. I will not melt, Smith." The coachman didn't look convinced, but offered an umbrella, which she accepted.

When Jocelyn reached the ground, she felt as though she had plunged into a tub of cold water, so drenching was the rain and wind, not to mention the height of water swirling about on the road. At least six inches of her skirt hem was immediately soaked with muddy water. The umbrella had been a kindly thought, not a practical one. The wind laughed at such a puny guard against its powers and turned the umbrella inside out in a trice.

Determined to show her fortitude to the driver and guards, all of whom walked before the carriage as the poor horses attempted to slog up the muddy, rutted road, Jocelyn struck out. She ignored the cold cling of her gown as it flapped against her legs. She ignored the wilting bonnet that drooped about her head or the feather that found its way to her cheek, sticking to her skin like a plaster. At least the bonnet gave her a modicum of protection. She was able to see a foot or two before her. The umbrella would have been welcome, she thought wistfully. She tossed it aside after a vain attempt to right it.

The road rose steadily before her, seeming to climb forever. She turned a foot on a stone, pausing to test the afflicted member before resolutely continuing. Right foot, left foot. Where was her hero? That champion of fair damsels in distress, the rescuer she needed? Not even a bitter laugh could escape her lips. They had to be clamped shut as she forged ahead, her head bent to somewhat shield her from the power of the rain and wind.

A trickle of water made its way beneath her pelisse and down her back, an icy snail trail. Her once elegant half boots squelched in the mud as she continued to slog her way. Anything would be better than this. Anything!

All this probably explained why she failed to see the man on horseback approaching *ventre a terre*. She was never certain what alerted her, some sound, perhaps a sloshing of the animal's hooves? She peered through the curtain of rain at the figure that now became visible in the gloom. He rode up to her side with a flourish.

"My lady, I am at your service!" he shouted to make himself heard above the rain.

Jocelyn did not question how he knew who she was. Half frozen, chilled to her very bones, all she could think of at the moment was: horse, rider, getting to the castle as quickly as possible. "Thank God!" she cried. He slid from his unsaddled horse, tossed her up, then within minutes was seated behind her. Her legs were scandalously placed across his left thigh, and she was wrapped inside his greatcoat, shivering with the encounter of his body heat and thankful her rescuer appeared not likely to quibble about a nicety of manners.

He wheeled about and commenced a return journey.

Jocelyn sank against him, comforted by the strength of his arms about her, his heat that he so generously offered.

Then her brain began to function again. She sniffed, absorbing the scent of his linen. Even in the rain she recognized that fragrance. How could she ever forget it? It had been unique, a part of only one man she had ever met. That he was also a man she had striven to forget made it now doubly potent.

She shifted within the confines of his arms, uneasy with the direction of her thoughts. She must be wrong in her judgment.

He would never come after her in a rainstorm. He had damned her to the netherworld when they last met. How foretelling he had been. Life had been rather grim for her since then. It *had* to be someone else.

"Sit still," he commanded.

That voice—she would know it anywhere, even after five years. It was rough, as rough as he, and it had a richness in it that had sent tingles to her toes when she heard him speak. Yet she obeyed him . . . this time.

"Well, well, is there hope for you yet?" The rough intensity of his voice lashed at her, bringing remembered pain.

The amusement in his voice made her long to punch him in the ribs. Oh, how she hated this man. He had torn her life to shreds, decimated her composure, and haunted her dreams far too often. Did he guess? She doubted it. He had left her, stalking from the library with determined steps, shutting the door behind him with excruciating quiet. He had said he trusted they would not meet again, and they had not. Until now.

"Peter?"

"So you still know me? I thought you would have forgotten my existence by now," he said, his mouth too close to her ear for her ease. He *was* amused at her.

"I am g-grateful you came to my rescue." How she hated her chattering teeth, a sign of fragility. She had learned she dare not reveal any weakness to this man. She sensed he would have taken advantage of any sign of disintegration on her part. And she had disintegrated—after he left her. She had crumbled into dull pieces, her outer defenses gone, her emotions shattered.

Her soaked garments or icy feet did not wholly cause her trembling. She had been held in his arms once before. Her reaction had terrified her, green girl that she had been. Surely such a sweep of sensation, of emotion, ought not be right? She had stiffened then, pulling away, and eventually lost everything through her own stupidity.

She knew shock at her thoughts. *Her* stupidity? Had she been a fool all those years ago? She had put him out of her mind, and no one had mentioned him in her presence. By design? Or accident? Her mind reeled with her muddled thoughts.

"I can hear you thinking, my lady."

He was still amused; she could hear it in his voice.

"It is not a moment for conversation, I think," she answered as well as clenched teeth permitted. She did not want to be a teeth-chattering imbecile while in his arms. She hadn't thought to ever be there again, for that matter. Not but what he couldn't reduce her to folly if he so chose.

"Indeed, we have much to discuss, but now is not the time," he said, his mouth again close to her ear. His breath warmed that appendage, and she just barely resisted burrowing further into his being. Never had she been so cold, not only outside, but inside. *Alone,* her mind shouted to her. She was alone, not only with him but without him. This shattering thought brought more tremors, whether from cold or emotions, she could not have said.

"We are here at last." Was that satisfaction in his voice?

"Relieved? Well, you have done penance for any sins you may have ever committed by coming to my rescue. I thank you," she managed to stammer as he slid from his steed, then plucked her from the horse with an ease she envied.

Expecting to be set on her feet by the man who had once made it quite clear he despised her, she was astonished to be swept into his arms. He strode into the castle, the door of which had mysteriously opened at their approach.

"She needs a hot bath, dry clothes, and I daresay a hot cider," he barked at the butler.

This man hurried off, and she was alone with Sir Peter, again. She shivered. Or trembled. She scarcely knew if she was on her head or heels. She stared up at his face, trying to understand what she felt. "You may put me down," she managed to say without teeth chattering.

"Oh, no."

She mistrusted the gleam in his silvery-blue eyes. She'd never seen that before.

"I have you just where I want you and will do as I please, Jocelyn." He said her name with deliberation, taking a familiarity she had never granted. And then he kissed her.

It was not a light touch, nor was it punishing as she might have expected. It was the sort of kiss that entranced, beguiled, turned a woman into soft mush. She felt as though a fire raged through her from her toes to her hair, every fiber of her being was aware of him, his power over her.

"I would wager that kiss warmed you as no amount of hot cider, but the drink will not come amiss." He looked so *knowing*, so sure of himself.

Once released from his spell, she reacted without thought, raising her hand to slap that confident face. Never mind that he had rescued her from possible illness and death. He took liberties denied to all. Her hand never connected with that handsome face, however. His expression stopped her in mid-swing. His eyes promised retribution. As to what form it might take, she dare not guess.

"Ah, Jocelyn, you could not treat an old lover so, could you?" he murmured, the seductiveness of his voice wrapping around her like a coating of warm chocolate.

It was humiliating how easily he intimidated her. "You, sirrah, are not a gentleman!"

"True," he admitted. "I am a lord now, and they get by with anything, or so I've been told."

"I did not know," she whispered, and would have asked him more had the housekeeper not arrived with Jocelyn's cousin trailing behind her.

"My lady! Oh, this dreadful weather! You poor thing, you must be half frozen. Lord Leigh, if you will follow me." It was apparent that Jocelyn was not to be turned over to some footman to transport. Well, she would get him soaked, and Lord Leigh was already wet. Lord Leigh?

"Jocelyn! We feared something had befell you when you were so late and this weather simply dreadful," Lora cried. "It was so kind of Peter to volunteer to hunt for you. How glad I am he found you. Was it so very bad?"

Jocelyn wondered how to best answer that. Evidently her cousin did not expect her to be coherent as she nattered on in a frantic manner.

"Once you have a hot bath, warm clothing, and a nice hot drink, you will feel more the thing."

"I can hear you thinking again," Peter Leigh murmured in Jocelyn's ear for a second time. "I promise you we shall talk later. And talk we will, you can be certain of that."

They traipsed up the wide staircase, its oak treads showing evidence of great antiquity. The magnificent portraits arranged on the walls did not even merit a glance from Jocelyn. All she could think about was a talk with Peter, now Lord Leigh. Later? What could they possibly have to say to one another? She wished no resumption of the hostility she had known in the library that day.

A brief distance along the hall brought them to the rooms assigned to Jocelyn. They entered the sitting room, but Peter did not pause here. Rather, he proceeded to the bedroom, that most intimate setting done in delicate rose and celadon green, all lace, ruffles, and rich damask.

"Where is Mercy?" Lora inquired. "She usually travels with you."

"She will be along soon, I trust. She has a streaming cold, and I feared her death on my conscience should she leave the coach," Jocelyn said carefully as Peter gently placed her on feet that were none too dependable.

"I am glad to know you possess a conscience, Jocelyn," Peter murmured while easing her soaked pelisse from her arms. "That ought to make our talk *most* interesting."

Was that a threat in his voice? Jocelyn shot him a questioning look but found no clue in his face. The chiseled perfection of that handsome visage revealed nothing of his inner thoughts.

"I suggest you remove your wet things as soon as possible. I intend to do the same," he said, gesturing to his own wet clothing. He turned to leave the bedroom and had reached the door before Jocelyn found her voice and manners.

"Peter . . . I thank you for rescuing me from who knows what fate. I doubt if I could have endured that dreadful walk for much longer. I appreciate it very much. I, er, thank you," she repeated, unable to express her feelings as she might like. He in turn bestowed a mocking look on her as though he was recalling that devastating kiss as vividly as she did. She knew she blushed, she could feel it spread over her like a rash.

And then he was gone, out of the door, and she was alone with her cousin and the housekeeper and their comforting concern. In short order she found her cold, dripping garments removed and was wrapped in a soft robe before a series of footmen marched in with pails of steaming water.

The housekeeper poured a bit of lily of the valley essence into the water, then drew Jocelyn over to the copper tub.

"There, now, my lady, into the water and mind you soak until all the chill is gone. There will be more hot water should you have need of it." She assisted Jocelyn in the tub, then left with the promise to return later with the hot cider Lord Leigh had demanded.

"Ah, I confess I wondered if I would ever be warm again. Chilled to the bone is not a pleasant state of being," Jocelyn quipped as she eased back against the rim of the tub. A linen towel had been placed at her back, and she drew comfort from that softness and the heat that surrounded her, then grew warmer yet as her thoughts wandered. Did Peter enjoy the same warmth—and the luxury of soothing scent in a tub of hot water to heat his chilled body?

"You said Mercy has a cold?" Lora said with bright sympathy. "How dreadful. I do hope you will not catch one as well. I have need of you in the coming days." Lora seemed to realize then how that might sound and amended her remark, "That is, I would not want you to be ill regardless, but I especially desire your help. Adrian plans to have an enormous party to celebrate the birth of his heir apparent. Baby Charles will scarcely be aware of all the fuss, but it will make Adrian happy."

"I shall be pleased to help you and your husband. And I never am ill. Father always said I had the constitution of a horse. A bit of food and drink, some dry clothes, and I shall be my old self again." Or would she? Could she return to that semi-alive woman she had been before Lord Leigh kissed her? One thing she had to confess was that he had made her feel more full of life than she had in many years. And that knowledge frightened her. If he could accomplish that with one kiss what else might he do?

"Well, I shall leave you to soak. As soon as the coach arrives, I will have your trunks brought up. In the meantime, why do you not put on that robe and snuggle under the covers for a time after your bath? I daresay you must be worn to flinders." With that remark, Lora rose to her feet and slipped from the room more quietly than Jocelyn expected from the girl who had once been so bubbly. Motherhood had made her more mature, but had also given her a harried, almost worried expression. Was something amiss?

Once the water cooled, Jocelyn stepped from the tub and rubbed dry with the elegant Turkish toweling provided for her use. As fine as her own home had been, it had not stretched to anything quite so new or luxurious. Feeling pampered, she donned the robe and crawled beneath the covers, intending to rest a bit. She was tired from her trek, beset by the emotions Peter, Lord Leigh, had stirred in her. And how had he become Lord Leigh? That was a question she longed to have answered, among a dozen or two others.

She fell asleep while debating which relative might have died and left Peter a title and fortune. That he now had a fortune, she did not doubt. His clothes were finer, his poise was greater, and he was more devastating than she remembered. And, she admitted, he had never been very far from her memory.

A stir at the door woke her some time later. Mercy entered to be followed by footmen carrying her trunks that they put down in the adjacent sitting room.

"My lady, I am so glad to see you abed. I worried about you all the way here. Saxby—he's the butler, you know—said Lord Leigh found you staggering along the road and brought you back on his horse." There was more than a hint of question in her words, although Mercy would never do anything so vulgar as to ask what had happened. She merely waited to see if Jocelyn chose to satisfy her curiosity.

"Do you recall a Sir Peter Leigh, Mercy? Well, he has become Lord Leigh now and do not ask me how, for I have yet to learn of it. Serves me right for removing myself from the gossips of Society. Had I paid attention, likely I would have learned all about him." Since this was one of the reasons Jocelyn had carefully avoided the women and men to whom gossip was lifeblood, there was little answer to this remark.

"Well, now, is not that a lovely thing, his getting a title and likely a fortune to boot?"

"I could not say," Jocelyn said primly. "I know full well that merely because a man inherits a title, it does not follow that a fortune goes with that title."

Mercy nodded, sneezed violently, then begged pardon until Jocelyn felt the beginnings of a headache appear.

"I would have you find the room assigned you and crawl into bed. I shall instruct a maid to bring you some hot bricks for your poor feet and perhaps the housekeeper has a nostrum to help your cold. No arguing, now," Jocelyn added as Mercy opened her mouth likely to do just that.

With patience, Jocelyn saw her maid on her way, although not before a bit of argument. It took but a few minutes to make her requests. Then she settled in her sitting room to sip the hot cider that the housekeeper had sent to sooth her chill. The chaise longue had been placed near the bay window, and from this excellent spot Jocelyn had a view of the rain-soaked lawn and lake beyond.

She didn't turn when the door opened, expecting a maid to unpack her things for her. It was not the maid, however.

"I see you are doing precisely as I advised," Peter said as he strolled across the elegant Aubusson carpet to stand before her. He looked down at her from his great height and never in her life had Jocelyn felt so helpless—or so feminine! She set the cup down with care.

Jocelyn sat up a trifle, disconcerted he should find her, alone, vulnerable. "You ought not be in here. I doubt it is the least proper. My lord," she added with a touch of provocation.

"The door is ajar, and I casually mentioned my intention to check on your state of health. That is considered admirable, since I doubtless saved your life, or so my valet tells me. And Dickman is never wrong about these things." Without asking her permission, Peter dropped down on the end of the chaise, examining her all the while.

"I thank you for your concern," Jocelyn said, thinking she must sound like a brainless twit.

"You are welcome," he gravely replied, but with that curious gleam in his silvery eyes once again.

Jocelyn picked nervously at the light throw she had drawn across her lap and legs, darting glances at him while wondering as to the real reason for this visit. He could have asked a maid as to her condition and learned she was quite fine.

"So we meet again, and after all these years," he mused, tilting his head back until his eyes were mere slits while he gazed at her.

"True," she whispered in reply, swallowing hard as he continued to stare at her.

"I had thought you to be wed long before now. It ought to be you having a party for your firstborn boy. Have you no desire for children?"

"Of course," she answered hotly. "I adore children and would love nothing more than to have half a dozen around me. Alas, it requires a husband; at least for me it does." She gave him what she hoped was a defiant glare.

"Hmm. I expected you to marry Simon before he left for the Peninsula. Why didn't you?"

"That is none of your business, but I shall tell you anyway." Jocelyn suspected Peter would worm it out of her should she try to keep the truth from him. "Simon did not wish to leave me with child in the event he might not return. I thought it most noble of him," she lied. Even if she had not loved Simon, she had wanted a child, a barrier against the world.

"I would have done the opposite—just to have had you in my arms and my bed before I marched off to war."

Jocelyn wondered briefly if he deliberately sought to anger her. "I can well imagine what you would have done in like circumstances, Sir Peter!" Unheeding of how her words might have been taken, she forged on, "But I must know how you turned from being Sir Peter into Lord Leigh."

"That will wait, I think. I have enough to mull over for the present, and so do you, unless I miss my guess." Slowly, with great deliberation, he slid along the chaise to capture her in his arms. Again, his kiss was most thorough, intimate, compelling.

Jocelyn thought she would melt before he released her. She could not manage the anger to slap his face as she ought. She was utterly sunk.

He rose and sauntered to the door. "I hope to see you at dinner. I believe Lora has partnered you with me. That ought to make our stay here most, er, provocative, to say the least."

Chapter Two

She would have to go down for dinner, even if she far preferred to remain in her room. She would *not* have him think her a coward, no matter that she would quake in her slippers! As well, he knew that she had suffered no harm from her wetting. How disgusting to be so hale and hearty when it was far more fashionable to be delicately wilting.

First she looked in on Mercy, to find her sleeping soundly. After arranging for a maid to check on her later, Jocelyn smoothed down her gown of soft merino crepe, the silk shot through the wool making the gown glimmer as she moved. The rich understated elegance of the celadon green was reflected in her eyes, which blazed green fire at the mere thought of confronting *that* man again.

A glance in the looking glass reassured Jocelyn that the maid sent to help her because of Mercy's indisposition had done an admirable business of arranging Jocelyn's hair. Her long dark hair had been plaited and wound about her head with a fluff of curls over her forehead and a couple of tantalizing curls by her ears. Indeed, the girl had talent!

Thus armed, Jocelyn draped a delicate cream shawl over her arms and left the security of her rooms to slip along the hall to the central stairs, then down a flight to the entry hall. This vast and chilly room led into the pleasant, if equally vast, drawing room, where the guests were to assemble before dinner. Jocelyn nervously clasped her white-gloved hands while surveying the room. She recognized a few people and expected she would shortly become acquainted with the others. Adrian Valletort was an excellent host as well as her cousin's adored husband.

A flurry of silken skirts brought Lora to Jocelyn's side. "I am so glad to see you looking so well, cousin. I feared you would have a cold or worse after such a dreadful wetting." Her soft blue eyes were anxious and almost pleading. How odd, *begging* Jocelyn to be well?

"Thank you, dearest, but you know how healthy I always am. It's such a pity, for I can never be interestingly pale," Jocelyn said with a mischievous gleam in her eyes.

"I should say that would be a definite plus for any gentleman looking for a wife," a lazy, rough baritone said from too close to Jocelyn's side.

She darted a glance back to see what she quite expected—a magnificently attired Peter looking down at her from his great height. She turned just enough to be polite, for she would never be rude to anyone while a guest. "You are looking well in spite of your heroic rescue this afternoon. It would seem that valiant deeds become you. Again, I must thank you for your deliverance from what could have had serious repercussions." She dipped a slight curtsy to support her words.

Looking *well*? What insipid words to describe the man at her side. Garbed in white satin breeches over white hose and the most elegant of patent slippers, a white satin waistcoat embroidered with wine roses topped by a long-tailed coat of wine velvet, he was quite enough to make a maiden swoon. How fortunate Jocelyn was not a susceptible maiden. She fixed her gaze on the deep red ruby that graced his simply tied cravat and took a deep breath.

"This promises to be an interesting party, does it not?" she managed to say before she realized how inane she must sound.

"Excuse me, please," Lora murmured. "Uncle Maxim and Suzanne have entered, and I must greet them."

Jocelyn nodded, watching her pretty cousin skim across the room to sweetly greet the latest couple to enter the room. The elderly gentleman Jocelyn had seen before. He was a sort of roué, but harmless as long as one made it clear one was not interested in dalliance. The girl at his side was breathtakingly beautiful. Rich black hair swirled about her head in an intricate style definitely French inspired, as was her gown of golden spider gauze.

"I gather you have not met the lovely Suzanne Fornier before? What a clever girl. Not, however, a hardy English miss." He raised one brow while giving Jocelyn a look she designated pure devilment.

"You make that sound like a curse rather than a blessing," Jocelyn commented absently, and ignoring his taunt, wondered why her cousin was so unlike her normal self. Unless Jocelyn very much missed her guess, something was more than a little amiss, and she would be compelled to wait until they could be alone to find out what it was.

"I expected to draw fire from those green eyes of yours with that remark. What has so captured your concern that you do not pay me the slightest attention?" He managed to sound like a little boy deprived of a sweet.

"I *am* concerned about my cousin," Jocelyn admitted, refusing to respond to his affront. "She is so unlike her usual self."

"Perhaps it is nothing more than the birth of a child and this monstrous party. I understand that having children can affect a woman in many ways." He reached forth to touch her arm, a very familiar and particular touch, almost a caress. It demanded a counterattack.

"Are you throwing my lack of family in my face again, Lord Leigh?" Jocelyn snapped, rising to his bating with predictable ire. "I can scarce cure that." She ran the delicate silk of her shawl through suddenly nervous fingers. Why did she permit this detestable man to taunt her in such a manner?

"Ah, that green fire I so admire." He smiled down at her; his dark eyes alight with amusement and something else she couldn't name. "Were it possible, I would see to it that you were aroused at all times, just to see that remarkable color. 'Tis most becoming, Jocelyn." His voice had deepened and assumed a rather intimate quality quite as though they were alone and not in the midst of a scene worthy of St. James's Palace. "As to a cure—you threw away a remedy years ago, as you well know."

"You are the most provoking man I have ever met!" She searched his face, those silver-blue eyes, trying to imagine why he was doing this to her. Aroused? He would see her aroused? Heaven help her, she was ready to fall into his arms without the slightest bit of help from anyone, least of all him, and he wished to keep her aroused?

"I intend to remain that, you may be certain." He executed a bow as slight as the curtsy she had given him shortly before. Just how he intended to provoke her was left unsaid for her imagination to work on. She could contemplate hours of fruitless speculation! She knew well he'd referred to what had happened years ago before she became engaged to Simon. Could she ever tell Peter the truth?

The spell woven by Lord Leigh was broken when another man approached them.

"Ah, Lady Jocelyn! How good it is to behold your beauty once again!" Pierre Valletort bowed correctly to her after bustling up to them in his pompous manner before turning to Lord Leigh and nodding rather distantly. "Leigh. Lora said you would be here."

"And so I am, and most fortunately so, for I was able to rescue a fair damsel in distress." The two men exchanged mutually hostile looks before returning their attention to Jocelyn. She felt like a marrowbone between two elegant dogs—poodles, most likely.

"It is true, Mr. Valletort," she inserted. "I was dreadfully soaked, tramping through the storm because of our problems with the roads when he rode to my rescue like a knight of old. It was most romantic, I must confess." She bestowed a twinkling smile at Pierre even though she was not in the least fond of Adrian's cousin. He was a brooding, cynical man, certainly not one given to easy friendship.

"Ah, Pierre, I see you have captured the attention of the loveliest of creatures, our cousin Lady Jocelyn," Henri Valletort exclaimed in smiling jollity. What a contrast between the two cousins—Pierre, the dark and solemn cynic, and Henri, the laughing and vibrant tease.

Jocelyn's smile at this cousin of her host was genuine. "How good to see you, Henri. I did not realize you were here as well."

"Had I known you were slogging through the rain, I would have raced to your salvation, *ma chérie*." He possessed himself of her hand and raised it to his lips. Even through her gloves Jocelyn could sense the kiss. It sent shivers up her spine.

"You are a rogue, Henri. I can't think you would wish to be wet." She grinned at him, knowing that he cared very much for his appearance when around women.

"Bah," Pierre exclaimed, "he rides out in all manner of weather. Hunting!" It was clear that Pierre considered hunting anything beneath his attention.

"But, cousin, hunting can be such pleasure." Henri gave Jocelyn a mischievous look, his brown eyes dancing with his usual rascality.

"I can just imagine what hunting you enjoy most," Jocelyn said lightly. Then she turned to Peter. "Lord Leigh, I believe it is time we drifted toward the dining room. I do not wish to set a bad example to others. Lora's chef throws a tantrum if dinner is not on time. I see Saxby at the door even now."

The other gentlemen promptly sought their partners; Henri finding the gorgeous Suzanne while Pierre escorted a lady of serious mien who ought to suit him well.

Jocelyn had intended to properly place her hand on Peter's proffered arm as other ladies were doing with their escorts. Rather, she found her hand tucked close to his side, necessarily drawing her closer to him. "Peter," she warned softly. "Behave yourself."

"But I do . . . *chérie.* I wish to make it perfectly clear to Adrian's cousin that he is not to poach on this territory." He gazed at her with a look that was more than warm. Good heavens, she could light a fire with it.

A thrill swept through her even as she said, "But you have no right to a say in *this* particular territory."

"I shall," he pronounced, and she could almost believe he would.

She mentally shook herself, restoring some semblance of sense to her disordered mind. This would never do. Years before she had determined her path, and it had not included Sir Peter Leigh, now Baron Leigh.

"You promised to tell me how you came to be Baron Leigh," she reminded as he assisted her to her dining chair. There must have been at least twenty-two sitting down to dinner, yet she had awareness only for Peter and couldn't have said who else was present.

"My grandmother." He sat at her right hand, his chair close to hers. He reached for his napkin, and his arm brushed hers, sending foolish tremors through her. "She was a baroness in her own right. My father was her only child and died before her. Hence, I acquired the title."

"I surmise a fortune as well. You are dressed in the very height of fashion, most tastefully as well." The man might drive Jocelyn mad but she had to give him credit where credit was due. He was male elegance personified.

"You took notice, *chérie*? By the way, I find I quite like that endearment. So much more courtly than 'my love' or 'dearest' don't you think?"

"I am neither to you, am I?" Jocelyn responded hastily. She did not wish him to use the term of affection casually as Henri did.

He did not reply, turning instead to the excellent soup set before him.

Jocelyn seethed as she calmly sipped her cream of asparagus soup, not tasting it. This was followed by course after course. It was too much food to consume especially because she was expected to eat. Most of what was placed on her plate was later removed.

"You must eat more. At this rate you will disappear in no time. Come, now . . . a bite of this excellent chicken and asparagus in cream sauce or whatever the chef may call it. It's good."

Jocelyn laughed as he had intended and did as told. It proved delicious, and she at least ate that part of her dinner. The sweet course Peter insisted she try was a concoction of whipped cream and almonds with chocolate swirled through.

"Eat or I swear I shall feed you," he threatened softly, menace clear in his deep whisper.

Jocelyn obeyed.

When Lora rose to indicate it was time for the ladies to leave the men to their port and gather in the drawing room, Jocelyn was quite thankful. A footman drew her chair back and she rose, a trifle unsteady, clutching her gloves in nervous hands.

"Good thing you do not remain for port. I did not know you were so affected by wine, *chérie*," he said quietly.

She glanced about, but there was so much noise she doubted anyone heard him. Smiling brilliantly she said, "I take great comfort in your concern, *mon chéri*. I no longer have my brother to look after me, as he has a wife to occupy his attention now. That was a very brotherly thought you showed, and I *do* appreciate it." She gave him a curtsy, then swept from the room in grand style.

Once in the drawing room, she welcomed her cousin with a smile, still seething inside.

"Jocelyn, you are not going into a cold, are you?" Lora inquired anxiously. "Your color is so high and your eyes are simply snapping. Poor dear, it would not be a surprise were you to take ill."

"I am quite well, thank you. How did you happen to invite Lord Leigh, dearest?" Jocelyn drew her cousin aside after seeing that all the other women appeared to be enjoying the usual gossip while one younger woman sat at the grand pianoforte to play a pretty tune.

"Adrian likes him, and we recalled you were once close friends with him. I feared you would not know many of the other guests. After all, you have not been much out among Society these past years." Lora frowned as though she feared she had spoken out of turn.

"That was most thoughtful of you dear." Jocelyn reminded herself that no one knew what had transpired all those years ago but the two involved. "Now I sense there is something troubling you. Can you share it with me? I'd not intrude, but I have this feeling, you see . . ." Her words faded away as she saw the haunted expression deepen in Lora's eyes. "Lora?"

"It is dreadful. Adrian removed the family necklace—you know, that medieval one with all the gems in it—from the vault for the fitting of my gown for the costume party. I am to be dressed as his ancestress for whom that necklace was made. Only . . . the necklace was never replaced in the vault. It is gone!" Her last words were whispered, with Lora looking pale and trembling like a leaf in high wind.

Jocelyn had seen the family heirloom but once and yet

clearly recalled the magnificence of the exquisite piece. Encrusted with pearls, rubies, diamonds, and sapphires, there had been a large pendant suspended at the very front that had an enormous ruby in the center surrounded by smaller sapphires and pearls. Emeralds had been included in that part as well, if memory served her right. There had also been a bracelet. "The bracelet is still in the vault?"

"Of course, it was only to see that the neckline of the costume was sufficiently low as to replicate the original and be correct in relationship to the necklace."

"And you did not tell Adrian?"

"It happened just before you arrived. How can I tell my dearest that I suspect one of his guests!"

"You have someone in mind?" Jocelyn found it hard to speak softly, so astounding was this knowledge.

"No, but who else would dare? None of the servants have the slightest idea what that piece is worth. Indeed, it would be difficult to sell to any jeweler, for it is well-known. Oh, Jocelyn, I am sick with worry. All this on top of so much company. It is almost enough to make me wish we had not had the baby! And my precious Charles!"

She sniffed into her handkerchief, looking as delicate as a lily. "I do love the baby, you must not think I do not. It is, just, well, I simply do not know how to go on."

"I think you ought to tell Adrian," Jocelyn advised.

"Tell Adrian what?" Peter inquired quietly.

"How did you get here so silently?" Jocelyn demanded. "I did not hear a thing."

"Never mind now, I sense trouble. What is it, Lady. Valletort? Is there anything I might do to help?"

Lora gave him a helpless look, then turned to Jocelyn. "I must mingle with the guests now. If you could explain to Lord Leigh, I would be grateful. I know Adrian trusts him." With that she drifted away to chat with the other ladies as though she did not have a worry in her head.

"If Adrian trusts me, I believe you may as well." Peter guided Jocelyn into the central entry hall and to the rear of the castle. "He has added a conservatory to the rear of this place. Suppose I show it to you while we discuss Lora's problem."

"I do not think . . ." Jocelyn began before he rudely interrupted her.

"Do not, I beg you, attempt to think just now. Allow me to think for both of us at the moment."

Docile as a lamb, she permitted him to lead her into an exquisite extension to the house that contained an abundance of plants, from what little she could see in the light offered by several Argand lamps. The outer wall was of glass, as was the roof. By day, it must be a pretty sight. Now it was but a place that offered privacy.

Peter halted beside a tall palm; looked about to make certain they were completely alone, then fastened a stern gaze upon Jocelyn. "Well?"

"Poor Lora. She had the necklace from the vault—an heirloom of some magnificence—and it has been stolen from her room. The theft occurred shortly before I arrived, so it must be one of the guests. And, she has not told Adrian yet. I advised her she must."

"You believe she ought not keep it from him? That there should be no secrets between husband and wife?"

"I do. I do believe there must be absolute trust and faith between a married couple. What kind of life is it, otherwise?" Jocelyn gave him a troubled look. She had not felt that trust or faith in any man who had sought to wed her. Yet she had accepted Simon. Fool! that little voice in the back of her head that often plagued her with unwanted advice and admonitions cried.

"Do not look so at me," he muttered before sweeping her into an embrace that turned her into a pliant willow of a girl again. His kiss put all else from her mind. It was that raging fire anew, and she no longer wondered that he had frightened her years ago with his passion. A green girl would find this man terrifying. She was no novice in some ways, and she found him intimidating, overpowering, and enormously compelling in an entirely masculine, virile manner.

When he at last released her, he kept her close to him, studying her face intently. What he saw must have pleased him, for he gave her a slow smile. "I believe we are making excellent progress."

Deciding the kiss had scrambled her brains; Jocelyn merely

stared back at him and shook her head as though to clear it. "I do not understand you in the least."

"That is all right, I do and that is all that is necessary, *ma chérie*."

"I want to help Lora recover that necklace, but how to go about it?" Jocelyn knew she had to put her mind to something other than this man in whose arms she was held, or she would lose far more than her sanity. "Who, of all her guests, would have taken such a thing?"

"More to the point, who knows of it?"

"Excellent thinking," Jocelyn commended. "The family all knew of it, for the painting hangs in the long gallery for all to see and the story of how it came down in the family to Adrian is repeated for any guest who asks."

"Oh, fine. Since the guests have either taken the tour of the house or they are relatives who already know the tale, that gives a great number of suspects—the entire list!"

"I cannot help that," Jocelyn flashed in return.

"That I know, dearest. I was merely commenting on the difficulty facing us."

"Us? I was unaware we intended to work together."

"I believe there are a number of things of which you are unaware, my dear."

"What are you up to, Peter? We have not seen each other for years, and you act . . . well, you act as though we are very, er, close."

"We are," he stated matter of factly.

"Well, I know I am in your arms at the moment, and what I am doing there is more than I can understand. I thought you hated me." There, she had said it, brought it into the open. How would he reply to that challenge?

He kissed her. It was a sweet promise of a kiss, no burning intensity, no fire. On the other hand, she couldn't label it mere. Then he released her, looking as smug as a cat in the cream pot.

"I feel like a mousefeather," Jocelyn murmured, and turned her gaze to a blue flower she couldn't identify, not that it mattered in the least.

"You aren't the least foolish, love. All will work out in due time. And we have a few weeks at our disposal. I shan't let you go from this place until you explain what happened five years ago."

"Peter, I was eighteen then. Young and foolish." Could she reveal how frightened she had been?

"So there you two are," Henri said upon entering the conservatory.

Jocelyn sought to move away from Peter, embarrassed at being found so close, with his hands on her shoulders. Peter refused to release her. If anything, he brought her closer to him.

"You sought us?" His manner dared Henri to question Peter's right to have Jocelyn in his arms in a secluded and dimly lit conservatory.

"In some circles it would be said you have compromised the lady's honor, my friend." Henri took a step nearer, crossed his arms, then stared at Peter in a hostile way that made Jocelyn shiver.

"Well, we are old friends, so he cannot compromise me," Jocelyn explained, not wanting complications. "We came out here to discuss something. And now we shall return, for I am beginning to feel the chill." Peter released her, and Jocelyn took him by the hand to go again to the drawing room. She didn't wish him to remain so that Henri could issue some sort of silly challenge. She was quite beyond that type of thing.

"I would like to know what was discussed," Henri murmured to no one in particular. "It must have been some discussion."

"Pity, my friend," Peter said with a sly grin, "that you shall never know. *Old* friends have much news to share."

"Is that what you call it? Hmm." Henri smiled and walked ahead of them, and once in the drawing room, immediately went to the side of the luscious Suzanne.

"Where do we begin?" Jocelyn asked, very aware of the hand she still held. It was like having a lifeline to grip when drowning. "And what on earth was Henri doing to come after us?"

"I believe he rather fancies you, my dear girl. Do you return his interest?"

"Henri? How absurd. He is most ineligible in every way."

"Does that apply to a lowly baron as well, Jocelyn?"

"A title does not enter into it at all. Do you know that if I loved a man, truly loved him and was loved in return, it would not make the slightest difference to me as to his title or status."

"You did not always feel that way, I think," he said with an intent look at her eyes.

Eyes reveal what the mouth refuses to say, he had once told her. Perhaps it was true. She prayed her eyes did not give her away now. She could not bear to have him know what was in her heart. "We stray from the point at hand, namely the missing necklace. I do not see how we will ever find it in this vast place with all these guests."

"I have patience and know this—you will not leave here until all is settled. As to the other, we shall ask Lora for a list of all guests together with the rooms to which they have been assigned. Adrian can supply a floor plan so we can match a room to a guest. Then all we need do is draw up a list of likely suspects."

"Oh, simple, indeed. Anyone could desire that necklace merely to admire if not to pawn." Jocelyn looked at him with disdain. "It is magnificent. Think what those jewels must be worth individually! That center ruby alone is quite something."

"Emeralds, I think."

"What?" Jocelyn gazed at him in confusion. Her wits were definitely going begging.

"I should drape you in the family emeralds." He stared at her décolletage with an assessing eye. "That skin fairly cries for emeralds."

"We were discussing the missing necklace, not my skin," she snapped, wondering if his wits had gone begging as well as hers.

"Well, you two," Adrian said, popping up at their sides, "I am pleased to see you getting along so well. Lora would have it that you ought not both be invited, but I was right."

"Indeed, old friend, and I am most grateful," Peter said with that sly grin in place once more.

"Adrian, have you spoken with Lora?"

"Is something amiss? You appear rather serious."

"I think perhaps you ought to ask her that," Jocelyn said slowly. She was sorry to have forced the issue, if she did that, but Adrian needed to know.

"Jocelyn merely wonders if Lora revealed her chef is furious again. Seems he does not feel appreciated. Perhaps if we consume the supper he sends up, he will be appeased?"

Adrian laughed, looking relieved, then sauntered away to chat with other guests.

"Why did you say that?" Jocelyn whispered furiously.

"Trust cannot be forced, my dear. It must come willingly or not at all." His sly grin gone, he gazed at Jocelyn with a strange expression in his eyes, and he looked incredibly determined.

Chapter Three

Oddly enough Peter remained at Jocelyn's side for the rest of the evening. She would have bet her next quarter's income that he would have hovered over the luscious Suzanne rather than stay by one who had supposedly wounded him so badly years ago.

They murmured opinions on likely suspects, exchanging knowledge about the various guests they knew anything about.

"What about the dour Pierre?" Peter inquired softly. "Do you know anything of his financial position? Does he need money?"

"Adrian is the only one in the family who seems to have any sense regarding money," Jocelyn replied with equal quiet. "Both Pierre and Henri are forever on the brink of bankruptcy, from what Lora has said. The earldom gave Adrian not only this castle but also the wealth to support him and a family in great style."

"I have the feeling that some of his relatives might resent that fact." Peter cast a look about the room, as though sorting relatives from friends of the family.

"There is little they can do about it. He has baby Charles who will one day inherit the title and all this," Jocelyn replied with a sweep of her free hand. The other remained quite captured close to Peter's side. And, oddly enough, she had no desire to pull it away. She might have been a fool once; she would do her best not to repeat past mistakes.

"Stealing a necklace would not necessarily put the infant in jeopardy, would it?"

"Oh, I cannot believe whoever would steal would also kill," Jocelyn said, almost forgetting to whisper in her horror.

"So, we must likely hunt for one who needs money badly."

Jocelyn chuckled with irony. "I believe that includes a great many of the guests. Is there not a tendency to live beyond one's means?"

"Tomorrow we shall meet—say in your sitting room, for we need utmost privacy, do we not? At that time we can cull the list for likely prospects. I have already asked the countess for a list of guests. Adrian can supply a plan of the house quickly enough. His steward would have such a thing readily available, I feel certain."

"I think it would be better were we to meet in the library," Jocelyn protested, the thought of being alone with Peter in her sitting room mind-boggling in complications, not the least of which was his being accused of compromise.

"Cold feet, Jocelyn? Is that a perpetual problem of yours? I seem to recall it occurring in the past as well."

"The state of my feet has nothing to do with this, and you should know that well enough. Do you not recall that but a short while ago Henri suggested that you might be accused of compromising me?"

"You are not a young miss," Peter protested.

"I am unmarried," she reminded with a pang.

"Indeed, I am well aware of that," he murmured with another of his heated glances.

"Must I ask you to behave yourself?" she demanded in a fierce whisper before she became aware of another at her side.

"Well, one could wonder if there will be an interesting announcement before we all depart from here," Pierre said, appearing like an unwanted spirit. "I vow you two have been living in one another's pockets all evening. When our dear countess gave you Lady Jocelyn as a partner for dinner, I doubt she intended to have you attached to her for the entire evening."

"Why, Pierre, you are so right," Jocelyn said sweetly. "Why do we not take a stroll about the room while you recount your recent doings for me?" She gave Peter a meaningful look to remind him they had a mystery and crime to solve.

"I shall allow you to one circle of the room, then we must

finish our plans for the morrow. And you promised to have supper with me, Jocelyn." His look would have melted steel, much less any resolve she might have had to elude him.

"Indeed, so I did." She drew her hand from Peter's arm, a feeling of loss inexplicably assailing her before she transferred her attention to the gloomy gentleman at her other side. "Come, now, do tell me what you have been doing these past months. I fear I have been utterly lost to Society for simply ages."

Peter watched her walk away on Pierre's arm, vowing she would make no more than one lap with that prosy bore before returning to his side.

"Ah, *chéri*," a dulcet voice exclaimed from behind him. "I thought I would never have a chance to chat with you. The hour grows late, and we have much to say. You must make me *au courant* with all your pastimes as of late. We will have an *intime* chat, no?"

"Miss Fornier, I was not aware that we were so well acquainted that I ought give an account of myself," Peter said somewhat stiffly. He glanced to where Pierre was pouring words into Jocelyn's ear and wondered what held her in such rapt attention. Drat the man, even though he was a pompous, dull dog, he had a certain presence that might appeal to a woman.

"I think you are a trifle shy, *chéri*," Suzanne Fornier said with a light laugh that also managed to sound a bit vexed.

Understanding that the beautiful young lady was not accustomed to being ignored for another woman who was at the very least three years her elder, Peter took himself in hand to play the gallant for her benefit. He also decided he might attempt to see in what state her finances might be.

"Your beauty is sufficient to stun most men, Miss Fornier," he said with a courtly bow that also managed to distance him from her clasp. "I cannot imagine that you lack for masculine favor for a moment. It must tax even your resources to be garbed beyond the elegance of every woman in the room. Your beauty is only enhanced by the refinement of your attire."

"Why, you are not shy, just with too much of that English reserve that is so charming," Suzanne dimpled up at him, leaning forward so he could not miss the view of her exceptional *dé-*

colletage. Not even a monk could fail to see the flirtatious invitation in her dark eyes.

"And I think you are a minx," Peter said instantly. He caught
sight of Jocelyn nearing, looking slightly harried, much to
Peter's relief. "Pierre approaches. He is your cousin?" Peter inquired, not certain of the complex relationship of that family.

She pouted before answering. "Pierre and Henri are from different branches of the family. Pierre is closer to me, being a first
cousin. However, he is not so close that he will lend me a few
pounds should I need it. Henri is, I think, a third cousin, or
some such." She frowned as though overwhelmed with the in-
tricacy of relations.

"And would Henri loan you a few pounds should you have
need of them?" Peter said with a grin to take away his desire to
know the financial state of these relatives.

"But of course," she said with an infectious giggle. "Henri
adores me."

All of which told Peter not a bloody thing.

Jocelyn looked up from the carpet she had been contemplating while listening to Pierre drone on. It was suitable punishment for wanting to distance herself from Peter for a while. And
now she had to see that gorgeous creature who was practically
falling out of her gown fawning over Peter as if she wanted to
consume him.

"Pierre, I suspect you will welcome a chat with your dear
cousin. Do you take her in to supper? Or does Henri have that
privilege?"

"Come, cousin. You will join me?" Pierre commanded. He
was quick to avail himself of Suzanne's arm. The pair strolled
off in the vague direction of the dining room, where a supper
awaited any who desired a late meal.

"Do not leave me with that woman ever again, I beg you,"
Peter said fervently.

"Well, I was amply rewarded for my efforts," Jocelyn retorted, hardly mollified by his declaration. "It would seem that
Pierre is well to grass from all the bragging he did. I had no notion that he had so many investments or was so interested in
monetary ventures."

"Even ventures can fail, and I meant what I said about

Suzanne Fornier. She is a predatory creature out to snabble a title if she can and a fortune as well, not necessarily in that order." Peter glanced at the door, then back at Jocelyn. "Are you hungry?"

"That all depends." She was wary of him and her attraction to his charm. "For food?"

He laughed, sounding utterly delighted with her little *bon mot*. "My dear delight, of course I meant food. We could have a bite to eat while we complete our plans for tomorrow that were interrupted by Pierre."

"I still say it would not be wise to meet in my sitting room. Surely there must be a room in this vast castle where we could go about our plans without causing eyebrows to raise?" Jocelyn reluctantly set aside the hint of kisses stolen in the privacy of her sitting room for common sense. If she didn't marshal her thoughts, she would be in a far worse state than five years ago.

"Why do we not ask our hostess?" Peter said in reply, gesturing to where Lora stood near the door.

"Excellent notion, I must say. Why did I not think of that?" Jocelyn murmured in vexation.

"Your wits are a bit addled, but that is quite understandable. You have not yet recovered from your wetting, I imagine. Perhaps you would rather go to bed than have supper?" Peter gave her a look of what appeared to be genuine worry.

"Such concern, my lord." Jocelyn raised her brows in surprise, then left him to go to Lora, only to find him still at her side. Ignoring Peter, Jocelyn quietly addressed her cousin. "We need the list of guests, a floor plan, and a place to study both in privacy."

Bless her heart, Lora did not inquire as to the reason for the latter. She nodded at once, then after a moment's thought said, "The muniment room. The floor plan should be there, and I will send Jocelyn a list of the guests in the morning. What excuse you may give others to be so private is up to you, however. I cannot think of a thing!"

"Very well." Jocelyn gave Lora an encouraging smile. "We shall find it, I promise."

"Now, off to bed with you," Peter murmured. "I want you

bright-eyed in the morning. We have much to do. I trust none of the guests will find it necessary to depart prematurely?"

"Good heavens! We should have to think of a reason to detain them until their room might be searched!" Jocelyn ignored his demand she retire. She would go to bed when she pleased, never mind that she was nearly asleep on her feet.

"Stubborn wench. I shall return for a late-night repast, my lady," Peter said to Lora with a polite bow. "Now I must see that Jocelyn finds her bed before she is unable to undress herself."

At Jocelyn's astounded look, he added, "You did say that Mercy is ill in bed. That means that unless you can borrow a maid, you will have to undo those hooks and ties all by yourself."

Not about to extend that thought one syllable, Jocelyn spun around and marched from the room, politely excusing herself as she wound her way through the clusters of guests.

When she reached the central hall, she could hear the click of shoes behind her, probably patent leather shoes, the latest style, worn by her sudden nemesis.

"I can see myself to bed without your help, thank you," she snapped before she realized how that might sound should anyone overhear her.

"The condition you are in? Why, you might take a wrong turn and end up in my room," Peter said while lightly clasping her arm as they walked up the stairs.

"Ha! That would be the day!" she said scornfully with an appropriate sniff when they reached the top of the stairs.

"Would it not?" Peter murmured with a wicked little chuckle.

Thankful she was not far along the corridor, Jocelyn paused before her sitting room door to face Peter. "Good night, my lord."

"Ah, *ma chérie,* you are tired and confused and need nothing more than sleep. I am cruel to tease you. But it is so difficult to resist now that I have you almost where I want you." He tapped her chin playfully, that odd gleam in his eyes once again.

Jocelyn stupidly asked, "And where is that, pray tell?"

"In my bed, of course. Is that not what you expected me to

say? Believe me when I state I want far more than that, al-. though I confess I anticipate bedding you with great pleasure."

"Never!" Jocelyn hissed, swirled about, and rushed into her sitting room, firmly shutting the door in his handsome face. In his bed, indeed. She wiped sudden tears from her eyes, deciding she must be far more tired than she suspected, and began to undress. She paused when someone knocked on her door.

"Yes? What is it?"

"Do you require assistance?" a too familiar voice queried in seeming concern.

"Not in the slightest, thank you, Peter. Go away!" She left the sitting room, tossing her gloves on the chaise as she went, kicking off her slippers in vexation with the difficulty she was going to have in removing her gown. Was it not a favorite, she would simply sleep in the dratted thing. She reached behind to grope for the first of the hooks.

"My lady?" the soft voice of the maid who had done her hair earlier whispered at the door to the bedroom. "May I help? Lord Leigh seemed to think you might have need of me."

The dratted tease! "Thank you. I could use a bit of help with these hooks." Jocelyn obediently turned so the maid could do the necessary. Within minutes the gown was off and placed in the wardrobe by the efficient maid. Jocelyn pulled her sheer muslin nightgown over her head with haste, not bothering to brush her hair after pulling the pins out. The plaits would untangle come morning.

Never had she been so glad to tumble into bed and close her eyes. She was far too tired to dream. She was haunted instead by silver blue eyes gazing at her with a hint of mischief and a promise. As to what *that* might be, she could not know.

Morning light was not welcome Jocelyn decided when she reluctantly opened her eyes. The same quiet little maid had slipped into her room to open the draperies, tidy the discarded items, and see to the fire. Never mind that it was June, Derbyshire could be quite chilly even in the middle of summer.

"Your chocolate, my lady? The gentleman thought you might like a bit of sweet. Our cook has a special way with hot chocolate," the maid concluded before setting a tray on Jocelyn's lap.

Not only was there a pot of hot chocolate but a plate of buns warm from the oven. Jocelyn poured, took a sip, then a bite of the roll and pronounced, "Sheer heaven! Please give her my heartfelt thanks. And my thanks to you for your care. Poor Mercy, she must be fretting herself to flinders."

"She is still very ill, I believe. The countess has requested the apothecary see her." The maid completed her tasks, then set out a gown of jonquil muslin trimmed with lace inserts in the bodice and three flounces at the hem. Jocelyn made quick work of her chocolate and buns, then slipped from her bed with haste. This morning she must assist Peter with the lists. She'd not put it past the dratted man to solve the crime without her! Not that she didn't wish a speedy conclusion to the theft. She wanted to be in on the solution.

The maid patiently untangled the plaits that had looked so pretty last evening and dressed the long shining length of hair in a most becoming style. Jocelyn studied the result and commented, "Did I borrow you from my cousin? You have extremely talented fingers."

"The countess has been training me to assist guests, although I am not her personal maid," the girl said with a blush before excusing herself.

Donning her yellow kid slippers, Jocelyn left the bedroom only to come to an abrupt halt in her sitting room. Peter lounged in the chair directly across from where she stood in shock.

"At least I can hear you wake up in a good mood. I had no idea you began the day so cheerfully, my love." He waved a folded sheet of paper in the air. "The list."

"What are you doing in my sitting room! Really, Peter, you cannot do things like this." She took a step backward as he uncoiled himself from where he had sat and reached her side in seconds.

"Good morning, my dear." He smiled, and she found herself foolishly smiling in return. Then he placed a light kiss on her mouth before grasping her arm. "Now, first I believe we shall have a good breakfast, then the muniment room, after which we may commence our sleuthing."

"I must check on Mercy first thing," Jocelyn insisted, ignoring the thrill of that kiss and the touch of his hand on her bare arm.

He waited by the door while she looked in on her poor maid, still miserable and apologetic for causing such trouble and denying her mistress her proper care.

"Not to worry your head about a thing. The countess has loaned me a maid for the time being, and you shan't leave that bed until the apothecary says you might. I shall be just fine." With the explosion of one of Mercy's finest sneezes in her ears, she left the maid to her misery and a good bed rest to rejoin Peter.

By the time he had outlined his plan for the day, they had left her room and were on their way down the stairs to the breakfast room.

"It ought not take us long to copy the house plan, then jot down just who is where," he concluded as they rounded the corner into the cheerful breakfast room.

Yellow-and-white-striped paper brightened the walls and showed the mahogany furniture to great advantage. Lora had redone the chair seats in a pretty yellow floral print, and the colorful array of tempting foods gracing the sideboard was enough to pull anyone from a case of doldrums.

Not having had her supper, Jocelyn was starved and not about to permit Peter to put her off her food. She ignored his murmured offer to assist her and helped herself to buttered eggs, a slice of ham, toast, and berry jam. The footman in attendance poured her a cup of steaming tea, and she surveyed her plate with satisfaction.

"A woman with a hearty appetite. I am glad to see you aren't one of those women who persist on living on air," Peter muttered as he set his plate near hers and requested a cup of coffee once he was seated.

"You will not spoil my breakfast as you did my supper, my lord," Jocelyn said primly. "I suppose you returned to the dining room and made a fine meal."

"Actually, I went to bed. All that dashing through the rain to rescue you took its toll. I had begun to worry when our countess mentioned you were due to arrive and wondered if you would make it, considering the roads and the weather, not to mention your brother's second-best traveling coach. I decided someone had better make certain you were not in trouble. And you were."

"I did thank you yesterday, but I am glad that you found me before I dropped of sheer anger and frustration, not to mention fatigue." Jocelyn spoke quietly, noting that the others in the room were not paying her much heed.

He glanced around the table, nodded to the gentlemen across from them who had finished and now rose to depart for the library. When they were gone, he turned his attention to Jocelyn again.

"What happened back then?"

She knew he was not referring to yesterday, but to a night five years ago. "I scarce know where to begin," she said to stall for time.

"Try the beginning. I understand that helps when searching for the truth of a matter," he replied with a wry tone.

"Very well. Do not say I did not warn you. What I say may not please you." She couldn't look at him, she was too embarrassed; her admissions were not easy for her to make.

"Consider me cautioned," he said with impatience and a glance at the door.

"Simply put, I was but eighteen, as green as a girl can be, and you frightened me out of my wits. Do you have the most remote idea what your kisses do to a woman? No, forget I said that," she said with a wave of her hand. "You are sufficiently arrogant as it is. But, nevertheless, I was totally unprepared for my reaction to you. The very thought of wedding someone who overwhelmed my emotions was not to be borne."

"So?" he softly urged.

"I took the cowardly way out and refused to see you again." She had never been proud of her timidity. She should have met Peter that final time and told him in person rather than send a message with her maid. But if she had met him, he would have seen her tearstained cheeks and perhaps guessed what was in her heart. Would that he had!

"I take it that Simon did not affect you so strongly?" he said with grim humor.

"Simon kissed my hand," Jocelyn admitted. "He posed no threat to my virginal peace in any way whatsoever."

"Did you love him?"

"No," she whispered, anguished she had to reveal such reprehensible conduct to the man who still had the power to stir her as no other ever had.

Silence reigned for some minutes while they applied themselves to the breakfast before them. Jocelyn resolutely forked cooling eggs to her mouth, chewed, and swallowed without tasting. The ham followed the eggs along with the toast and jam. She washed the lot down with her tea, then simply sat, waiting for what Peter would say next. That he would say something, she was certain. It was what he said that mattered.

She was startled when he chuckled, shaking his head as though surprised at her words.

"You have no idea what thoughts have raged through my head these past five years. What a fool I was. I ought to have known you had to be led to passion gently. So, who taught you?"

"Excuse me? What do you mean, *taught me*?" She pushed her chair away from the table, preparing to rise and flee the room.

He rose as well, towering over her. He tenderly wiped a corner of her mouth before grinning at her, a hateful grin, she thought. "My dear girl, had you responded with as much passion five years ago as you did yesterday, we would probably now be wed with several children about us."

"I do not believe my ears. You conceited oaf! I have led an utterly blameless life, full of good works for my brother's tenants, church matters, and simple pleasures. I have not kissed a man since I last kissed you," she admitted in an unguarded outburst of fury.

"Ah. Then, it is simply that you grew up. I hoped something of the sort might happen when Simon failed to return and you remained in what many claimed mourning all these years. I thought it strange when you did not return to Society and seek another marriage. I shall be a gentleman and not inquire as to *what* you actually were mourning. Shall we go to the muniment room now?"

Jocelyn shut her eyes and shook her head. "I shall never understand men if I live to be two hundred." She swept past him and out the door only to halt when she realized she had no idea where the muniment room might be.

"This way. Adrian gave me directions last evening. By the by, your cousin took your advice and informed her husband about the theft. He comforted her as best he could at the moment, given the throng of guests around at the time. I trust he was able to extend more generous comfort in the privacy of their room."

"I don't believe I shall inquire too closely into what you deem generous comfort." Jocelyn marched bravely at Peter's side, wondering if she was headed for her doom.

"Cheer up, *ma chérie*. One day you shall know the comfort of a husband's embrace."

He spoke with such confidence, Jocelyn could almost believe him.

The muniment room was small, lined with shelves stacked with papers and boxes, and possessed a slanted table in the center before which stood two stools. Peter gestured to them, saying, "Take your pick. Adrian told me where to find the plan of the castle. Here, take the list of guests. I believe nearly all are arrived, even if we have not met every one of them as yet. Your dramatic arrival rather precluded a proper introduction."

Jocelyn fingered the list, watching as Peter dug through a particular stack of papers, then turn to her with a neat rendering of the castle floor plan.

"He said there are several of these and we may write on this one should we please. Now, read the names and the rooms to which they have been assigned. I shall mark them." He found a pencil and poised, waiting.

Jocelyn pulled herself together and began to read. She had admitted to him that no man had kissed her in all these years, not even her fiancé. It hadn't seemed to affect him much. He knew, as did no one else, that she had never loved Simon, poor man. So now what? She was open, vulnerable, and caught in a web not of her making. If her brother had not married, and if Lora had not begged her to come help out with the costume party, and if . . . so many other things had or had not happened.

She sighed and read another name from the list and the room to which he had been assigned.

When all names had been ticked off the list, she straightened, wondering what her nemesis might say or do next. She had not long to wait.

"We need costumes, you know. Or did you bring one in your trunk?" Peter inquired, tapping his pencil on the desk while awaiting her answer.

"I had not the least idea what to wear. I'll not be Cleopatra, nor a shepherdess with one of those silly crooks to carry about."

"Perhaps we should take a page from the family history and come dressed in medieval garb, fitting for the restoration of the necklace."

"Do you really think we will find it?"

"We must." He met her worried gaze with one equally concerned. "The thief must *not* be permitted to get away with the fabulous jewelry."

Chapter Four

"How on earth do we go on from here?" Jocelyn looked at the neatly labeled plan of the castle and grimaced. "Every guest room is assigned, and we now know who is where."

"I trust you took note how close my room is to yours? You have a sitting room, and I do not—so we shall meet in yours to confer."

"I do not think that is such a wise idea," Jocelyn began, only to be swept to her feet and out of the muniment room by her partner.

"Nonsense. Think, girl! We must talk and privately at that. It would never do to have someone overhear what we have learned. Either they would think we are mad or we should tip our hand, and reveal what we have uncovered to the wrong person." Peter ushered Jocelyn past the breakfast room, now quite empty, to the central entry hall, equally devoid of people. He brought her to a halt at the bottom of the broad oak stairs.

"They might also get ideas about us—quite erroneous, I am certain," she pointed out with what she considered excellent reasoning. She would not allow herself to be shattered by this man again. Once had been more than enough. And he could scarcely want to be paired with her in view of their past.

"Do you still enjoy a morning ride?" he inquired.

"With you?" Jocelyn asked rather irrationally. But then, he could have been sending her away so he could ferret out what he might on his own. "That is, you might wish me elsewhere so you can discover a clue or something of that sort," she explained awkwardly. Heavens, she hadn't been this ridiculous in years. Why did he have the power to reduce her to a blathering idiot?

"I would welcome your company at any time, my dear girl, but I thought it would be an opportunity for us to talk without someone overhearing what we might say."

A part of Jocelyn melted with his tender look. The other part was screaming at her to beware of this man. He was just a little too ready with the soft words and loving look, not to mention those kisses he disbursed with such devastating results.

"What I thought we might do was to take the floor plan with us so we could best decide which rooms each could search." He tapped his pocket, and she noted how superbly his bottle-green coat fit over that comfortingly masculine chest that she had snuggled so tightly against.

"Search?" she whispered quite as though it was some word utterly foreign to her.

"You have another idea as to how we may find the necklace? Come, you will change into your habit, and we will go out for a nice private ride. Do not tell a soul we intend to go out, much less anything else," he said quietly into her ear.

There was no one around that she could see, but the effect of that soft baritone so close to her ear did strange things to her. It turned her into mush.

"Indeed, I can quite see that it would be the best thing to do." She hurried up the stairs to the door of her suite, her breathlessness having nothing to do with her rush. It unnerved her that he kept pace with her. Here she paused. "I'll be as quick as possible, given that Mercy is still abed with her cold."

"I don't suppose you would accept my assistance? No? Ah, well, I shall bide my time, *ma chérie*. I shall fetch you as soon as I am ready. I do not intend we be joined by anyone else, you may be sure."

She gave him an uncertain glance before entering her sitting room. In her bedroom she did the best she could to slip from the jonquil muslin without damaging it. She tossed it on her bed, pulling her hunter-green riding habit from the wardrobe, then found the other necessary items to go with it. The habit shirt was simple to don, and was quickly followed by the skirt and jacket.

"Need help with your boots?"

Jocelyn paused, boot in midair at the sound of his voice. Walking stocking-footed into her sitting room, she scolded, "You really ought not be in here. What will the other guests think!"

"Precisely what we wish them to think," he said with deliberation and a rather calculated look at her. "If they believe there is a romance between us, it will make it all the easier for us to track down the missing necklace. Think how we can slip through the halls at odd hours and it will be seen as a romantic rendezvous."

"Oh. I see." She sat down on the chaise with an inelegant thump. Not that she was the least concerned about that at this point. She hadn't anticipated all the ramifications of this partner business. "So," she concluded in a most prosaic manner, "you may as well help me with these boots. The ones ruined by the rain were my favorites. These do not fit as well and are stubborn to put on." She gave the polished leather half boots a skeptical study.

"Allow me, my dear." He knelt before her and within minutes had eased the half boots onto her feet. It seemed to Jocelyn that his ministration required exposing a great deal of ankle and leg. She hadn't paid much attention when Mercy helped her, so perhaps it was necessary. "Try that for comfort."

She rose and was surprised to discover that the old boots were amazingly not too ill fitting. "Not so bad after all," she said with surprise. "Thank you."

"My magic touch, ma'am." He offered his arm, and Jocelyn accepted it, even as she swept up her skirt into the other hand. They left the room and were out of the house before they saw another person. Since this was the groom, all had gone well.

"Did you work your magic to keep the other guests away while we slipped from the house?" she inquired with an amused glance at him as they rode down the drive.

"No, we were merely very lucky. Now, let us canter away from here before Pierre or Henri spot us. I believe I see them back there." He pointed with his riding crop, and Jocelyn could just make out a couple of gentlemen riding in their vague direction.

Obedient to his suggestion, she nudged the well-mannered roan mare that she had been given to ride, and they soon distanced themselves from the house and any others.

Once they reached a high point from which they had a commanding view of the terrain, Peter drew his chestnut gelding to a halt. Jocelyn followed suit with her mare.

"Adrian said there was a viewing bench in this area. Ah, over there. We shall dismount, I think—if that is agreeable to you. 'Tis a pleasant day with nary a sign of rain. I believe it safe from intrusion." He did as he said, then assisted her from her mount, holding her firmly in his strong hands before allowing her feet to touch ground.

Jocelyn was acutely aware of his touch, their proximity. "Safe. Yes, indeed. Quite safe, I am sure." From what, she wasn't quite certain. Peter? Her own inclinations?

"I imagine you have been kept busy since your grandmother's death," Jocelyn said while they crossed to the bench. She paused to watch him tie the reins for both horses to a post Adrian had thought to erect for that purpose, then resumed her pace. "I expect there have likely been a great many demands on your time. Did you take your seat in Lords?"

"My grandmother had a capable steward those last years, so it was not as dreadful as it might have been. And yes, I did take my seat in Lords. Did you not read *any* newspapers these past five years?" He gave her a speculative look, as though wondering how she had occupied her hours.

"I seldom had the time. Odd, how most people seem to find the country boring and believe there is nothing to do. I seemed to fill my days and never lacked for interests." She surveyed the scene spread below them, seeing greenery and wildflowers in abundance, yet heeding nothing.

"I expected to read the notice of your marriage. I never did and confess I wondered. Then Simon was listed among the dead and wounded. I waited to see if you would marry another. You didn't. Why? Rumor had it Lord Izard wished to be your groom."

Jocelyn gave a mirthless laugh. "He ran quickly once he learned I had no intention of sharing his attentions with the dozen or so other women he enjoyed."

"So you did know what was going on in Town."

"To a degree. I have good friends who sought to make me *au courant* with his shortcomings."

"Interesting. And none of the others who beat their path to your brother's house met your standard?"

"You pry, sir. I might well ask the same of you, except that I doubt you find the women waiting on your doorstep. Or do you?" She allowed him to seat her on the stone bench, then shifted uneasily as he sat close to her side.

"One or two. After coming into the title and fortune, it was amazing how eligible I suddenly became. Mothers with daughters of age found me much to their liking." He grimaced, and Jocelyn found herself patting him on his hand in comfort, understanding what he meant only too well.

"Yet we are both expected to marry, and well," she mused. Then recalling how she had turned down his proposal of marriage five years ago and that he had thought her no better than those girls who sought fortune and title, she snatched her hand away as though burned. He studied her while he leaned back against the bench, looking at ease, yet as though tightly wound.

"I admit I thought ill of you for some time, my dear. You see, I thought we were admirably suited. I would have sworn that you returned my regard." He leaned forward to rest his arms on his legs, turning his head so to look up at her.

Her smart riding hat with its short cream feather above a trim brim offered her no concealment. She was exposed to his scrutiny. "Perhaps we were. It is all past, however," she said with a sigh.

"And now we have a mystery to solve," he said, the resignation clear in his voice.

"I pray we can find it in time for the costume ball. It is a week away. That does not offer us much leeway. I suppose if worse comes to worse, Adrian can announce the theft and insist upon a complete search of all rooms. Think of the scandal that would bring! I imagine he would prefer to keep the theft quiet in the event it is a relative. *That* would really be the outside of enough."

"You also think it might be a relation? What of the beauteous

Suzanne? She looks expensive to keep. I fancy she requires a fair sum of money to dress in the latest stare of fashion."

"You are aware of the costs of a wardrobe! Your future wife will be fortunate, indeed, to have an understanding husband." Jocelyn had forced herself to utter those words, wondering if he might reveal intentions to marry someone in particular. He had agreed, more or less, that they both must wed.

"Thank you. That is an encouraging remark. Now," he said sitting back on the bench to pull the castle floor plan from his pocket, "I can't think why Adrian's family thought to call this place a castle. It is merely a very large Palladian-style home—overlarge and a trifle ornate to be sure, but hardly what I would call a castle."

"There was a true castle here once, ages ago," Jocelyn said, recalling what Lora had written. "The ruins offered building stone to some degree, but true, this is not the original castle built by the first earl." She leaned over to study the first-floor plan of rooms. "Suzanne is conveniently close to Henri and Pierre. I find it curious that Lora did not separate the ladies and gentlemen to separate wings as sometimes is done at these house parties."

"It makes intrigue so much more tantalizing," he said with a half smile.

"Well, it will also make it awkward to examine each room. I would *not* wish to be found in Pierre's room, for example!" She gave Peter a rueful smile, sharing her horror of that fate.

"That is indeed reassuring, my love. Now, as to particulars . . . you take the women and I shall take the gentlemen. We shall divide the couples between us. Do you want to do Suzanne's room immediately? If so, I could possibly entertain her, keep her out of the way until you have finished."

Memory of that exposed bosom offered so temptingly for Peter's perusal last evening returned and Jocelyn just barely agreed that Peter would be doing her a service. "It will be good to know she will not waltz into the room whilst I am digging through her bureau drawers. Where do you think it might be hidden?"

"Bureau drawers are a good starting point. I wonder about the storage area—the trunks and cases, that sort of thing. Think you that the thief would have stashed the necklace in the box rooms?"

"It is possible, I suppose." She looked at the sky and angle of the sun, then added, "I think we had best return to the house and begin our hunt promptly after luncheon. I shan't relax until that necklace is back in the vault."

"Right. Allow me to help." Again, he assisted her on her mount, then rode at her side until they reached the front door all the while discussing ways and means of entering the guest rooms and likely hiding places for the priceless necklace. A groom appeared shortly after Peter had helped Jocelyn from her saddle. The fellow left with the horses in hand. Jocelyn stood facing Peter, curiously uncertain.

"No one will ever believe we rode off to the distance to admire scenery and chat," Peter said with a sudden grin. "They will be certain we had a romantic tryst. Shall we give any watchers reason to sustain that belief?" Peter asked, that silvery gleam present in his look once again.

Jocelyn eyed him warily. "I was not under the impression we were actually required to foster the illusion of a romance. I believed we would merely let them think what they would."

"I am a firm believer in action, my dear."

Before Jocelyn could move, he had gathered her in his arms and kissed her thoroughly. Which, of course, shattered her poise quite as he probably intended it should.

"Someday . . ." she sputtered once she had collected her poise again. "Someday your behavior is apt to plunge you into trouble."

"I believe it already has, *ma chérie*." He led her into the house, where the first person they saw was Henri.

"Thought that was you riding off across the grounds. Wanted a touch of privacy, did you?" His handsome face wore what would have been a leer, had he not laughed immediately. "You're a sly dog, Lord Leigh. Staking your claim for one and all to see, eh?"

"Sir," Jocelyn began, wishing she might slap that calculating expression from his face.

"You may have the right of it, old man," Peter replied with a grin that didn't make Jocelyn any more pleased.

Deciding she was not going to remain to be insulted, Jocelyn gathered her skirts in hand and hurried up the stairs until she reached her rooms. No one had followed her, so she was able to enter without undue haste.

The young maid was again there to assist her, turning from her task at making the bed and tidying the room.

With help, it was but a short time before Jocelyn was presentable in her jonquil muslin again. Pacing back and forth beside the chaise longue, she considered the house plan, recalling precisely the location of the gorgeous Suzanne's room. Would Peter undertake the distraction of the beautiful young woman so Jocelyn might search her room now? Or when?

The door opened, and Peter stuck his head around it to inquire, "Are you ready to begin our quest?" At her nod, he continued, "Very well. I shall seek out the lovely Suzanne at once. Perhaps she will be down for a light luncheon. She has to sustain that figure, you know. How do I signal you?"

Jocelyn ignored the remark about Suzanne and her figure to concentrate on her task. "We shall eat what we would, perhaps see if Lora has plans for the afternoon?"

"Excellent notion, my dear. And Suzanne?"

"Simple. I will follow you and as soon as I see you have her charmed, I will immediately return to this floor and her room. How long do you think you can keep her entertained?"

"How long do you think you will need?" He sauntered across the room to gaze at her, a disconcerting look, intent and assessing.

"Perhaps thirty minutes should do? I cannot say I have any experience at this sort of thing, so I may be slow or miss something," Jocelyn cautioned.

"I can always do another search," Peter said reassuringly. Jocelyn felt a stab of what only could be jealousy at the thought of Peter entering that woman's room for any reason. Impossible! How could she be jealous when she did not like the man!

"Undoubtedly," she murmured as she slipped past him and into the hall.

They chatted amiably about nothing at all while going down the stairs to the dining room, where sound told them most of the guests were gathered. A magnificent buffet was set forth with

every delicacy one might wish to tempt the appetite. Pierre had
Suzanne in tow, lecturing her on what she ought to eat, while
Henri eyed the other young ladies present with what Jocelyn
thought a predatory eye.

Considering what she faced after luncheon, the meal had little appeal for her. She managed to eat sufficient to appease her
cousin, then sipped tea. She looked up when Lora wrapped on
her glass to gain attention.

"We are to have a game of bowls," Lora announced gaily.
"The gentlemen must choose their partners, and there will be a
prize for the winner."

There was a general move in the direction of the perfectly
maintained bowling green, one that had been there likely a hundred years or more. Since bowling had been a sport enjoyed by
Adrian's great-grandfather, the green had not only been carefully sited, but also kept clipped to a perfect level all these
years.

Before Henri reached her, Peter had claimed Suzanne's hand
and her society for the afternoon. Henri turned to where Jocelyn had stood moments before, only to find she had vanished.
With a grace that Peter could only admire, Henri then sought
the company of a young miss not long from the schoolroom but
possessing a handsome countenance as well as dowry.

Peter glanced at the doorway through which he had seen Jocelyn disappear and wondered how she would fare. It would be
the first test of his theory. He strongly suspected one of the relatives. It made the most sense. They above all would know the
value of the necklace and the likelihood of it being removed
from the safe for the costume party. A glance at the luscious
Suzanne brought an appreciative smile. His share of the afternoon's work would not be all that bad.

Jocelyn cast an anxious look about her as she quietly walked
up the stairs to the first floor. Not even a maid was in sight, nor
a footman, either. Jocelyn prayed it would remain that way for
as long as needed. Most of the servants' work was accom-
plished in the early morning, knowing that the guests would be
in and out of their rooms the remainder of the day.

Now, if Suzanne's maid were only off pressing her evening gown or doing a bit of laundry, it would be perfect.

Jocelyn tapped lightly on the bedroom door, listening with care for any sign of the maid inside. Hearing nothing, she slipped inside, tightly closing the door behind her. Should the maid return, it would be awkward but Jocelyn would deal with it if it happened.

She found the drawers exceptionally neat and orderly, high praise for Suzanne's maid, indeed. Drawer after drawer Jocelyn searched, trying to leave things as she found them. Finding nothing in the bureau, she turned to the wardrobe. Here she plowed through costumes for every conceivable occasion in a vast selection of hues, all calculated to enhance the beauty's charms. Jocelyn noted there were a goodly number with the same *décolleté* as viewed the previous evening. Well, with the ample curves and bounteous blessings Suzanne possessed, it was not surprising.

Hatboxes were stacked with care, and Jocelyn went through each and every one of them. She well remembered how she had hidden things in them when she traveled.

She found nothing there, either. She prepared to leave the room, quite discouraged. As reprehensible as it might be, she had been hoping the thief would prove to be Suzanne and her search ended. After checking to see that all was as it was when she entered, she paused in her steps at the sound of voices in the hall. Tiptoeing to the door, she listened with great care. "Suzanne!" she whispered.

The bed was the sort with a solid frame to the floor, obviously no place to hide. She could see no other place in which to take refuge, either. The window beckoned, open to the afternoon breeze, the draperies moving slightly in the gentle wind.

Without another thought, Jocelyn dashed to the window and spotted a narrow ledge, part of the design of the structure. "Well, I have no wish to explain why I am in here, so I had best make a stab at this," Jocelyn said under her breath. Looking down was not to be done. She bravely stepped to the ledge, grimly hanging on to the window surround as long as able. She slid one foot before the other, hands damply plastered to the stone surface of the house, clinging, hoping that there was no obstruction, that no one on the ground should look up to see her idiotically making her way where she had no business being. Thank goodness the bowling green was on the other side of the building.

Inch by inch she made her way, Suzanne's voice floating from her room, with complaints about a headache, demands for a tisane, a cool cloth.

The sound grew more faint as Jocelyn continued, trying to recall who had been assigned the adjacent room. Pierre, she thought. Would he likely be there at this time of day?

"Great scot, girl, what in heaven's name are you doing?"

Jocelyn clung to the stone, forcing her body against it. She really did not need to look down. What was Peter doing on this side of the house? She carefully waved at him with the hand that presented itself most outward, then continued to inch her way to the next window.

"Whatever you do, do not fall. I cannot catch you," she heard next. She made no attempt to signal him at that stupidity. Did he think she intended to jump? Idiot!

The silence that followed his inane remark made her long to look down. Was he still there watching her progress? It had been his idea to search Suzanne's room, and he was to have kept her occupied until Jocelyn returned to the group.

Her hands were damp, her brow near dripping with fear, and her heart pounding so fast she was almost faint with anxiety. Yet she kept on, for there was really no other choice. Glancing ahead she caught the welcome sight of Peter's head as he leaned out the window, watching her progress.

"Give me your hand, love," Peter said, stretching out his strong arm, his hand held upward for her to grasp.

"When I am sufficiently close," she muttered, teeth clenched. She would take no chances. As soon as her left hand touched the window surround, she bent slightly to reach for his. She found her hand strongly clasped, and she was guided into the room with great haste. Then she was swept into Peter's solid embrace, and hugged closely to his lean frame.

"I do not think I have ever been so terrified in my life," he said to the top of her head, not releasing her to so much as look her in the eyes.

"And what was I to do? Tell Suzanne I had gone to the wrong room? She might be a featherbrain, but she is not precisely stupid. What happened at the green?"

"She got a headache. I gather I was not sufficiently flirtatious."

Jocelyn was tired, still frightened, but all receded at the thought of Peter not being flirtatious enough to please the charming Suzanne.

"Poor man," Jocelyn said in a mock soothing manner.

"I tried, God knows I did. I just hoped she had stayed there long enough for you to be in and out by the time she went to her room. I thought my heart would stop when I glanced up to see you making your way along that wall. Please, dear girl, crawl under the bed next time."

"Couldn't," Jocelyn replied into his cravat. Then she pushed herself away from him, looking about at the room. "We had better get out of here at once. What if the person in this room returns?"

"Oh. Right." He pulled her to the door, paused to listen, then opened the door to cautiously peer around the edge. "All clear," he whispered even as he drew her after him, walking along the hall with quiet steps quite as though they had not been trespassing.

Once in the safety of her sitting room, Jocelyn sank down upon her chaise, unsure of whether she wanted to collapse or scream at Peter. "I do not think I could do that again."

"Good. My nerves couldn't take it."

"*Your* nerves!"

"Did you find any sign of the necklace?"

"All I learned is that Suzanne has a remarkably neat maid. She also owns an excellent collection of gowns and hats and assorted other paraphernalia. Curious. From what Lora said, I had not believed Uncle Maxim so well to grass."

"Well, what next?"

"Your turn, I believe?" Jocelyn said quietly, the strain on her system catching up with her.

"You are still pale. Allow me to summon a maid with tea and toast for you."

"By all means. Announce to the world that you have taken residence in my sitting room while you are at it."

"True," he said, rubbing his jaw with one firm hand.

Jocelyn thought of the strength offered in his hand when she had reached out to him and he had proved to be her almost rescuer again.

"Thank you for your help. Moving around that window into that room could have been tricky." Jocelyn leaned against the chaise, watching as he restlessly paced about the sitting room.

"I had not considered this search might involve danger," he said at long last with a rueful look at Jocelyn.

"Neither had I. We had best not tell Lora. She would insist we stop, and I am quite determined to find that necklace. It has become a matter of honor."

Peter stared at her, a bemused expression on his face. "Indeed. A matter of honor it is. All we must do is refrain from being trapped in the room we are searching. Will you stand guard for me?"

"Of course," she said promptly. "But in the hallway."

"Naturally. There shouldn't be any danger *there*, love."

Chapter Five

A soft rap on the door brought Jocelyn alert. She exchanged a look with Peter, wondering if scandal was about to break over their heads.

"Who is it?" She fingered the jonquil muslin draped over her knees with nervous fingers that had nothing to do with her hair-raising escapade.

"Lora. May I come in?" Without waiting for an invitation, Lora slipped into the room, swiftly shutting the door behind her when she observed Peter standing near the fireplace. "Oh."

"Peter and I have been discussing how to go about the search of the various rooms, Lora. I attempted to hunt through Suzanne's room but without much success. The neatness of her possessions was not disturbed by the concealment of the necklace."

"I confess I had hoped it would be hidden there. She is such a likely suspect, you see. She needs money and, well, stealing a necklace is such a simple thing for a woman to do. If someone were to come upon her, all she would have to do is drop it in her bodice."

Thinking of the low cut of Suzanne's dress tops, Jocelyn wondered precisely how much could be concealed therein.

"Well, I think we shall need help. Can you find something that will occupy the guests and possibly take them away from the castle for the entire afternoon tomorrow? Better yet, the entire day?" Jocelyn looked at Peter, who nodded in agreement with her suggestion.

"We could organize an outing to some ruins not too far away

from here. It is some distance, but manageable within one day.
And I fancy the women would enjoy an excursion to the little
market town not far from here, where they could browse
through the shops. Adrian could take the men fishing or something."

"Yes, yes, anything to draw them away from the house," Jocelyn concurred. "I shall be sorry to miss all this gaiety. Once
we recover the necklace, I shall insist upon proper recompense
in the form of shopping and interesting jaunts!" Jocelyn said
with a grin. It was a trifle forced, for she suspected that by that
time Peter would be long gone and she would be alone again,
searching for a place she might live. What a pity she could not
simply buy a house, bring in an elderly indigent aunt or cousin,
and be left in peace. Amazing how something so improper
could sound so boring, but that couldn't be helped. Such was
life for the spinster, and she could make the best of it if needs
be. It was something to consider, even if deemed unseemly.

"We must have time to investigate without a worry that the
guest will return to the room," Peter inserted into the ensuing
quiet. "I can enlist Dickman to help, and I imagine Mercy
would if she is sufficiently recovered?" he added with a questioning look at Jocelyn. "I suspect Jocelyn is not going to tell
you the whole of her tale. She did investigate Suzanne's room,
but that young miss thwarted us by claiming a headache and returning unexpectedly to her room. Jocelyn was there with no
place to hide. She took to the ledge outside, inching her way
while clinging to the wall until she made the next room, where
I caught her."

"After he had called up to me from the terrace," Jocelyn reminded him with a grim smile, "and frightened me half to
death. I dared not look down at him, lest I fall. I was very
tempted to toss a brick at him, however."

"Sorry, my dear," Peter said handsomely.

Lora had turned pale and groped for the nearest chair. Sinking down, she stared at Jocelyn with wide-eyed astonishment.
"You actually made your way along that ledge? Good heavens."

"You see why it is so important that the guests be drawn
away from here?" Jocelyn decided she must take a firm stance.

She would not be placed in such a position again, nor could she risk another enfolding in Peter's arms. That way led to greater danger than the ledge possessed.

"Indeed. I will make every effort to do precisely that, you may be certain." Lora shook her head in wonderment. "I cannot believe what you did. When Adrian hears of this, he will be most upset."

Peter cleared his throat, looking at Jocelyn, then Lora. "It is nearing the dinner hour. Perhaps we should dress and meet Adrian in the library as soon as may be?"

"A council of war?" Jocelyn said with an attempt at humor. It fell flat as the others merely stared at her.

"You are certain you do not need to rest in your bed? I vow I would have had an attack of the vapors had I been in that circumstance!" Lora said softly, a delicate frown marring the perfection of her brow.

"I believe I would be the better for company," Jocelyn said by way of denial. "If I remain here by myself, I will think of a thousand things that might have happened to me, none of them good. Just go, and I shall change into something suitable for the evening."

"I salute you, my dear. You do not cease to amaze me." Peter gave Jocelyn an elegant bow, then escorted Lora from the room, sticking his head back around the corner to add, "You promise not to change your mind? I am terrified of that man-eating woman, into whose clutches you gave me this afternoon."

As intended, this bit of humor made Jocelyn smile. "I cannot see you as intimidated. You strike me as a man well able to fend for himself." She rose from the chaise, ready to change to her evening attire.

"You do not know the half of it, my dear. We men are every bit as vulnerable as any woman." With that astounding comment, he closed her door.

Jocelyn stood stock-still for a few moments, absorbing what Peter had just said. Men—vulnerable? Nonsense. They were the rulers of the world, the controllers of women's destiny. There was nothing they might not attempt, there were no constraints on them—other than Polite Society might place. And that, she reminded herself as she made her way to the wardrobe in her bedroom, was more of a problem with every passing hour.

"You," she addressed the image in the looking glass, "are an utter nodcock to continue to permit Peter Leigh in the sitting room, regardless of what foolishness he spouts about consultation and the like."

"Talking to yourself, ma'am?" Mercy peeked around the corner of the door, looking confused.

She was pale and looked the worse for her ailment, but Jocelyn imagined that Mercy would insist upon assisting with her evening dress.

"Indeed, Mercy, is that not the hallmark of an old maid? I am becoming a thornback, a maiden past praying for, an apeleader."

"Bite your tongue, my lady. You must not even think such things." Mercy sniffed into the huge white handkerchief she had found.

"You seem better," Jocelyn said while submitting to Mercy's tender care. The jonquil muslin was gently removed, and Mercy took the taffeta gown that Jocelyn intended to wear from the wardrobe.

"The tisane Mr. Dickman sent up to me was most efficacious. I ceased my sneezing and now feel as though I may recover quite soon. When I met him at noon meal he said it had some sort of flower. It is remarkable."

"How thoughtful of him. I trust you will not mind assisting Lord Leigh and me with a matter, in that case. It will involve working with Dickman."

"I shan't mind in the least, my lady," Mercy said primly, but with a faint pink creeping into her pale cheeks.

Jocelyn quickly explained about the missing necklace and the need to avoid a scandal. "Lord Leigh thinks it is likely to be a family member, for one of them would be more apt to know of the jewels and their value."

"Likely that Miss Fornier," Mercy said with a sniff.

"I searched her room this afternoon and found nothing.

"I'll wager you simply did not know where to look," Mercy said with a nod and a knowing gleam in her eyes.

Jocelyn was not about to argue with Mercy regarding whether or not there was a lack of skill in her own ability to search. "Well, if you think you can do better, you have my leave to investigate on your own," Jocelyn said before thinking of the possible ramifications of such an act.

"The others think I am still in bed with my cold. I could slip into Miss Fornier's bedroom while you are all at dinner. It would give me pleasure to see that haughty lady brought to her comeuppance," Mercy declared firmly.

"I was not aware you knew anything about her," Jocelyn said with a frown.

"Mr. Dickman told me all," Mercy said with her usual aplomb well in place.

There was nothing like a superior lady's maid, Jocelyn reflected as she eased onto the seat before her dressing table. Mercy deftly arranged Jocelyn's long, dark hair into a becoming chignon, twining a strand of pearls through the tresses with her usual skill.

When Jocelyn rose to leave for the library, she saw in the looking glass a calm, collected young woman garbed in a simple deep green taffeta gown trimmed with knots of matching riband and seed pearls. Perhaps she did not reveal the *décolletage* that Suzanne Fornier displayed, but Jocelyn thought her own gown quite elegant and respectable. Besides, she was not in competition with that young woman, she reminded herself.

"Be careful, Mercy," Jocelyn urged before she left the sitting room. "Do not take any chances."

"Mr. Dickman said as how you did. I can do no less."

"At least remain inside," Jocelyn said with resignation. Mercy was a treasure, but at times her devotion became a trifle wearing.

There were several other women about to descend to the main floor. Jocelyn joined them. She said little, replying with circumspect vagueness to their queries regarding her absence that afternoon.

"Lord Leigh seemed most distracted," a Miss Murray said with a coy glance at Jocelyn. "I fear Miss Fornier was not best pleased with his lack of attention whilst they played at bowls."

"Gentlemen have their little spells of preoccupation," Mrs.

Murray said with a curious glance at Jocelyn. "I believe you are a cousin to Lady Valletort, Lady Jocelyn?"

"Indeed, I am. It is most gracious of Lora to wish me to be the baby's godmother." Jocelyn offered this information with the hope of luring them to another topic.

"Really? A maiden lady for a godmother? How unusual. And who are to be the godfathers?"

Jocelyn well knew that a boy had but one godmother but was given two godfathers, whereas a girl had the opposite. She didn't know who had been chosen as godfathers, however.

"You shall have to ask my cousin regarding that, I fear. I do not know."

Miss Murray giggled and was only silenced by a look from her mother.

At the door to the library, Jocelyn murmured something about joining them later and left the others, closing the door firmly behind her lest the inquisitive Miss Murray decide to follow.

"You look beautiful, but slightly harried, *ma chérie*," Peter said. He stood by the fireplace, garbed in a dark blue superfine coat over biscuit pantaloons that fit to utter perfection, she noted. His waistcoat of cream and blue stripes was in elegant taste.

"Miss Murray was a bit curious, that is all. By the way, Mercy is up and about this evening. She said Dickman sent her a splendid tisane and later exchanged the latest gossip. You told him of my escapade on the ledge?"

"Dickman knows all, my dear. Most servants do. You must be aware that it is impossible to keep anything from a trusted servant or, for that matter, any servant."

"Good grief! Mercy insists that she should examine Suzanne Fornier's room, declaring that I did not know what I was about."

"Well, there are times I would agree with her, but inspecting a room for jewelry is not one of them."

Jocelyn gave him an inquiring look, but was not gifted with any other comment.

Within moments Adrian and Lora joined them, intent upon

covering as much ground as possible in the least amount of time.

"Jocelyn," Adrian said with a firmness that reminded her of her late father, "you are not to take such dreadful chances again. Bluff your way out of the situation, but no daring escapades. I must insist!"

"I shall second that motion," Peter added with a fierce look at Jocelyn that weakened her knees.

"Very well, but I shan't promise not to do what I deem necessary—should the situation arise for a creative solution." She darted a glance at Peter to see if he swallowed her equivocation.

He watched her, but made no comment.

"Well, I intend to take the men out shooting first thing following breakfast tomorrow," Adrian announced while making his way to the door. "And I believe Lora should take the lady guests to Melbourne. That town is sufficiently large that it ought to offer something of interest to them."

"In the meanwhile we shall snoop," Jocelyn said with a wry smile.

"Hunt, my love," Peter corrected gently. He led Jocelyn past Adrian and Lora into the hall and along to the blue drawing room. All the guests were now gathered here, and as Jocelyn looked them over, she murmured to Peter, "I wonder which one it is."

He cast a contemplative look at the assembled and agreed. "Indeed, my love."

"Peter," she murmured, "you must be more discreet. Someone might think you are serious."

He looked down at her, a half smile playing about his lips. "Hmm, that is interesting." But he did not say he would cease teasing her nor whether or not he was serious.

There was a fitful fire burning in the elegant but simple fireplace, just enough to take the chill off the June evening. It was a pleasant room, Jocelyn reflected. She ambled across the rather pretty Turkish carpet to stand near where Mrs. Murray had settled in a rose damask-covered armchair not far from the large window through which one could view some of the fine gardens around the house.

"Are you pleased with the thought of a day spent shopping, ma'am?" Jocelyn inquired with civility. She might be of higher rank, but she had always felt strongly about showing proper respect to one's elders.

"Of course, although it cannot be compared with London."

"No, but it offers a diversion," Jocelyn replied with composure.

"And what do you wish to buy, Lady Jocelyn?" Miss Murray inquired with a giggle.

"We shall have to see what is found," Jocelyn said evasively. She glanced to the door to view the sight of Saxby with grateful eyes. An interrogation by the curious Miss Murray was a thing to be avoided.

"Lady Jocelyn said she is to be godmother to baby Charles," Miss Murray said to Lora. "Who have you chosen for the godfathers?"

Lora met Jocelyn's interested gaze and said in a soft but clear voice, "Lord Leigh and Uncle Maxim have agreed to serve in that capacity."

"Mama said it is most unusual to have an unmarried lady as godmother." There was more than a hint of query in Miss Murray's voice.

"Well, we shan't worry about that. I intend that Adrian live to a ripe old age, you may be sure," Lora answered easily, and Jocelyn felt like applauding.

Saxby announced dinner, and Peter appeared at Jocelyn's side at once. "How fortunate I am to partner you again. I am most thankful that Lora saw the sense of a permanent arrangement for her dinner table."

"You mean you put her up to this?" Jocelyn strolled at his side, keeping her distance but remaining close enough to hear what he said with ease.

This evening Jocelyn was more herself and was able to assess each of the dinner guests in turn. Uncle Maxim sat across from her, his mischievous gaze slanting down at Mrs. Murray, offering some witticism that made her blush.

Beyond Mrs. Murray, Henri sat next to Suzanne Fornier.

"I see Miss Fornier recovered from her headache. I wonder what manner of tisane cured it?" Jocelyn turned her head to study Peter, who seemed oblivious to the dark looks sent his way by the beautiful Suzanne. "I believe you have offended the lady, Lord Leigh," Jocelyn murmured under cover of a hastily applied napkin to her mouth.

"Umm." He seemed not the least affected by the observation. "I shall guard my back in that event."

"You still believe it to be one of the family?"

"Well, it isn't likely to be Miss Murray or her patient mother."

Jocelyn had to admit that he had a point there. Neither of the women looked the sort to be thieves. "On the other hand," she observed, "do we know what would mark a thief?"

"I wonder if any of Adrian's dogs are good at tracking by scent?"

"Oh, excellent notion, my lord." Jocelyn looked at her cousin's husband, thinking it likely he would have such a dog. "There is to be shooting tomorrow, he may wish to take the animal with him, though."

"I'll ask him about it later. And for goodness sake, do stop my lording me to death. We are long past that, Jocelyn. Would you not agree?" He placed his soupspoon down, turning to cast her a look she found difficult to judge.

"As to that, we must work together in some degree of closeness for the next few days. I agreed I would call you by your Christian name when we are alone. We are not alone now, however."

Her attention was demanded at that moment by the gentleman at her other side, Pierre.

"Indeed, the country hereabouts is quite fine this time of year, is it not?" he said politely.

Happy he was not in one of his more dour moods, Jocelyn agreed, pursuing this train of thought throughout the next course until she had exhausted her knowledge of gardening, the scenery to be viewed nearby the castle, and the great houses in the vicinity.

"Curzon has built a sumptuous place not too far north of here from all I've heard. Have you seen it?"

Jocelyn had viewed the elegant mansion the year before and was happy to elucidate about that visit, which got her through the remainder of the course.

When it came time to change the direction of her conversation, she turned to Peter with marked relief.

"Enough to make you wish you were alone?" Peter murmured as he accepted a helping of excellent-looking trout.

"It is most fortunate that I found him interested in Kedleston Hall, Lord Curzon's country home."

"Interesting. You have been to Chatsworth?"

"Indeed, I went with Margaret Mercer Elphinstone one year ago. Simply because I was in the country does not mean that I was totally out of Society," Jocelyn said sweetly.

"Miss Elphinstone found time to escape the Princess Charlotte? I am amazed," Peter commented, aware as all were of the close connection between the two. Margaret had been a confidant of Charlotte's for years, and it was well-known how Charlotte was apt to demand her company on a mere whim.

"The princess is insecure, I think. She finds Miss Elphinstone of great comfort. Have you given any more thought to how we are to proceed on the morrow? Even if Adrian whisks the gentlemen away and Lora takes the women off shopping, that still leaves the servants in the house."

"I suggested that all personal servants be given leave to go to Melbourne as well. Something about possibly being needed or the like." Peter looked at her as though he expected some sort of reply.

Jocelyn placed her fork and knife on her plate, studying the remains of her fish and potatoes with a supposedly fascinated eye. "Excellent. With only the other servants around, we ought to be able to skim through a goodly number of rooms."

"Not skim, my dear. Inspect with great care."

"Indeed." She looked at where his hand rested lightly next to hers, finding that his mere proximity had the power to disturb her.

The remainder of the meal continued course after course, Jocelyn finding the conversation with Pierre rather heavy-going. However, he appeared to mean well and sought to keep the discussion on general topics he thought might be of interest to her.

The armless chairs were comfortable, being of a recent design and added to the room when Lora took the reins of running the household. Yet Jocelyn was not sorry when Lora rose to signal the time had come for the women to retire from the room.

"Enjoy your port," Jocelyn whispered to Peter as she rose from her chair, gloves dangling from her hand.

"I shall see you soon enough," Peter replied with a warm look.

The richly paneled walls beautifully reflected the candlelight, especially now the women were departing to leave the men at the table. The covers had been removed, and Saxby was bringing in the port and other wines that might be desired. Jocelyn cast one last admiring look at the pretty little arrangements of spring flowers Lora had contrived for the table, then followed her from the room.

"Well, Lady Jocelyn," Suzanne Fornier said, bustling up to Jocelyn's side while they entered the elegant saloon at the far end of the main floor, "what do you plan to do tomorrow? I fancy you would like a new bonnet to replace the one ruined by rain the day you arrived? How gallant of Lord Leigh to go to your rescue."

"A new bonnet?" Jocelyn repeated, thinking of the amazing number of bonnets she had seen in Suzanne's room. "Indeed, I should like a new bonnet above all things. I may wait until I order a new pelisse, though. For you must know that the rain and mud ruined it, too. It was not the easiest of walks, I must confess."

"But to be retrieved by his lordship must have been some compensation," Suzanne persisted.

"As you say," Jocelyn murmured by way of reply, not wishing to discuss the matter with Suzanne much less have her dig more deeply into a past association.

"I trust seeing him again after all these years has not been painful?" Suzanne dared to ask, her gaze falling before Jocelyn's astounded look.

"I cannot think what interest it could possibly have for you, Miss Fornier. Lord Leigh and I have known one another for many years. I was surprised to see him, but not, I believe, pained."

With a whirl of taffeta Jocelyn left Suzanne's side and walked over to stand by the fireplace, where a small coal fire

took any chill from the room. Overhead both the lovely crystal
chandeliers had all dozen candles lit offering pleasant light, together with braces of candles here and there about the room.
Miss Murray and a young matron, Mrs. Hastings, had seated
themselves at the pianoforte and commenced to play a pretty
duet.

"Your expression could curdle cream," Lora said quietly as
she joined Jocelyn by the fireplace.

"Small wonder. She is beyond belief. I cannot like Miss
Fornier. She is *most* coming. The nerve of her to ask me if I
found it painful to see Peter after all these years. It is simply not
done, Lora." Jocelyn's voice shook very slightly as she informed her cousin of the conversation. Had she known pain?
Not precisely. But whatever she had felt was not a topic of discussion with that pert young miss.

"She didn't!" Lora whispered, obviously shocked.

A stir at the door brought the gentlemen into the room, and
all conversation picked up in gaiety and manner. While the
women had been somewhat listless before, they were all ani-
mation now.

Jocelyn soon found Peter at her side, staring at the glowing
coals in the fireplace. "Good heavens, girl, what happened?"

"I had not thought it showed now. I am merely vexed with
Miss Fornier, that is all. Her manners are much in need of
mending."

"She offended you?" He cast a frown at the luscious brunette
who hung on Henri's arm.

"I do not wish to talk about it. Everyone seems to believe I
shall go with the women tomorrow. I expect you are supposed
to go with the men as well. What excuse can we offer?"

"I do not know at the moment. Allow me to think about it,
will you?"

Jocelyn nodded, then turned aside when Mrs. Murray sought
her attention. However, she did not fail to note that Peter sauntered across the room in a roundabout way to reach Suzanne
Fornier's side.

Drawn to the lovely green damask sofa that faced the fireplace, Jocelyn resolutely turned her back to where Suzanne
now flirted with Peter.

"That young woman sadly lacks a mother's guidance," Mrs. Murray said quietly.

Jocelyn was tempted to suggest that Miss Murray could use a lesson in tact as well, but refrained—knowing well it was none of her business. "It must be difficult for Uncle Maxim to show her the proper way to go on."

"Hmm, he would not be my choice as a guardian of a beautiful young woman. I fear he is more interested in his own appetites."

Not about to hazard the topic of the gentleman most kindly termed a roué, Jocelyn merely offered a smile and changed the subject.

While listening to Mrs. Murray natter on about one thing and another in a surprisingly good-natured way, Jocelyn shifted on the sofa until she could see Peter and Suzanne from the corner of her eye, if she chanced to make the effort. Odd, she found she quite trusted him with Suzanne. It wasn't just that he had joked about not leaving him alone with what he called a man-eater. Jocelyn felt that he would never pay her the attentions he had and still foster an interest in another woman.

She trusted him! Perhaps not completely, but nearly. The thought overwhelmed her with its shock. She had hated him all these years, and yet she could now trust him? Her gaze shifted to the pattern of the carpet, tracing the designs with a toe while contemplating this turn of mind.

"Ah, the dear girls have finished playing," Mrs. Murray said, rising from the sofa. "I have enjoyed our chat, Lady Jocelyn. It is agreeable to find a young woman of your position who is not the least high in the instep."

Jocelyn shook herself from her peculiar reverie and uttered thanks, although she had not the slightest idea what the woman had talked on and on about. She had risen out of respect for the older woman and now stood lost in thought.

"You look as though you had stumbled upon something that surprised you," Peter said at her other side.

She turned, then looked back to where Suzanne now flirted with another young gentleman Jocelyn had not met as yet.

"I thought you were back there," she said, confused.

"I get around, my dear. Suzanne Fornier is a transparent creature. I believe she knew my thoughts were elsewhere this afternoon and was not best pleased."

"That has nothing to do with me," Jocelyn pointed out.

"She queried me about our past. I believe I satisfied her curiosity. I don't think she'll bother you again."

"She angered me, but I held my tongue. At least I tried to be polite. I should think we had better search her room again. I do not trust her in the least. Perhaps the you-know-what is in one of her dozen bonnets?"

"She brought a dozen bonnets along? Maxim is indeed generous when he is sailing close to the wind himself. I have it on good authority that he is in dun territory."

"And thus a likely suspect? I should feel sorry for the man Suzanne marries. He will have to have deep pockets."

"I have no doubt but what he will. She would wed no other."

All of which left Jocelyn wondering if Peter had learned something of Miss Fornier's intent. At least Jocelyn was confident it did not include Peter, and that was an amazing comfort to her. What it meant was something else.

Chapter Six

"We have used up two of our days," Jocelyn reminded her accomplice the next morning when he found her at breakfast.

"I looked for you upstairs, and you had gone," he said with an air of complaint.

"So I feared. I wish to eat before the others come down, so I am beforehand in my meal. The men will want to have an early start, I suppose?" Jocelyn glanced from her plate to the man who stood by the excellent spread of food set forth on the sideboard.

Rather than the food, he stared at her. He said nothing, merely frowned, then made a selection from the array set forth. There were a few servants about, otherwise not even their host and hostess were present.

"Well, it is a good thing to . . ." He paused, then continued, "Tell me, are you always thus this early in the morning? Neatly, nay, attractively garbed, hair in place, and disposition as well?" He settled across from her, looking rather appealing with the quizzical expression on his face.

"Well, I did think there might be someone about, but yes, I am one of those who awake and are instantly alert. I am not prone to lounge in bed, and if I did, I feel certain I would spill my chocolate, if you see what I mean."

What he might have said to this was not to be known, for Adrian bustled into the room, a surprised expression crossing his face when he saw the pair at the table. "I vow you take this quite seriously, considering it is not your necklace that has been filched."

Jocelyn glanced at Peter, then said, "Of course, we care. I think it utterly reprehensible that someone might steal such a gem from his host, much less get away with the crime. That is quite beyond the pale."

"We have wondered the best way to avoid going with the others. I thought I could be about with the men, then sort of fade into the stables while they continue on with the shoot, but what about Jocelyn? Is she to hide in her room until they depart?"

"Indeed, although Miss Murray might insist upon finding out why I do not go with them to enjoy the pleasures of shopping. And Miss Fornier believes I *must* want to purchase a new bonnet to replace that one that was ruined by the rain."

"I see what you mean." Adrian selected his food, then joined them. "Stay in your room, and have Mercy answer the door should anyone be so bold as to inquire about your business. Offer no excuses."

"Mercy has enough brass for a duchess," Peter said with a grimace.

Jocelyn concealed a grin by looking down at her plate. "Very well. It is settled. Peter goes to the stables, and I hide in my room until they are gone." She finished her meal with haste, and before any of the ladies had made an appearance, she was settled with a book on her chaise longue.

Mercy, instructed as to the true reason for the retreat of her mistress, stood ready to repel all intruders.

Jocelyn listened to the bustle of the departing guests with a longing to join them. She truly would adore a new bonnet, and she did not shop all that often. Once that necklace was found, she intended to indulge herself. The reason for desiring a more attractive headgear was not admitted, naturally. Her wish to look her best had nothing to do with Peter Leigh!

Suzanne Fornier insisted she be allowed to see Lady Jocelyn. Suspicion could be clearly heard in her demand. That had no effect on Mercy. She was not one whose resolve would melt like an icicle before a fire. The young miss was denied and sent on her way, presumably satisfied that Lady Jocelyn had suffered a setback from her wetting and could not join them.

When the house gained relative silence, she sent Mercy out to make certain all was clear. When the maid returned, Peter was with her. Mercy looked as though she had eaten a sour pickle.

"His lordship is ready to begin the search, my lady."

Peter waved the house plan in the air with a decided manner of one who wants to get down to business at once.

"We shall begin at one end of the house and work our way down the hall to the other end. Mercy will help, as will Dickman. I thought we could have them check the rooms first to make sure no servant is about. Once each room is free, you and I can begin our search."

"I should like Mercy to remain with me," Jocelyn said thoughtfully. "We ought to be able to go faster with an assistant. Besides, she says I may not think of some hiding places known to servants."

"You think that whoever has done this deed would allow his or her servant to be aware of the theft?"

"I think it might be possible," Jocelyn said, considering the beautiful Miss Fornier. She might be gorgeous, that did not mean she had the brains for craftiness.

Within minutes they headed for the east end of the hall, Dickman standing ready to assist in any way he could.

"The Hastings are in the corner room—labeled the yellow room on the plan. You and Mercy take that while Dickman and I do young Tremayne. I believe Lora intends him for Miss Murray. Certainly, he would never do for Suzanne."

"And why not?" Jocelyn demanded, instantly ready to defend poor Mr. Tremayne.

"Money but no title," Peter replied. Dickman returned to assure him that all was ready to examine the belongings in Tremayne's room. Since Tremayne agreeably shared his room with his good friend, Hugh Fordyce, it was unlikely either would prove to be the thief. However, as Jocelyn well knew, it was possible to be in and out of a room in a trice, stashing something away if you didn't want anyone to see it.

Alone, Jocelyn stared at a rather pretty landscape on the wall between the rooms. She turned when Mercy beckoned from the door.

They worked in silence. Jocelyn felt as though she violated Mrs. Hastings privacy by fingering the silks and muslins in the bureau drawers. No matter how often she reminded herself that it was for a worthy cause, indeed an important one, she felt an intruder. It was one thing to search the luscious Suzanne's belongings when she felt in her bones that the girl was guilty. It was quite another to inspect all that Mrs. and Mr. Hastings had brought with them. They seemed an innocuous pair.

The search did offer an insight as to their character.

Mr. Hastings was obviously a cheeseparer. He had brought elegant items of clothing for himself, but his wife possessed few gowns and they were of inferior stuff. Jocelyn exchanged a look with Mercy as she held up a gown obviously made over from another, then continued to search the recesses of the wardrobe.

"Find anything?" Peter said from the door. "I must say, the décor of that room across the way is quite something, all hand-painted Chinese paper on the wall and two elegant walnut beds. Adrian and Lora have done a splendid job of decorating."

Jocelyn looked up from where she knelt before the wardrobe. "Other than some dust missed by the maid, I have found nothing of interest. Certainly the necklace is not here. For that matter, Mrs. Hastings seems to have brought little jewelry with her. Very likely she fears to be robbed while traveling," Jocelyn concluded, thus sparing the niggardly Mr. Hastings any censure.

"Those two chaps travel with only what I would expect. Dickman said they are up to snuff with their garments and other items. Surprisingly neat fellows, as well. The room isn't littered from one end to the other."

"That bespeaks superior servants, I fancy," Jocelyn said, noting that Mercy nodded in agreement.

"Well, it made it easy to search the room."

"I keep wondering if we are overlooking an obvious hiding place," Jocelyn said, rising to her feet to confront Peter with her fear. "I recall seeing that necklace once, and it is not small. It seems to me that it could not be concealed easily if loose. But if it were kept flat, and in a thin box, it might be slipped inside a traveling case or portmanteau." She watched while Mercy peered beneath the large four-poster bed, shaking her head when she arose to signify that she had found nothing. "I must confess that I detest examining the belongings of others. It is horridly intrusive." She gestured to the bureau and wardrobe she and Mercy had inspected.

"Faint heart will not win the day, my dear," Peter said in what she supposed he intended for a rallying manner. It merely depressed her.

"What is next?" she asked as they returned to the hall.

"According to your notation, Pierre and Henri occupy the green room, which is the next on this side. Mrs. and Miss Murray are across the hall in the blue chamber." He gestured to that one while Dickman opened the door to the green room.

"I hope they do not unexpectedly return. You realize that if one of the men decided he had quite enough, there is nothing Adrian could do to prevent him from returning to the house?" Jocelyn said urgently in a near whisper.

A footman appeared at the top of the stairs, and Jocelyn was thankful that both Mercy and Dickman were not in the hall with them. It would look most peculiar if the four stood in seeming consultation.

"Is there something?" Peter said in a manner guaranteed to intimidate the loftiest servant.

"Ah, no, milord. Mr. Valletort, that is, Mr. Pierre, wanted his room aired while he was away."

"Very well."

Jocelyn shot Peter a warning look. Dickman was in that room even now. How would the footman cross to open the window without discovering the valet?

Peter shook his head ever so slightly, and she waited.

The footman entered, and the sound of the window being cranked open was heard. Within minutes the servant returned, begged their pardon—not questioning their standing in the hall in the middle of the morning—then disappeared down the stairs.

"He will report we are about here, and so the others will stay away, I believe," Peter said softly.

Dickman opened the door and smiled a trifle grimly. "That was a near one, sir. I had very little warning. But whilst I hid in the wardrobe, I found something that might interest you."

Peter quickly crossed the hall, followed closely by Jocelyn. Mercy had gone into the blue chamber to begin a look at what the Murrays had brought with them.

"This is empty, but it has the look of a jewel case."

"I am certain I have seen that before," Jocelyn stated. "I would swear that it is the case for the missing necklace! Recall I said it would require a thin, flat box? Here it is." She reached out to touch the box with a tentative finger.

"It certainly looks suspicious. But if the box is here, where is the necklace?" Peter held the dark blue box with care, examining it from all sides. The name of the jeweler who had most likely last cleaned the necklace was in delicate silver script on the top of the box. Inside, it was empty. "This is not the original box. Is it possible that there is another box with the necklace in it?"

Jocelyn leaned against one of the bedposts to consider the matter. "I agree. Then, it must be here. But just to be safe, I shall join Mercy to search the blue chamber across the way. Maiden ladies ought not enter a gentleman's room, even for a worthy purpose."

Peter merely chuckled in a rather nasty way that lingered in her ears as she hurriedly left the green bedroom for the blue chamber across the hall. While she went through the belongings modestly placed in the bureaus and wardrobe, she wondered if it had been Henri or Pierre who had filched that box. And, more importantly, where was the necklace that had been inside?

It did not take them long to complete the inspection of the Murray room. Neither mother nor daughter had brought much jewelry with them. Their garments were of high quality, and Mr. Murray had been most generous to both wife and daughter, unlike the parsimonious Mr. Hastings.

Jocelyn stood uncertainly in the hall, waiting for Peter to join her when she heard the unmistakable sound of someone entering the house and shortly began the walk up the stairway. Wondering who it might be, and not a little worried that it might be a guest come back to interfere with the search, she signaled to

Mercy to retreat to her rooms and sauntered to the top of the stairs. She held a handkerchief to her nose as though prepared to blow it.

"Pierre!" she cried loudly. "What a surprise. Did you tire of the shooting so soon?"

"I thought you were in bed, Lady Jocelyn." He came to a halt at her side. "I am glad to see you up and about."

"Yes, well, I had just decided I might go downstairs for a light nuncheon when I heard you come in the house. Would you join me?" She smiled coyly and invited him with her eyes to join her in a private repast.

"I should rid myself of this dirt," he protested.

"We would be alone. Your hunting clothes do not offend me," she declared stoutly, as though accustomed to having a gentleman join her while still in his hunting garb. To be sure, he did not reek of the kill, nor were his garments soiled. They must have walked, for she could not detect the scent of the stables about him.

They had begun their descent when a door slammed shut. Jocelyn paused, a frown wrinkling her brow. She devoutly hoped it was Peter and that he intended to join them. She had no wish to fend off the unwanted attentions Pierre looked to offer. It had been stupid of her to flirt with him, but she had not been thinking clearly.

"Ah, Valletort! Good to see you, sir. Had enough of the shooting for a day?" Peter sauntered down the stairs to where Jocelyn stood just one step above Pierre.

Pierre swiftly concealed a look of anger with a bland regard. Had Jocelyn not been quick, she might never have known how annoyed he was.

"I thought the sun a trifle hot, and the notion of a cooling drink on the terrace seemed most agreeable."

Jocelyn smiled widely and nodded. "I vow, it does sound appealing. Shall we all venture forth to the terrace? I feel certain that Saxby can conjure up not only a cooling beverage but a light repast as well."

Peter watched Jocelyn skim down the stairs, then disappear along the hall toward the dining room. He was thankful she had spoken so loudly, but sorry to leave off investigating that room so soon. He and Dickman had just begun to dig. By now Dickman should have tidied the room and whisked himself out. What a blessing that his own room was nearby!

"You elected not to join in the shooting this morning?" Pierre inquired suspiciously.

Peter thought it odd that the fellow should be so distrustful. On the other hand, Jocelyn was here as was the purloined necklace. Perhaps Pierre had good reason to be wary.

Jocelyn had flirted with the man, something that had annoyed Peter even if he had to applaud her quick thinking. But surely there must have been a way to detain him, lure him to the main floor without flirting? Yet Peter didn't think she was the slightest bit interested in the man. It was his own sense of *amour propre* that objected.

"Lady Jocelyn is *sans pareil,* is she not?" Pierre said admiringly as they strolled forth to the terrace.

"Without a doubt," Peter agreed warmly. She was also possessed of an income that would keep a family in style, not to mention pay any gaming debts that had accumulated.

It was a beautiful June day, one of those rare times when the scent of roses drifted across the gardens, the clouds in the sky did not threaten rain, and the breeze was but moderate.

"Come," Jocelyn invited. "I am feeling so much better, I almost wish I had gone with the other women to town. However, if I had . . ." She smiled, dimples appearing in one cheek. Peter hadn't noticed that before and found it entrancing.

There was ale and chilled lemonade, plates of sandwiches, salads and sliced beef, a bowl of fruit, and to one side an apple torte.

"I believe the cook has outdone herself," Jocelyn said gaily. She handed plates to the others, then helped herself to a couple of sandwiches, some salad, hothouse strawberries, with a promise that she would sample the torte later. It had been made of dried apples, obviously, but it looked appetizing nonetheless.

She found a chair that was turned away from the sun and sank onto it with what she hoped was sufficient grace.

Conversation was general, as might be expected with people who did not know one another well. Jocelyn wondered what would have happened had she been alone with Peter. Perhaps it was a good thing that Pierre had returned to the house. It had likely prevented a difficult situation. Not but what there were servants in the house. That did not make a difference when it came to the problem of compromise, she suspected.

She had about finished her slice of apple torte when the sound of a carriage could be heard. She looked to Peter Leigh first, then at Pierre Valletort.

"More guests?" she wondered aloud.

They sat, chatting aimlessly, all the while wondering just who Saxby would usher out to the terrace to join them.

"Ah, my friends," Suzanne Fornier exclaimed as she drifted out from the house, wearing a froth of muslin and lace with a delicate parasol in hand, a superb bonnet perched on her dark curls. "I am so pleased to see Lady Jocelyn from bed and in the sunshine. You are feeling more the thing!" She glanced at Pierre, saying nothing to him. Rather, she turned to the remaining gentleman and smiled, gliding forward to extend her hand in fulsome greeting. "Lord Leigh, you are returned as well?"

"As you see," Peter began, only to be halted by Pierre's interruption.

"Chap never left. Although why, I do not know. You never did say." Pierre shot a hostile look at the man he apparently deemed a rival for either of the women on the terrace.

"Well," Suzanne declared as she sauntered over to inspect the table laden with the inviting food, "I was not the least surprised to see Pierre. He loathes walking, and when I learned the men were to be on foot, I surmised he would much prefer to lounge on the terrace. And I was right!"

Peter said nothing for a moment, exchanging a look with Jocelyn. She wondered how he would extricate himself from this spot. She need not have worried. He appeared adept at anything.

"Some paperwork that Adrian wanted me to look at. He seemed to think that I'd had a similar situation on my estate, and that I might have a solution." Peter took a long pull at his glass of ale, looking as though he had done nothing more than peruse a few papers since arising.

"And did you?" Suzanne said with a lilt, peering at him from beneath her new and elegant bonnet with a fetching smile.

"I think the solution to his problem is at hand," Peter replied somewhat enigmatically.

"He is so discreet!" Suzanne cried with delight in her voice. "I do admire a discreet gentleman."

Jocelyn could not help it, the thought flashed in her mind that the luscious Suzanne would want a man who was discreet were she to engage in the flirtation she invited.

Suzanne took a plate over to sit close to Peter. She placed the parasol on the stone below her chair, then fluttered her lashes at Peter with coy allure. "I could not carry the lemonade, *chéri*. Would you be so kind?"

"Allow me, cousin," Pierre said instantly. He was on his feet and pouring lemonade before Peter had a chance to say a word.

Jocelyn thought Suzanne looked delighted at this clash between two gentlemen over her. Never mind that Peter hadn't said a thing. No doubt that young miss imagined all men at her feet. Trouble was, they were. Except, Jocelyn fancied that Peter was immune. What was it he had said? That he wanted Jocelyn to keep that man-eater away from him? Well, she would certainly try her best.

"Peter, you promised to show me the roses you sent to Adrian last year—you know, the red ones with such fragrance?" She rose, set her empty plate on the table, then extended an inviting hand to the man whose gaze twinkled at her a brief moment.

"Indeed, I did. I am dismayed to think I forgot it even for an instant. Forgive me, Lady Jocelyn?" He crossed to her side in a few steps, and before she knew it they were far down the lawn, coming up on the rose beds that Lora had written about in her letters.

"I think we got out of that fairly well," he said quietly with a glance behind them at the couple on the terrace who now appeared to be arguing.

"You looked as though you wanted rescuing. It was the least I could do." Jocelyn accepted his proffered arm and strolled at his side, admiring the roses. "Did you perchance send rosebushes to Adrian? I have no idea if you raise roses on your country estate or not."

"You would like my home, I think. My grandmother kept it well, insisting rooms be decorated, nothing was allowed to

decay. She was a curious old lady, wanted the latest of everything. The décor is most up-to-date! She didn't dabble much in
gardening, but kept to the old partierre style. There are a number of roses, however. I couldn't say if Adrian has the like or
not. I did not send him any, but thank you for saying I had."

"Well, they are not to know, unless Adrian says something of
the matter. I cannot think he will talk of roses to either Pierre or
Suzanne." Jocelyn paused to study a deep red rose nearing the
end of its bloom. The rich scent was enticing, a perfume worthy of a queen.

"Indeed. Especially to Suzanne Fornier. A man scarcely
thinks of gardening with her around."

Jocelyn looked up to see a teasing light in Peter's eyes, and
smiled as she supposed he intended her to do.

"What a pity. I fancy she misses a great deal in life."

Peter gave a shout of laughter, but wouldn't explain why
when Jocelyn nudged him in the ribs.

"So," he said shortly once he had sobered, "how are we to get
back into Pierre's room to hunt for the necklace?"

"I refuse to volunteer as a lure," Jocelyn said lightly, but with
meaning. "There is only so much I will do to obtain that necklace. If needs be, we can tell Adrian what you found and let him
handle it. After all, Pierre is his relative," she said reasonably.

"True, but I hate to quit now. There is something most satis-
fying about completing a task you have set out to do."

He met her inquiring look with an expression she couldn't
begin to understand. She was not about to ask him, either. There
were times when he gazed at her with the strangest look on his
face. He offered no clue to his thoughts, but she would have
given a great deal to know what went on in his mind.

It was impossible to hate him anymore. They had been tossed
together by fate—and her scheming cousin. And, Jocelyn concluded, it was more than time she release those memories of a
much younger and somewhat foolish girl.

In the distance she could see the men returning from their
shoot. The beaters walked behind, carrying bags and extra
guns. The dogs trotted at their sides. Before them the men ambled, arms waving while talking sixteen to the dozen, it appeared.

"I suppose they had a successful day," Jocelyn murmured. "What will Adrian do tomorrow to entice them from the property?"

"You are willing to continue?"

"Well, I fancy it will seem strange if we are absent from all the entertainments. Can both of us stay here?"

"I would as soon not see you go off with Pierre or Henri."

"Not Mr. Tremayne or Mr. Fordyce?" she teased.

"Leave them to Miss Murray and Miss Osmond, although if that young lady has a word to say for herself, I would be very much surprised."

"Yes, she could have passed for a statue last evening. Perhaps I ought to make an attempt to draw her out? I remember how painful it was at that age when I was around witty, older people. I dared not own to an opinion!"

"Truly? I never would have suspected. You always seemed so cool and assured. I suppose that is why I approached you as I did." He kicked at a clump of dirt, sending it into the depression of a rose bed.

Jocelyn didn't know how to reply to that statement. It seemed as though he had viewed her in a most unlikely manner, one far from reality!

A fluttering of color appeared on the terrace. "Look, the ladies have returned from town. It would seem they are in a good mood. I wonder what excuse Suzanne gave to return early. She must have made it crowded for a few of them, taking a carriage for herself."

"I doubt she considers anyone else," Peter said with a look at the colorful grouping. Suzanne remained, standing close to Pierre and not talking, unless her eyes failed her.

Jocelyn suggested they ought to return to the terrace, and it seemed to her that Peter agreed with reluctance. To tell the truth, she wasn't too pleased to go back, either.

"I trust you are feeling more the thing now?" Lora asked brightly when they joined the group.

"My daughter's old nurse always advocated fresh air and sunshine for a summer ailment," Mrs. Osmond declared, nudging her silent daughter toward the equally speechless Mr.

Fordyce. "It has stood Alisha in good stead, for she is ever in good health."

It was impossible to say anything to that as Miss Osmond looked as though she would willingly sink into the ground.

Peter left Jocelyn on her own to admire the bonnet Lora had thoughtfully bought for her delight. He crossed to stand by Adrian, raising his brows to alert his friend that something of significance had occurred while they were gone.

"There is something in those papers you asked me to check that I wish to show you," Peter said casually.

Adrian agreed at once, excused them from the others, and drew Peter down to the vastness of the library. "Well? What did you find?"

"Not the necklace. But we did find the box in which it had been stored. Jocelyn recognized it. It means that the necklace *must* be around here, and I suspect it is in Pierre's room. He returned before we could dig it out."

"Bad luck," Adrian said with a frown. "I hate to accuse my cousin until I am certain he is guilty."

"If you can get them away from the house tomorrow, perhaps I will have a better chance. Jocelyn will have to go along, or it will be too suspicious."

"I agree. So be it," Adrian replied with finality. "I do not look forward to what tomorrow will bring."

Chapter Seven

Dinner proved to be a festive event. The gentlemen were full of the day's shoot and how well all had gone, the number of birds bagged and the splendid weather. Over roast pheasant and stewed partridge they compared their shots, how many they had hit on the wing and the plentitude of game to be found on Lord Valletort's acreage.

The women exclaimed over the delicious birds, and expressed satisfaction at the excursion into town. And any number of men wondered what their sport had cost them, with perhaps the exception of Mr. Hastings. Since he had not given his wife more than a few shillings to spend, he had no worry that he had been impoverished.

Lora had been most pleased with the news of the found case, even if the necklace had not been inside. She had smiled at Jocelyn when offering the truly gorgeous bonnet with a fetching green bow to one side.

"This is to recompense you for having to remain at home. I trust that tomorrow you will be able to join us?"

Knowing that she would not willingly return to examine Pierre's room, Jocelyn was able to agree, albeit reluctantly.

She consumed her partridge and pheasant with muted pleasure. When the syllabub was served, she ate with little appreciation of the fine flavor. Tomorrow would be another tedious day, and she had known far too many of those. The knowledge that it would be dull because Peter would not be with her was instantly repressed.

"Circulate among the gentlemen this evening, Jocelyn,"

Peter said in an undertone when Jocelyn rose to leave the dinner table following the sumptuous meal.

Thinking she would be glad for a chance to move about for any reason, Jocelyn murmured her acquiescence.

Miss Alisha Osmond joined Jocelyn on the walk to the saloon, where the ladies were to await the gentlemen. Then Miss Cordelia Murray slipped up next to them.

"We are the only unmarried women here," simpered Miss Murray, with a superior glance at the tongue-tied Miss Osmond.

"How fortunate we are, in that event," Jocelyn said smoothly. "Considering that Mr. Tremayne and Mr. Fordyce are single gentlemen, not to mention Pierre and Henri Valletort as well. Even Uncle Maxim is a happy bachelor." Then she added, "You forget Suzanne Fornier, my dear. She is still unmarried, and I doubt she will remain a spinster for long. She is quite beautiful," Jocelyn concluded with a pang. No matter how Peter might hover over her, she could not help but realize that she was only assisting him with the recovery of the necklace. And Suzanne at her flirtatious best was incredible to behold. Never mind that Peter had begged Jocelyn to keep Suzanne at bay. Like a woman, a man was quite able and often willing to change his mind.

Lora fluttered over to join them once they entered the lovely saloon. "I hope you will like my surprise. I engaged a group of musicians to play for us this evening."

"For dancing? Oh, I quite adore a ball," Miss Murray squealed. "We will be at least ten couples, and that is surely enough for a ball? I hope the gentlemen do not linger over their port this evening!"

"I trust Lord Valletort will see they do not," Jocelyn said, exchanging a look with Lora above the fluffy blond head belonging to Cordelia Murray.

It was as Jocelyn said; very shortly the gentlemen began to saunter into the room. Lora led them all to a set of doors that, when opened, revealed the lovely and seldom used ballroom.

The soft rose walls had festoons of gold riband swagged from sconce to sconce, with streamers hanging simply at each sconce. Between sconces hung unpretentious but simply ele-

gant gilt-framed looking glasses. The several crystal chandeliers were lit, the many candles lending the room a golden,
rose-tinted hue—most flattering to the women, Jocelyn
thought. Even Mrs. Whyte's many wrinkles seemed to disappear.

The musicians played a sparkling minuet from behind the
pots of palms brought from the conservatory for the occasion.

"This must be why we saw so little of the servants today," Jocelyn remarked to Peter when she had slipped away from the
two younger girls.

"Clever of Lora to think of such an excellent diversion," he
said with an appreciative look at Jocelyn, who was attired in a
becoming rose and cream sarcenet gown.

She fingered with unfeigned eagerness the diamond necklace
that matched the simple earrings she wore. "I do love to dance."
She did not add how seldom it was she enjoyed this pursuit. "I
believe all shall enjoy it excessively. I feel guilty that I did not
help."

"I suppose you would ask your favored guest to assist you if
you held a ball?"

"Of course not," Jocelyn responded slowly. "I see what you
mean." Lora had wanted Jocelyn to be at ease and most likely
wanted to show her own skills as a hostess. "Most thoughtful of
her."

"May I suggest you flirt with the other single men, and learn
what you can from them? Discreetly, of course."

"What? You do not wish me to make a cake of myself over
Hugh Fordyce?" She glanced at the shy young man who
seemed to turn brick-red if a girl so much as looked at him.
"Well, I shall begin with him. Be warned, sirrah, I intend to
meddle."

Before Peter might stop her, Jocelyn glided away from him,
coming to a halt before the aforesaid Hugh.

"I believe a country-dance is a most delightful occasion, is it
not, sir?" Jocelyn thought he stammered an agreement, but she
wasn't positive.

"Although, I do feel sorry for poor Miss Osmond. She is so
very shy, you know. Dear girl is so sweet, yet when confronted

with a gentleman of the *ton,* she seems terrified to open her mouth. Can you imagine?"

Since Mr. Fordyce felt precisely the same, he was able to agree—this time to be heard. "Poor girl."

"I do wish some kindly gentleman would take pity on her. If only you might assure her that she need not be afraid of you."

"Me?" sputtered the amazed Mr. Fordyce. "I did naught to her! I swear it."

"Well, of course you did nothing to her, poor girl. Most gentlemen turn to someone like Miss Fornier rather than a shy violet like Miss Osmond. She is a pretty little thing, I think."

"Do you think she might dance with me?" Mr. Fordyce mumbled clearly enough for Jocelyn to understand him.

"Why do I not devise her assent? I shall think of something, you may be sure." Leaving him, Jocelyn sidled up to Alisha Osmond. "Is this not a lovely scheme? The room looks so pretty." All she received for her efforts was a look of misery from the chestnut-haired girl.

"Alas, poor Mr. Fordyce. Such a pity *he* is so shy. I believe he needs a kindly lady to put him at ease. I was wondering if you might help him? I sense in you a woman of compassion, one who would be willing to help a gentleman so afflicted."

Miss Osmond was so astounded to be petitioned for help that she was quite overcome and said in a heartfelt voice, "I know what he must suffer. Indeed, I sympathize. Would you . . . ?" she asked Jocelyn, unable to give speech to her request.

"Of course," Jocelyn said, guiding the girl along with her to where Mr. Fordyce stood in silence not far away, looking quite as miserable as it was possible. "Miss Osmond, may I present Mr. Fordyce as an agreeable partner?"

The two young people exchanged shy looks, then with a fortifying breath, Alisha Osmond commented on the weather and wondered if Mr. Fordyce had enjoyed the walk in the woods. He smiled with encouragement at her efforts.

"That was most kind of you, Lady Jocelyn," Uncle Maxim said when Jocelyn had retreated some distance.

"I had not thought anyone noticed what I was about, but I do think they are definitely a pair."

"And who would you pair me with, my busy go-between?" he said with twinkling gallantry.

"Mrs. Murray is keeping an eye on her vivacious lamb, while Mrs. Osmond sits staring at dear Alisha with an astounded expression on her face. Perhaps you had best divert the lady?"

"Meddling, my dear? This is no more than a party to celebrate the birth of the heir-to-be, not a matchmaking mart."

He smiled, but Jocelyn felt there to be an irony in his voice she did not understand. She frowned, looking at him in confusion. "Every ball and assembly is an occasion for encouragement of an interest, perhaps particular attentions, sir."

"There is a regrettable undercurrent to this one. It ends the hopes for Henri. He was the heir apparent before the infant Charles came on the scene." Maxim Valletort gave Jocelyn a narrow look. "You did not know this?"

She looked off to where couples now assembled for a dance, taking note that Miss Osmond and Mr. Fordyce were deep in conversation. "No, I had no idea. I fancy that alters his prospects some?"

"He is but a year or two younger than Adrian, but one never knows about the future. Anything can happen."

Jocelyn felt a chill sweep over her, and she drew her shawl about her shoulders for warmth. "I pray that Charles will be a healthy little boy and grow up to emulate his worthy father. I am very fond of my cousin Lora, her husband, and her son."

"I trust your kind nature extends to the Valletort family as well?" This time he was most definitely eyeing her with a predatory look.

Jocelyn darted a glance to where Suzanne Fornier flirted quite blatantly with Peter and Adam Tremayne. "You are an interesting family, to be sure."

"Suzanne is trying her wings," Uncle Maxim said complacently.

"I believe she does very well, if she is a novice," Jocelyn replied politely, while thinking that if Suzanne was no novice, she was born a coquette.

"I understand Lora intends to display the family necklace at the costume ball. Is that so?"

Jocelyn was startled to hear him speak of the thing that had so occupied her thoughts since shortly after her arrival. "I believe that is her plan. Do you not approve? It has been some time since I saw it, but I thought the necklace quite lovely."

"Lovely? My dear Lady Jocelyn, it is magnificent! I do not believe either Lora or Adrian properly appreciates the family heirloom," he grumbled. "To wear it for a mere costume ball is an insult. That necklace is worthy of a queen at the very least." He darted a frowning look at Lora, who sparkled up at her husband in the turn of the dance.

"I believe it now belongs to Adrian, however. Surely he may do with it as he wishes?" Jocelyn felt compelled to point out.

"Bah," Maxim said in disgust. "I would treasure it properly were it mine. You would grace that necklace nicely, Lady Jocelyn. You are a lady born and bred, not some upstart." He smiled at Jocelyn, the smile of one who would flirt and beguile a lady to his arms.

"You forget yourself, sirrah. Lora may have been merely the daughter of a viscount, but she is a lady through and through, besides being a favorite cousin of mine. Excuse me, please."

Jocelyn turned and walked rapidly away, concealing her ire as best she could. In such a small group it was imperative she not reveal her annoyance to mar the harmony of the party.

"Is that smoke I see seeping from your ears, Jocelyn?" Peter asked.

"How did you get here, Lord Leigh? The last time I looked, you were fawning over Suzanne." Jocelyn stopped by one of the palms to survey Peter Leigh. She could sense her cheeks were flushed with high color following the exchange with Uncle Maxim. It was a wonder she hadn't slapped his face!

"And you have been arguing with Uncle Maxim. May I ask why? It is unlike you to come to verbal sparring with a gentleman, particularly at an evening party like this."

"Excuse me, I have been sorely tried." She examined the fronds of the palm at her side, trying to calm her breathing and not succeeding very well.

"Uncle Maxim? The sly old dog. He flirted with you?"

"You need not sound so astounded," Jocelyn snapped. "I am not quite past praying for, my lord."

"It is just . . . Uncle Maxim?"

"He finds Lora not worthy of wearing the necklace, if you can believe that. Once Adrian made her his wife, she was immediately deserving of the honors due to a countess. She is the daughter of a viscount and not an upstart, as he said."

"Maxim Valletort talked about *the* necklace? What else did he say? Think, Jocelyn," Peter said urgently.

"He said *he* would fully appreciate the necklace's beauty. He also mentioned that Henri had been Adrian's heir apparent before Charles was born. So it would seem that Henri has little joy at this birth!"

"I had forgotten that bit about Henri," Peter mused. "What else did Uncle Maxim say?"

"Well, it was not so much as said as implicated," Jocelyn hedged.

"Come, woman, before I shake it out of you," Peter said with more than a trace of impatience.

"He implied that if he had the necklace, I would make an acceptable woman to display it. My rank, you see."

"I am astonished, I must say. I'd not thought that of Maxim. He did not actually seek your cooperation in obtaining the necklace, did he?"

"What? He made an overture to seduction, nothing beyond that, but that was quite sufficient, I believe," Jocelyn said with a huff.

"Poor Jocelyn, to be opportuned by an elderly roué." Peter took her arm. "Let us join the Hastings for the next set."

"I do not wish to dance, my lord," Jocelyn whispered ferociously.

"Indeed, splendid weather we are having. Would you not agree, Mrs. Hastings?"

The meek Mrs. Hastings in a plum sarcenet gown that had seen several seasons allowed as how it was most splendid. She looked gratified to have the elegant Lady Jocelyn as one of her set, offering a quiet smile when they exchanged looks.

Any irritation Jocelyn had felt melted at the sight of Mrs. Hastings, bravely wearing her elderly gown, offering a bit of friendship. Jocelyn returned a smile of muted brilliance.

She intercepted a look between Suzanne and Peter and could not interpret what it might mean—anything and nothing, in her estimation. The evening was coming to have all the appeal of a nightmare. But at least it would appear that her effort on behalf of Miss Osmond was bearing fruit. She certainly could not be counted as animated, but she conducted a demure conversation with Mr. Fordyce with pleasant amiability.

"I think you may have been successful there," Peter observed when they chanced to stand beside one another during the pattern of the dance.

"Does everyone believe I have been dabbling at matchmaking, sir?" Jocelyn said with slight exasperation.

"No. I doubt anyone—with the possible exception of Uncle Maxim—paid you the slightest attention. I always know where you are and what you are doing when we are in the same room, my dear girl."

"Remarkable," Jocelyn said with wide eyes before stepping off again to circle with Mr. Hastings. She had time to mull over the implications of this remark during the more complicated steps of the pattern.

"I can hear you thinking," Peter said when the dance concluded and he led her off to where a punch bowl reigned supreme over a table laden with cakes and pastries.

"Am I so transparent, then?" Jocelyn asked absently.

She would have to confess that she could not understand Peter Leigh. Years ago she thought she had. He had been wretchedly poor, yet handsome, winning more than warm glances from Jocelyn. Then her elder brother had pointed out to her that as a husband Peter would control what fortune his wife possessed and it was possible he might wish to marry an heiress for that reason. That she might be courted because of her wealth and rank had occurred to Jocelyn. That the man might be Sir Peter Leigh broke her heart.

She had refused his offer of marriage with a curtness he had not merited. Yet she knew that if she'd softened at all, she would break down in tears and her pride forbade that.

"You are far away from me, Jocelyn," Peter said quietly. "Where have you gone that I may not travel?"

"The past," she replied without thinking.

"I go there often myself," he mused, before setting his punch glass on the table and leading Jocelyn from the room to the terrace now lit with lanterns.

"A romantic setting for a little romance, I should think." They walked to the edge of the terrace from where they could inhale the scent drifting from the rose garden. "Indeed, most appropriate."

Not bothering to explain this remark, he took her unresisting hand to lead her down the steps, only to stroll on the grass.

"My slippers shall be ruined," Jocelyn observed without concern.

"You can buy new ones. So can I now. What were you thinking about that made you look so sad, my dear?" Peter halted, turning to face her. No moon blessed the garden. There was but faint starlight and the glimmer of the distant lanterns to offer illumination. Jocelyn could make out very little of Peter's face, only the shape, and the shadows from which his eyes undoubtedly watched her.

"I do not believe it is a good thing to rake over dead coals," Jocelyn said with an air of resignation.

"But are they so dead?" Peter whispered before taking her into his arms in a gentle embrace that was all a part of the rose-scented air and the still night.

She yielded with grace and was rewarded with a kiss to stir her soul and warm her memory on cold nights to come. She would never understand how such a gentle kiss came to have such a passionate conclusion. The intensity of that so gentle embrace shook her to her fingertips and toes.

"I should say that the coals are not dead at all, merely coated with ash. They need but to be fanned a bit to glow with the fire they once knew."

Jocelyn heard the trace of a tremor in his voice and knew he was not unaffected by their kiss, that gentle embrace.

Laughter coming from the direction of the terrace prevented her reply to his remark.

"We had best return before we are missed," Jocelyn said quietly.

"Allow me to pluck a rose for you—a red one that will likely clash with your lovely pink and cream gown, but is a testimony of my affections. It will also still any question of what we have been doing on our stroll, will it not?" Peter broke off one of the red roses that Jocelyn had admired before. He handed it to her, then turned back, guiding her up the steps into the soft light from the lanterns.

Jocelyn studied the rose he had given her. Was it truly a token of affection as he had so lightly claimed? Or was it more a ruse to prevent any unwanted conclusions? Was he so wealthy now that he feared being compromised, even by one such as her? What irony, if that be so. Her reflections were shattered by the approach of Adrian's uncle.

"Lady Jocelyn," Uncle Maxim exclaimed, "had I known you wished a stroll in the garden, I would have sought a lantern. It is difficult to see in the dark," he said with unkindly laughter.

"There are times when starlight and distant lanterns are sufficient, sir." Jocelyn turned to Peter and dipped a curtsy, hoping she was as graceful as she wished. "I thank you for your gift, sir. I shall carry its fragrance with me the remainder of the evening." With that, she walked swiftly into the ballroom.

Lora beckoned to her, and Jocelyn was thankful to be swept into another's concerns.

"A rose?" Lora inquired when she saw the splash of red held in a white-gloved hand.

"Peter plucked it for me. I trust you do not mind—there are so many out there. The fragrance is wonderful."

"Not in the least," Lora said.

Jocelyn endured the searching stare from her cousin. "May I be of help?"

"Oh, yes. Can you maneuver Suzanne away from poor Mr. Tremayne? I should like him to dance with Cordelia Murray, and she has had to endure one snub after another from my husband's gorgeous cousin. I cannot think why she had to be invited. I hadn't wanted her to come, for there is always trouble when she is around, one way or another." Lora gave a stricken look at Jocelyn. "Forget I said that, please. What I feel toward Suzanne ought not be said, even to my dearest cousin."

"Never mind, dear. I agree with you, and you may forget I said that as well. I shall sally forth to do battle. Perhaps Suzanne would wish to take a cup of punch to the terrace?" Jocelyn walked purposefully around the edge of the room, nodding to Lady Thynne and smiling at Mrs. Hastings, the poor dear. Then the thought occurred to her that Mrs. Hastings might make wonderful use of a valuable necklace, prying the gems to sell one by one. For anyone so circumscribed in her situation, it would be temptation beyond belief.

With another glance at the now suspicious Mrs. Hastings, Jocelyn approached the invincible Miss Fornier. Tucking the red rose into the low neckline of her gown, Jocelyn smiled at Suzanne. "It is a glorious evening out. Would you not like a cup of punch on the terrace? I fancy Mr. Tremayne has been wishing to dance with Miss Murray this age. Henri looks as though he might enjoy a bit of fresh air. We are truly blessed with a lovely evening. It will probably rain by late tomorrow."

Jocelyn had never been so blunt in her maneuvering in her life. It was amazing what she would do to please her dear cousin.

Suzanne's gaze darted to the rose now tucked deeply into Jocelyn's décolletage and from there to her face, which probably still glowed with the aftereffects of that wondrous kiss in the garden. There was no way a woman could disguise such emotion, no matter how skilled she be as an actress. And Jocelyn was a poor actress.

Henri looked as though he was going to laugh, but he sobered enough to whisk a now-willing Suzanne off to the terrace, pausing on the way to gather two cups of punch.

"What are you up to now, my love?" Peter inquired as he led her away from a puzzled Mr. Tremayne and a pleased Miss Murray.

Jocelyn looked back to see the younger couple take the floor in the dance now forming and sighed with satisfaction. "It is not often people do as I plan. So gratifying when they do. Lora asked for my help and help I gave. I shan't explain beyond that. You might not approve."

"You never cease to amaze me," he murmured. His gaze fell on the red rose now tucked so cozily against her skin. "I am honored that my offering merits such regard. I envy it."

"I enjoy the fragrance it offers." Drat the blush she felt skim over her skin. She could think of nothing to add to her poor words, then spotted Mrs. Hastings and motioned Peter off to one side. "I just happened to think of poor Mrs. Hastings. Her gowns are old, and I doubt she receives much in pin money to spend. Would it not be a strong temptation to snatch a valuable necklace were she to see one?"

"Nonsense. Mrs. Hastings?" He paused, looking at the sweet-faced lady who so graciously wore an out-of-date gown she likely knew others could see as old. "On the other hand, you may have a point there. Did you not search her room?"

"Indeed, and found nothing other than a pathetic collection of gowns and simple belongings. The only jewelry she brought along is what she wears now."

"I should think her room merits a second look."

"Indeed, I thought so as well."

"What are you two in such deep discussion over?" Adrian asked, coming up to where Jocelyn and Peter had been standing quite out of the way.

"Gauging your guests and who might most be in need of the necklace," Peter murmured.

"I wish I had not thought of a costume ball. Yet what good is a piece of jewelry if it cannot be used? Lora wore it at our wedding, and I would see it complement her gown again." He looked at his wife with such loving devotion that it brought sudden moisture to Jocelyn's eyes.

"What are you going to wear, Jocelyn?" Peter inquired, quickly breaking the spell cast by sentiment.

"I fear I have not given it much thought. Are there old clothes in trunks up in the attics as there are at my former home?" Jocelyn inquired of Adrian, aware that Peter had given her a look of surprise when she spoke of her home as now her former abode. And so it was.

"My family is one like yours, then. Nothing is ever thrown away. If you would like to hunt there, you have my permission. Only, say nothing to Suzanne. I would not wish her to put her hands on anything belonging to my forebears."

"Sticky fingers, has she?" Peter said with a lazy regard for the lady mentioned.

"You might say that," Adrian agreed before he excused himself to visit with another guest.

"I think we shall find the necklace in her room," Jocelyn

vowed. "I truly had not completed my search. Perhaps tomorrow you may be able to ferret out something of interest, if you know what I mean." Jocelyn gave him a look of significance, then continued. "I must go to the ruins tomorrow, but I cannot think it will take all day. I intend to go to the attics first thing before the others are up. Once I find a suitable costume, I can forget about that aspect of this visit and concentrate on helping you find the jewels."

"And while you are in the ruins, take care. I'd not wish someone to cause you an accident."

"Now it is my turn to say nonsense. Is it not?" Jocelyn gave him a worried look.

"Anything is possible. You really were serious about not returning to your brother's house?"

"Indeed. It is his home, and I know I am welcome—but to visit. I made a list of my belongings, and once I find a place in which I may put them, I intend to send for them all."

"Brave words, indeed, my lady."

Anything else he might have said was lost when Pierre came up to ask Jocelyn for a dance. Mindful she had promised Peter to encourage any of the men to talk, Jocelyn instantly agreed. She left Peter with regret. The dour Pierre could scarcely compare to the other man when it came to charm. Since Pierre had never kissed her, she couldn't comment on his ability in that line.

It was not difficult to persuade Pierre to talk, for he would converse about himself.

Jocelyn found herself murmuring replies to words she didn't hear while she turned her thoughts back to the garden and Peter Leigh's kiss. The red rose was now wilted against the heat of her skin. What was in her future? Where would she go when she left here? She couldn't stay very long after the costume ball and the baptism of baby Charles—perhaps a week or two. Hospitality could be imposed upon just so long. It would have to be the indigent relative if she might find an agreeable one. She dare not think in another direction. She had poured water on those coals five years ago.

Chapter Eight

Clouds hovered over the horizon early the following morning, casting a promise of rain later in the day, quite as Jocelyn had predicted. She had hurried down to the breakfast room, eaten what she wished, then left.

She was returning to her room when she encountered Peter leaving his. With the door open, she could see the rumpled covers on the vast oak bed, the tapestried walls offering a warm, inviting background to a night's rest.

"Good morning," she said, veering her thoughts in another direction. "I intend to hunt for a costume. Shall I see you before the women depart for the ruins?" She had whispered, unwilling for any to know what she was about, as well as mindful that some still slept.

"I understand a few of the men plan to join you on the excursion. Promise you will be careful?"

"Of course. I have no intention of departing this earth in an untimely manner." She made to move on, and he detained her with a touch on her arm. Jocelyn looked up into his face, wondering what he was thinking.

"If possible, I shall see you in the storeroom."

She nodded, then whispered, "In the event I do not see you before I leave, please consider Uncle Maxim as another suspect. Upon reflection, he has as good a motive as Suzanne, Pierre, or for that matter, Mrs. Hastings." She gave him that thought to consume with his morning meal.

Jocelyn donned the oldest thing she'd brought along with her, the still wearable dress in which she had traveled. Mercy had done her best with it, and Jocelyn thought it fit to wear while searching the storeroom.

The stairs proved quite nice, for there were guest rooms on this floor as well. There was no true attic as at her home. They had merely set aside two rooms for storage and into the first of these Jocelyn entered. Lora had instructed her to look for black trunks, and it did not take long to find them. The room was incredibly tidy, boxes stacked in order, everything labeled neatly. Her brother's attic should be so meticulous.

Rummaging through the clothes proved interesting. Jocelyn had just decided upon a gown of some forty-odd years ago when the door opened. Thinking it was Peter, she called, "Well, shall I do with this? The color is rather pretty, I believe." She rose, holding the patterned, peach, silk gown before her. She thought the tight sleeves with the cascade of chiffon frills and sack-back style vastly becoming. "The tight-fitting waist is so different from the loose-hanging styles of the present."

Not receiving an answer, she turned to look at the door.

"Having a look about?" Henri inquired as he sauntered across the room to stand before her.

"As you see," Jocelyn replied, puzzled as to his presence. "Did you intend to look for a costume, too?"

"Is that what you seek? I wondered. There are bedrooms on this floor as well as the one below. For all I knew, you were intending to pay a visit to the Corshams or Uncle Maxim."

"I didn't realize he was on this floor." That was a lie, but she did not think it wise to let anyone know she was so aware of the room assignments.

"The owl room, Lora calls it. It has fantastical owl paintings on the upper walls above the wainscoting. I thought perhaps he had attracted you last evening."

"You must be joking! He is old enough to be my father!" Jocelyn wanted to laugh, but something in Henri's expression suppressed that desire.

"He is a distinguished gentleman, and I understand you need a roof over your head when you leave here."

"Listening at keyholes, Henri? I have not made that public knowledge. However, I shan't wed merely to acquire a house. Do not entertain such a notion for a moment."

"You could always choose me, if you wished," he offered with insulting diffidence. "I have a respectable home, and with your inheritance we could live simply but well." He strolled closer to where she now stood clutching the pretty silk gown to her chest, quite rooted to the spot with the incredible proposal.

"How lovely—to be asked to marry you for my money. It is what every woman longs to hear." Sarcasm dripped from her voice, and she shot him a look of pure dislike.

The door opened, and Peter entered the room—to her great relief.

"Ah, Henri. Good to see you. You as well, Jocelyn. I gather I am not the only one sent to the storeroom to find a costume?" He sent Jocelyn a quizzical look, glancing first at Henri, as though he sensed something amiss.

"There is a gentleman's coat just below the gown I found. It is an elegant green with a great number of brass buttons. You might be able to pair it with something you already have," Jocelyn babbled with haste to cover the awkward silence.

He crossed to the trunk, peered inside, then looked at her. "We should make a fine couple, in that event. The green matches the green in your gown." He picked up the coat, holding it against him. "Acceptable, do you think?"

"Perhaps they belonged to a long-ago husband and wife?" Jocelyn said. "I think we will do splendidly," she continued without considering how her words might sound to Henri.

"Is that the way the wind blows?" he inquired, his manner curt, eyes hard.

"I do not know what you mean," Jocelyn said quickly to cover her lapse. "I am talking about the party costumes."

Henri merely stared at her, then left, slamming the door behind him.

"Do I sense a rejected suitor? How many have you racked up over the years?"

"That is a cruel thing to say! I have not made a game of refusing gentlemen. However, when a man makes me an insulting offer, I do not scruple to worry about his sensitivities." Jocelyn bent to gather the white muslin apron that appeared a part of the ensemble, along with a flat straw hat she thought she recognized from a painting on the stair landing.

"Jocelyn, I'm sorry. When I saw Henri standing so close to you, and you looking as though you were stunned, I jumped to the wrong conclusion. But he insulted you? The fool! What did he say that so repulsed you?"

"First he thought I had come up to the owl room *and* Uncle Maxim! Fancy that, a man old enough to be my father—not but what it isn't done by some. Then, he offered me his hand and house, as I need a place to live—it seems Henri is not above listening at keyholes, for I have not made it widely known that I am not returning to my brother's home when I leave here."

"The cad—that insult is so outrageous it is laughable." He shut the lid on the trunk, then guided her to the door. They walked down the stairs side by side.

Jocelyn made no reply to his remark. She simmered at the memory of his accusation. Was that what he thought of her? That she would be so rude, so cruel to any man who sought her hand—and wealth?

At the door to her rooms, he paused, gesturing to the green satin coat in his arms. "I suppose I can manage with this, but I may have to make another trip up there."

"Be on your guard if you do. Who knows what woman may follow you, so to offer her hand and home," Jocelyn said, still angry at his assumption that she had made a game of rejecting her suitors.

"Jocelyn," he began.

In no mood to listen to a pointless explanation, Jocelyn swept into her sitting room. Casting a cold look at the man who stared at her from the hall, she firmly shut the door in his face.

What a blessing she had agreed to go to the ruins with the others today. She did not think she could be polite to Peter after what had just happened. His accusation of her behavior to suitors cut deeply.

Peter stood by the window in his room, watching the guests disappear down the drive in a collection of carriages. He still smarted from Jocelyn's cold glare, and the door closed ever so firmly in his face. It was scarcely what he wished.

What in the world had prompted him to insult her with the taunt about the proposal? It was a wonder she hadn't slapped his face. Likely the only thing that kept her from doing so was the gown she had held in her arms.

He looked at the green coat he'd tossed across his bed. "Dickman, can you find the breeches and anything else that ought to go with that coat? 'Tis for the costume party four days hence."

"Indeed, sir. From one of the trunks upstairs?"

Peter explained where he had found the coat, then went out to the hallway with his valet. While Dickman went to the storage room, Peter thought to explore Uncle Maxim's chamber. He joined his valet on the walk up the stairs, listening all the while for any sound of activity.

From the main floor could be heard expected noise, the maids cleaning and the footmen rearranging furniture for whatever Lora had planned come evening. There had been no one around on the first floor, and he thought he had accounted for all guests when he watched them depart.

"I believe it will be safe," Dickman said quietly as they parted company.

Upon opening the door, Peter was surprised at the interior. Owls peered from the walls here and there, perched on painted trees. It was fantastically beautiful, if one enjoyed owls. White ceiling and wainscoting offset the wild painting, to the eye's relief.

After his swift perusal, he set to work. With methodical care, he began next to the door and worked his way around the room, searching the bureau and the two closets he found at the far end, much to his surprise. One held clothing, the other, a shaving stand and the chamber amenity so necessary.

Maxim was untidy, with papers strewn over the small desk provided for a guest. Peter had no scruples about examining these and found them of interest. It would seem that dear Uncle Maxim had not a feather to fly with, judging from the letter to his banker, who apparently had demanded funds be deposited or else.

That might well explain why he had offered for Jocelyn. The mere thought of her married to that old roué was enough to make his blood boil.

He did not find the necklace or anything indicating that

Maxim had anything to do with its disappearance. But the reality remained that Maxim needed money and hated that Adrian possessed the necklace.

From there, leaving each paper precisely as he had found it, he went across to the room occupied by the Corshams. Yellow-and-white-striped walls above the white wainscoting and simple furnishings greeted him. The massive bed took pride of place, draped with more yellow.

Peter didn't think they would steal the necklace, but mindful of the demure Mrs. Hastings and her surprising motive, he made the same careful search here as he had in Maxim's chamber.

With the same results.

Not about to quit, he proceeded back down to the first floor to Suzanne Fornier's room. Mercy had promised to keep the personal maids occupied with something or other. It seemed she had succeeded with Miss Fornier's maid, as the room proved empty.

Since Jocelyn had examined the room in haste, Peter went over it as he had Maxim's chamber. He was about to leave when he espied a box on the floor of the wardrobe. It looked to be identical to the one they had found in Pierre's room. He quickly picked it up to examine and was more than a little surprised. Unless he much missed his mark, it was the same one. He doubted there would be two such boxes in this house.

Hearing a noise in the hall, he replaced the box, then hurriedly walked to flatten himself against the wall next to the door. It opened, and Peter wondered how he would get out of this spot. He could hardly say he had bumbled into the wrong room!

Then whoever was about to enter apparently changed her mind, for the skirt Peter glimpsed disappeared, the door left ajar.

Wiping the sweat from his brow, he slipped from the bedroom to saunter down the hall. He paused near the room occupied by Pierre and Henri only to encounter their man as he left the chamber. He was holding two pair of breeches, and Peter guessed he was off to do some pressing.

"Good day, sir," the man said politely.

Peter nodded politely. He was not one to snub servants, and he always left more than adequate vails upon departure, figuring that he had made extra work for them.

He sighed. This was more risky than he had figured it would be. With the hall clear, he slipped inside the chamber he wanted to examine again.

The room was neat. Peter headed for where they had found the necklace box to find precisely what he had expected. It was gone—which meant it had been transferred to Suzanne Fornier's room. Why?

On that note of mystery, he escaped the room to slip into his own. He leaned against the door with unfeigned relief.

Dickman looked up from where he worked over the green coat. He had added a mustard yellow pair of breeches that matched a knee-length waistcoat. "I believe your own hose and patent slippers will do with this. I'll add a bit of lace to one of your shirts and that ought to finish it. Did you find anything of interest, milord?"

"We have a mystery upon our mystery, Dickman. The jewelry box we found in Pierre's chamber is now in Miss Fornier's room, placed neatly on the bottom of her wardrobe. There is no necklace inside it, unfortunately."

"That is a pity, sir. A real pity. What do we do next?"

"Let me think. This place is a hive of servants. I shall have to wait a bit, I believe."

"Just so," Dickman agreed. He suggested a spot of coffee in the library would not come amiss. Peter nodded agreement and was off in a trice.

Jocelyn left the carriage with reluctant feet. Her anger with Peter had dissipated with every yard she had traveled. Now she wanted nothing more than to make peace with him.

"I trust you will not allow our little misunderstanding to come in the way of friendship, *ma chérie,*" Henri said quietly, offering her his assistance over a ridge of unscythed grass.

"I shall behave as I would to any of Lora and Adrian's guests, even one who insulted me, sirrah," Jocelyn replied with quiet dignity.

"I see I am not to be forgiven easily." He looked affronted, to her surprise.

"I do not see why I should," Jocelyn replied with what she deemed a most reasonable manner. Then she remembered he was in the room with Pierre. Perhaps he knew something of his cousin's difficulties or feelings regarding the necklace. "But I shall—in the interest of peace."

"You are most gracious," he murmured, taking her hand to place on his arm.

She made no comment on his assumption that she would also welcome his attentions. She wanted to learn something from him and now she had to wonder how.

They strolled about in the ancient church, possibly Norman in origin. Jocelyn knew little of ancient history, and it appeared Henri knew even less. The roof was gone and the windows out. Grass grew between the slate on the floor. One could only guess where people had once stood or sat for worship. Jocelyn dimly recalled her father telling her that before they had pews, the people had stood—sometimes for hours—in the chilly, bare sanctuary.

"The sun is pleasant, but this has a feeling of ancient cold about it," she commented as they paused in the center of the nave. It was a narrow building, and not very long. Once, someone had added an ell near the door, as though the congregation had grown before it disappeared.

"It does make one realize how short our span is on this earth." She removed her hand from his arm, ostensibly to examine some carving on a wall. "I suspect this is a name and a date with some saying, but I cannot read Latin," she said with a rueful look.

Henri contrived to look superior. He studied the words and numbers etched into the stone wall. "Denis is the name, and the date is 1162 and the words are to the effect that this man was a law unto himself."

"So long ago. It would seem that people do not change much over time. I see Pierre is escorting the quiet Miss Osmond today. I believe she has an enormous dowry. Would that make a difference to him? Is he in need of funds?"

Henri gave her a surprised look, as he rightly ought, she

thought with an inward grimace. It was not like her to phrase a question like this, or to pry in such a manner.

"Is there any man who would not welcome additional fortune? I fancy Pierre more than others. He has known severe losses of late. But then, any woman of wealth must expect some fortune hunters after her."

Jocelyn would have liked to ask if Pierre would steal to attain money. "I imagine that is so. Why frequently gentlemen who scarce know me ask me for my hand. It was not so difficult when my father was alive to order them away. Even my brother has been careful to vet them on my behalf. However, now I am to fend for myself, it would seem. I cannot say I like it in the least."

"I shan't remind you of the obvious solution, for I value our peace too much."

"Thank you, Henri. Why do we not join the others?" She doubted she would learn anything more about Pierre from his cousin. Were she to probe too deeply, she might bring unwelcome mistrust on her head.

The clouds gathered overhead, yet the expected rain held off, to Jocelyn's relief. Lora gathered them all under her wing, promising a nuncheon at a pleasant little inn not too far away.

Once seated in a carriage, Jocelyn surveyed the assembled guests one by one as the vehicles left the church ruins. Who had stolen the necklace? It had to be one of these, surely. Pierre? Mrs. Hastings? Perhaps the elegantly attired Suzanne was the one? Uncle Maxim, possibly? Or was it another?

Adrian entered the carriage to sit at her side.

"Have you learned anything of use?"

Jocelyn exchanged a smile. "Nothing surprising. Both Uncle Maxim and Pierre are under the hatches, according to what Henri said. And I suppose he would know just how they are situated. I must admit, I was confounded when Uncle Maxim exploded into a fury of ill-usage that you should have the necklace when he felt you did not properly appreciate it." She glanced across at Lora. "He also cast aspersions on Lora, and you may be certain I cast them back at him in full force. I cannot recall when I have been so angry."

"We appreciate what you are doing. Do you suppose Peter is having any luck while we are gone?"

"Oh, I devoutly hope so."

Their low-voiced conversation was interrupted when the carriage drew to a halt in the yard of a pretty country inn. There were a few long boxes of early summer blooms along the ivied walls, and straw was strewn over the earth so as to protect the shoes of any lady who happened to appear.

They all straggled into the inn, prepared to enjoy the repast set forth. Jocelyn chanced to look out the window and grimaced when she saw a gentle mist falling.

"How fortunate we are inside. Do all the carriages have tops?" she asked Adrian. She thought most of the landaus would be no problem. Any gig or curricle would be something else.

He assured her that all would be well, and she relaxed to enjoy her meal. And wonder about Peter. How did he fare? They would soon leave here to return to the castle. She could hardly wait to consult him, quite forgetting she had left him in a snit of anger.

Peter stared out at the mist drifting across the gardens. How it suited his mood. He had searched as many of the rooms as he dared, given the servants that seemed to persist in coming and going. Was it always thus?

"Dickman, is it unusually busy around the house today?"

"Aye, milord. They take advantage of the absence of their masters and mistresses."

"I went over rooms of the Corshams, Maxim Valletort, Miss Fornier's room as well as the Thynne's. I should like another look at the room where the Hastings stay. Lady Jocelyn noted how poor Hastings keeps his wife."

"A motive if ever I heard one," the valet replied quietly.

"I wonder what Henri Valletort was doing upstairs earlier? We thought he came to harass Lady Jocelyn. But what if Henri intended to look for something in his cousin's room and entered the storage room instead? I believe I shall go upstairs again and ferret out what I may."

"Aye. A body gets restless when it is raining and there is little to do. Now if the gentlemen were to come home, you might enjoy a game of billiards."

"I suppose you have things to do here, and I keep you from them?" Peter grinned at his valet.

"Nay. Anything I need to do is done regardless." Dickman sent a look of affection mingled with respect for his longtime employer. He had been with him many years before he came into the title and all the money. There had been months when things were a trifle dicey, but they had hung together in spite of it all. And now it was clover.

Peter wandered down the hall, climbing the stairs slowly, looking about him as he went. Clues. There had to be something he was missing. But, what? The jewelry box had been in Pierre's room, and now it reposed at the bottom of Suzanne's wardrobe. Why the switch? And who had done it? And, would it stay there? A traveling clue!

At the top of the stairs, he looked down the hall to where Maxim stayed, the Corshams as well. Turning aside, he entered the storage room and went to the shelves. Could Henri have come up here to conceal the necklace in a location where it was unlikely to be looked for? People—like Jocelyn and himself— might come up to hunt for a costume. They were unlikely to examine the contents of the shelves.

He began at the far end of the room, systematically checking box contents one after the other. He had reached the middle of the wall of shelves when he heard the door open. He did not bother to turn, believing it to be Dickman come with a glass of welcome ale for him.

That was the last he knew. One blow, and he collapsed on the floor, senseless.

The ride home from the inn was hurried. Several of the ladies who had come in a gig or curricle joined those who had ridden in one of the landaus, while the gigs and Henri's curricle dashed on ahead, hoping to avert a dire soaking. It meant a crowded ride, but no one complained.

Umbrellas were put to good use. Jocelyn was thankful that she had remembered to bring the largest one she could find, a red oiled-silk of large proportions.

Rushing from the carriage to the house, Jocelyn could not help but recall the previous time she had come here in a rain, drenched and carried in Peter's arms. Much had altered—including her feelings—since then.

Upon entering the house, she handed the umbrella to Saxby, shook out her shawl, then joined the others in the saloon, where a marvelous fire burned to welcome them. Within minutes Saxby came with the makings of a punch. A footman followed with a tray of savories.

Henri entered the room behind the footman, brushing moisture from his coat as he walked.

"Ah, *chérie*," she heard him say to Suzanne. "I missed you on the drive back here."

Jocelyn shamelessly eavesdropped.

"Well, you found plenty to occupy your time this morning. I had not expected rivalry for your attention from a woman so past her prime."

"*Ma chérie,* I am desolate you are displeased. I shall devote the rest of the afternoon to charming you."

Jocelyn mulled over that little conversation, then edged over to where Saxby stirred a fragrant punch.

"Where is Lord Leigh, Saxby?"

"I could not say where the baron is, my lady. I have not seen him for some time. He had coffee in the library some hours ago. I doubt he is in there now." The butler nodded respectfully, then returned to pouring out cups of punch for the thirsty.

"He ought to be here," she replied, then drifted across the room to stand by the fireplace. Perhaps he had fallen asleep, bored with the hunting and lack of clues.

She sipped her cup of punch while thinking about Peter. It simply was not like him to be absent when they were all gathered.

"Shall we have a game of billiards, gentlemen?" Adrian asked. He smiled at the warmth of their response.

Jocelyn watched them leave in clusters of two and three until they were all gone.

"You look somewhat forlorn, Lady Jocelyn. Do you miss the gentlemen? You have not sought any man's company this afternoon. Rather, you have been staring at the fire for some minutes," Lady Thynne said. The baron's good wife was not thin, as her name might imply. She was just right, with a kindly face and an air of concern.

Jocelyn thought she detected a note of commiseration in her voice and promptly denied an attachment to any of the gentlemen who had just departed. "It is the rain that puts me into the megrims. There ought to be a law that it may only rain at night," she concluded with a smile.

"Your cousin mentioned that you had once been engaged and that your fiancé was killed in Spain. I am sorry to learn that, for you ought to know the happiness found in a good marriage."

Jocelyn privately thought there were a great number of marriages that were anything but happy, yet said nothing to that. She merely smiled and murmured, "I have found solace in the ensuing years doing charitable work and enjoying the children of my friends. Now that my brother has married, I look forward to nieces and nephews to dote upon."

Mrs. Hastings called to Lady Thynne to join her, Mrs. Osmond, and Mrs. Whyte in a game of whist. Suzanne flounced off, ostensibly to her room. Mrs. Corsham, being somewhat younger than the other married ladies, joined Cordelia Murray and Alisha Osmond on one of the sofas before the fire to talk about fashions and gossip, as was much the custom at house parties.

Restless and wondering why Peter had not made an appearance, Jocelyn decided to investigate. It took her but minutes to go up the stairs, then along to Peter's room. It took courage to rap on his door. As there was not a soul around, she felt reasonably safe, yet it was not her custom to do such a thing.

Dickman answered. "I've not seen Lord Leigh in some time. He said he was going to check the attic room again."

Jocelyn exchanged a worried look with the valet. "I believe we'd best investigate. Something may have happened."

Chapter Nine

Jocelyn pushed open the door to the storage room with caution. She did not see Peter and was about to leave when she heard a groan. Glancing at Dickman, she searched the room more carefully.

"Perhaps he has fallen, my lady," the valet said, moving past Jocelyn into the room to look about.

Jocelyn also walked into the room, quite certain she had heard something that sounded like a groan, although she supposed it might be the house—unlikely, but possible.

When she approached the far wall, where neatly arranged shelves housed all matter of items, she saw an arm. Within seconds she had rushed forward to find Peter crumpled on the floor.

"He is stirring, Dickman. Fetch some cool compresses and a bit of brandy," she ordered, looking at Peter with horrified eyes. "And say nothing to anyone unless you happen to find Mercy. She is very good at helping, and she knows what is going on— or at least as much as we do."

"Very good, my lady," the valet said as he left the room with obvious reluctance.

Alone with Peter, Jocelyn bent over him to examine the wound, which did not appear serious. There was no blood seeping from it. He stirred, albeit fitfully. Deciding he needed a softer cushion and finding none, she gently eased his head and shoulder onto her lap, thinking it was better than a hard wooden floor.

He groaned.

"Peter, dear Peter, speak to me," she implored, afraid she might have caused him injury, yet still convinced he was better for a softer headrest.

His eyes fluttered and then closed again, but it seemed to her that he made an attempt to speak.

"Peter! Peter, darling! Oh, please wake up. Look at me, scold me, only say something."

He stirred again, as though he might try to rise. Horrified, Jocelyn clutched him against her. He must not do a thing until Dickman had cleansed the wound and he was restored to his rational self.

Then he opened his eyes; those silvery-blue orbs warm with an emotion she couldn't guess.

"Peter, what happened?" she begged. "Can you speak to me? You poor man, to be so wounded."

"I must say this is the nicest pillow I can ever recall," he murmured, his baritone raspy.

She moved with indignation, and he gasped as though in pain.

"I hurt you! Oh, this is dreadful. Be still, and Dickman shall be here in a few moments with a bit of brandy and some cool compresses." She gave him a watery smile; worried she had done more harm than good with her well-meant intentions.

"Both will be welcome," he replied in that husky rasp, then cleared his throat. "You looked for me?"

"I long to know what has happened, but I do not think you ought to talk just now," she said, conflict raging within her. She wanted to know who had knocked him out, yet she felt reluctance to urge him to speak. However, he seemed fit otherwise. Could a rap on the head cause such fearful damage? She didn't know. For a moment she wondered at his incapacity, then felt certain Peter had no reason to feign an inability to move. That lump on his head was proof.

"Someone came into the room. I thought it was Dickman. Got conked over the head by someone. Couldn't see if it was man or woman. You wouldn't hit me, would you?" He gave her a bleary smile, then shut his eyes as though that bit of speech had been too much.

"Peter? Don't slip away from me, please. I need you." And,

Jocelyn realized, it wasn't merely to help her solve the theft. She needed Peter in her life, every day and always. But—she had rejected him when he was poor and how would it look were she to encourage him now that he possessed a fortune? He would think no better of her than she had thought of him five years ago. What a maddening mull this was!

He opened his eyes again, staring at her with what seemed to be curiosity. "Talk later, my dear."

She smoothed his hair away from the lump on his head with gentle hands. "Of course, we shall. Rest, now. Dickman will be here any moment." She hoped. Or did she? There was something very appealing about holding Peter in her arms.

"Like it here," he murmured, with a hint of a grin tugging his mouth.

Then the door opened, and Dickman bustled in with a tray holding a bottle of brandy—Adrian's best—a glass, some damp cloths, and a look of concern on his face. Mercy followed him.

"Oh, my gracious," Mercy whispered. "The poor man!"

Dickman set to work, offering the brandy to Peter first, then handing Jocelyn the damp cloths so she might cleanse the wound and inspect the area.

The brandy appeared to help him enormously. There seemed to be an improvement at once. His eyes flashed open, and he stared up at Jocelyn with disconcerting intensity.

"He does not seem to be mortally wounded—at least the skin is not broken, and we need not fear infection."

"Good," Peter said in a stronger voice. "I should like to go to my room if you think we could manage it?"

"Should you attempt to walk?" Jocelyn stared down at the man in her arms with alarm. "I would not want you to collapse."

"Mercy can make sure there is no one about. Dickman and you can walk on either side of me, hold me up. I would like to be in my bed." He looked so pathetic, she hadn't the heart to refuse his request.

"Very well. It shall be as you wish."

Dickman moved around to assist his master, easing him up to a sitting position. Then he nodded to Jocelyn, and they slowly helped Peter to stand.

"Are you sure this is a good thing to do?" Jocelyn asked Dickman, a worried frown creasing her brow. "If he were to fall, I should never forgive myself." She slipped one arm around Peter, then walked slowly at his side until they reached the door.

Without prompting, Mercy slipped from the room, only to pop her head around the door in a few seconds. "I can't see a soul, and it is as silent as the grave down the stairs."

"Not the best choice of words, I expect," Peter murmured to Jocelyn while Dickman opened the door so the three could exit as one.

"At least no one shall see you to ask awkward questions," Jocelyn whispered.

How they made it down the stairs, Jocelyn didn't know. Peter leaned on her heavily while Dickman eased him along.

"'Tis better than going up, my lady," the valet said quietly.

"True, true," Jocelyn replied absently, relieved beyond words when they reached the bottom step. She never would have admitted it, but Peter's weight had been considerable, and at one point she had feared she might fall herself instead of supporting him. Another man ought to have assisted, but to call Adrian might have raised questions none wanted to answer at the moment.

Fortunately, Peter's room was not very far from the stairs. Within a brief time they had him in the room and helped him to his bed.

Jocelyn was barely aware of the gorgeous tapestries on the walls or the elegant half-tester bed. She clasped her hands before her in concern as Dickman and Mercy helped Peter back on his pillows. Wanting to do something, Jocelyn found a light throw, and spread it over him.

"Do you feel like talking yet?" she wondered.

"I can give you no clue as to who knocked me out. I heard footsteps, but paid them little heed. With enough of a swing, even a woman might have managed to render me unconscious. I do not recall being aware of any scent."

"Which eliminates Suzanne," Jocelyn said, recalling the strong fragrance used by the younger woman.

"Who would wish you unconscious, my lord?" Mercy queried.

"There are too many, I fear." He exchanged a worried look with Jocelyn. "There was something on that shelf that someone did not wish me to find. I fancy it is gone now, so do not think of going back to the storage room to investigate."

"I believe I will heed your advice, for I suspect you have the right of it. Whatever was there is long gone." Jocelyn turned to Mercy. "We must leave Lord Leigh now so he can rest. If possible, he may want to join us for dinner, and that is but a few hours away." She took a step toward the door, then motioned for Mercy to open it so to see if the hall was clear.

"Thank you, Jocelyn," Peter said with deliberation, "for all you have done. I shan't forget it."

Jocelyn felt the heat rise in her cheeks. If only she didn't blush so easily! "Think nothing of it, my lord. You rescued me. It is only right I help you, is it not?"

With that, she whisked herself around the door frame and out of the room.

Peter looked at his valet and sighed. "Fine kettle of fish this is. I have no idea who came up there after me. Perhaps if I talked with Adrian, I might at least discover who was downstairs and who left for any time. Would you find him for me?"

Dickman nodded and immediately left his master upon reassuring himself that the head wound was responding to the cool cloth treatment.

Once alone, Peter gingerly sat up, pushed himself against the headboard, and mulled over the situation. Nothing was so bad but what it wasn't good for something. He had heard Jocelyn softly call him her darling, cradling him to her bosom in a rather endearing manner. It wasn't the least like the way Suzanne used the word, as a casual fondness that might be given to anyone. No, Jocelyn had meant it when she referred to him as her darling—even if she was not aware that the depth of her feelings could be heard by him.

He could make use of that knowledge later to achieve his goals. For the moment he had to concentrate on gaining mobility. He needed to sit at the dinner table, study the expressions of those who were suspect, particularly when he entered the room just a trifle after the others. Who would show surprise?

The door opened, and Adrian strode in to stand by the edge of the bed and confront Peter. "Good grief, you have had a time of it. Dickman told me some of it while we came up here. Perhaps we had best call off this investigation? I do not wish my son's godfather to go aloft while he yet has need of him."

"My lord," Dickman admonished when he observed Peter sitting up, "ought you not be on your back?"

"No, no. I am feeling more the thing by the minute. These cool cloths are helping famously. Perhaps more chilled water?" He glanced out the window to where rain now pounded against the window. "That rain looks cold enough."

"Indeed, sir," the valet responded. If he thought Peter ought to just tell him to leave them alone, he said nothing.

Once the valet had gone, Peter turned to gingerly put his feet on the floor and sit more erect. "Who has been with you? You played billiards?"

"Indeed, billiards. Thomas Hastings and Edward Corsham were a team with Philip Whyte. George Thynne, Adam Tremayne, and Hugh Fordyce played as well."

"What about Uncle Maxim, Pierre, and Henri?"

Adrian wrinkled his forehead in thought. "I believe they were all there as well, at least most of the time. Uncle Maxim fancies himself an expert in the game, more than willing to offer advice whether one desires it or not."

"Pierre? Henri?" Peter wanted to know with what he felt was good reason.

"I was distracted from time to time—not expecting I should pay the slightest attention to which of the men remained and which went in and out," Adrian said ruefully. "I truly do not know for certain. Even Adam and Hugh disappeared a bit at one point—not at the same time, however."

"Ah, yes, the call of nature," Peter said, bitterly disappointed. He had hoped his friend would have noticed who was absent and when. It was too much to expect of a host, and he ought to have known it. Easing himself to his feet, he made his way to the window, where he leaned his head against the cold glass.

"I should simply declare the entire house suspect and demand a search," Adrian declared when he watched his friend wince at a sudden movement he'd made.

"Think of the scandal that would spread, especially if it proves to be a relative? No, we shall persist until the last moment. One good thing about this weather—no one is likely to take off with the necklace. He'd be drowned before he got one mile."

"That's a rather macabre note." Adrian thought a moment, then continued. "You believe you will feel up to joining us for dinner?"

"Another glass of that brandy, and I think I might dance a jig," Peter quipped, thankful he'd not be called to put that to the test.

"Lora had planned charades for this evening. You ought to be able to sit quietly to the rear of the room if you wish to remain downstairs. I imagine Jocelyn will conspire to see you are kept quiet. Dickman said she behaved with great common sense while tending to your wound. Helped you down the stairs, too."

"Perhaps we might think of a charade to make use of my wounded noggin?" Peter gave his friend a conspiratorial look. "Think of something clever, will you? I'm not up to it at the moment. Better yet, ask Jocelyn."

"You are rather free with her Christian name, Peter. How do matters fare in that direction?"

"Better than I'd hoped, but I shall say no more on that score now, lest I jinx it."

Adrian laughed quite as Peter intended and shortly left the bedroom.

Adrian reported Peter's good progress to Jocelyn and she was relieved beyond measure. She turned to face Mercy after Adrian had left. "I cannot like that he is sitting up, much less walking about. I should think a thump on the head such as he has known could have serious repercussions."

"Gentlemen are ever thus, milady," Mercy said in a soothing way her mistress knew well. It made Jocelyn feel about ten years old.

"I am not a child, Mercy. I am well aware of the dangers to

the head should one take a beating. 'Tis not the least pleasant."
Jocelyn suspected she sounded a trifle petulant, but her concern
for Peter had left her in a shaken state. She did not think he had
been aware of her spoken endearments while in the storage
room. She hoped he hadn't heard her. What he might think if he
had heard her slip did not bear contemplation.

There was a faint tap at the sitting room door, and Mercy answered it before Jocelyn could ask who might be there. Peter
entered, walking with care, using Dickman as a cane.

Jocelyn jumped to her feet, closing her eyes in disbelief.
"Are you out of your mind? Here," she said to Dickman, "help
him to the chaise longue, where he can put up his feet and relax
against the pillows."

"I wanted to talk with you, and it seemed a better idea for me
to cross over here than for you to be seen coming out of my
room." He sank down on the chaise, allowing Jocelyn to tuck
an extra cushion beneath his head and fuss over him a bit before touching her hand. "Enough. Sit down, I wish to discuss a
matter."

Mercy made to leave the room and was halted by a wave of
his hand. "No. Both of you remain here."

Jocelyn knew she ought to be grateful he had the sense to
think of propriety, but it made her very aware that he had no desire to be compromised with her, nor marry if needs be.

"What must be discussed?" she inquired, taking a seat on the
chair Dickman drew up for her.

"I shall go down for dinner. Even Adrian admitted that it was
a good idea if I felt up to it. I should like to watch a certain few
faces when I stroll into the room with you on my arm after all
are seated."

"And you, milady," Dickman inserted, "will be a gentle assistance for Lord Leigh."

"I see. You suspect someone who will be at the table and
want to see them in spite of a lump on the head and being scarce
able to negotiate the level floor much less a stairs. Of course. It
makes perfect sense. Idiot!" she exclaimed, though softly, lest
one who liked to listen at keyholes overhear her.

"What would you have me do? Hide in my room until my

head is better? May I remind you that we do not have the luxury of time?"

Jocelyn slumped against her chair. "You are right, of course. Well, I shall do my best to assist you without appearing to lend support."

"Adrian was going to wander around the billiard room to see if anyone asks questions about me," Peter said, relaxing a trifle against the chaise.

"Would anyone dare?" Jocelyn wondered.

"Not if he had conked me over the head. But the others might wonder where I am." Peter shifted his feet on the chaise, and Mercy hurried to place a light shawl over his legs.

"Perhaps the man who hit you might ask just to avoid suspicion?" Jocelyn suggested.

Peter turned to Dickman, "You see now why I wished to discuss this with Lady Jocelyn. She has an excellent head on her shoulders." Before Jocelyn might allow herself to get puffed up, he continued. "Adrian said Lora plans to have charades this evening. Can you think of a charade we might do that would allow me to recline—or at least rest?"

"Oh, dear," Jocelyn said with true dismay. "I have never been very good at charades. Think of something, please."

"The course of true love never did run smooth," Peter began, only to have Jocelyn finish the Shakespeare quotation for him.

"But either it was different in blood—" she concluded the line. "You think Lysander meant her class in that instance? That Hermia must resign herself to a marriage in keeping with her position?" Jocelyn queried, thinking back to what her brother had said to her when Peter had sought her hand in marriage. Her brother had reminded Jocelyn of the difference in their rank—Peter being poor and the grandson of a baroness, while Jocelyn was the daughter of a marquess. It had not mattered to her in the least, but she had allowed her brother to prevail upon her and been sorry ever since.

"I think Lysander offers consolation to poor Hermia, unable to wed the man she wants. What would you do? Obey your father, as Hermia must, or follow your heart?"

"I think it depends on the woman—is she given to an independent spirit or is she obedient? Has someone planted seeds of doubt in her heart or is she full of resolution?"

"Hmm. At any rate, it is not a line that lends itself to portrayal very well."

"We might use a title such as 'Sense and Sensibility,'" Jocelyn suggested. "You could be Sensibility reclining on a chair while I portray Sense somehow."

"What about the proverb, 'Revenge is sweet'?" Peter asked with a frown. "Confound it, I cannot think of a thing. I think my wits were addled when I got hit on the head. But you must confess that revenge on that thug would most definitely be sweet?"

"Possibly. How about, 'He sleeps with his eyes open'?" Jocelyn asked, thinking her own wits had gone begging.

"Aye, I could do that one, and you announce it as a proverb. That would allow you to avoid being in a charade if you so pleased."

Jocelyn looked at him and smiled. "How well you see through me. I do not like charades. Perhaps it is too much like life—when we are all playing a role we hope others will not discern."

Peter studied her a moment, then carefully swung his feet to the floor. Dickman hurried to assist him, and within a short time the two men were gone, leaving behind the admonition that Jocelyn be prepared to go down for dinner with Lord Leigh.

Jocelyn suspected her acting ability would be far more needed when she went in to dinner than at the charades. Nevertheless, she was dressed and waiting when Dickman rapped on her door, urging her to join Lord Leigh and himself for a walk down the stairs to the dining room.

The dinner gong had long since sounded, and Jocelyn had almost abandoned the thought of dinner. Her stomach had protested at the very thought.

Peter appeared to approve her garb—a pretty blue muslin, simple and feminine. He, in turn, looked rather splendid in his royal blue coat of Bath cloth over dove-gray pantaloons.

"I shan't offer you my arm, *ma chérie*. I rather think I will welcome your support."

She nodded, and the three of them cautiously made their way down the stairs and almost to the dining room door. Here Peter removed his arm from Jocelyn's shoulders and slipped from

Dickman's grasp. He stood as though squaring himself for an ordeal, as indeed it might be.

"Ready?"

Jocelyn nodded, and together they entered the dining room. A few looked up at them. She skimmed her gaze over the assembled. Not a soul seemed surprised to see them, although Uncle Maxim looked rather vexed at something. Pierre also appeared annoyed. Was that the reaction Peter sought? Jocelyn guided him without seeming to, and within seconds they were seated at the table, ready to partake of the first course.

"What did you observe?" Peter inquired in an undertone as the noise increased with social chatter about them.

"Maxim and Pierre," was her terse reply.

"Indeed. I noticed them as well. We shall compare findings later." He applied himself to the meal, and perhaps only Jocelyn noticed that he ate little.

She hated to leave him when it came time for the women to depart, but he merely nodded. He could scarce leave now, and she certainly might not remain. She glanced at Adrian, who nodded in reply. He would take care to see that Peter did not come to harm.

"I thought we might do a few charades," Lora announced brightly to the ladies in the saloon. "Can you all think of something? You may join together if you please, or include a gentleman if he agrees."

"That rhymes, Lora," Jocelyn said with a laugh. "Why do you not limit our charade to an old proverb. It will be difficult, but surely not impossible, and offer a challenge to all."

Mrs. Thynne sought Mrs. Hastings, and they put their heads together. Alisha Osmond and Cordelia Murray sat near the fire giggling. Jocelyn wondered what they thought so amusing. It seemed some time since she had giggled at foolishness. The solution to the theft hung over her like a shadow.

"What about you, Lady Jocelyn?" Suzanne demanded. "Surely you can think of something dashing? I do not think you so very old that your brain no longer works." She laughed most unkindly.

Jocelyn seethed but could do nothing until Lora happened to invite her to offer tea around. She did so with ease until she came to Suzanne when she appeared to stumble and the tea went sloshing down the white muslin gown that was demure only in color. The neckline of this dress was as daring as any Suzanne possessed.

"Oh, oh," Suzanne cried, jumping to her feet and nearly causing Jocelyn to drop the cup and saucer.

"Dear me, Suzanne, that pretty gown! What a dreadful thing to happen. I insist I help you to your room and assist you to change into one of your other becoming gowns. That is the very least I can do," Jocelyn declared in a voice and manner that would not brook no for an answer.

Looking somewhat bewildered, Suzanne found herself rushed from the room and up the stairs before she could think of a reply. "But," she sputtered, "it is not necessary for you to do this. I am quite capable . . ."

"I must, or I should not forgive myself," Jocelyn declared firmly. "Your maid will be at dinner, and you cannot manage the back of your gown. I would never pardon myself were it to be ruined!"

Once in Suzanne's room, Jocelyn whisked the not-so-innocent muslin from Suzanne's shapely form, then opened the wardrobe ostensibly to find a clean gown. While searching she took pains to take note of the wardrobe floor. There was no blue box on it anywhere!

She grabbed a dress at random, holding it up for approval. Since it was a rich cream jaconet trimmed with knots of brown velvet riband, Suzanne seemed more than willing to make the change. It took but minutes to arrange the gown to satisfaction, then smooth the hair that had been mussed. Jocelyn cast surreptitious glances around the room as she assisted Suzanne. She could see no other evidence of the blue jewelry box anywhere.

Once the change of attire was complete, the two young women returned to the hall, prepared to rejoin the others.

"I trust your maid will be able to remove the tea stains? If not, she must ask Mercy, for she is rather clever at that sort of thing," Jocelyn offered, wanting to atone for her misdeed.

"I believe my maid is quite capable," Suzanne answered, in what might be called a snub.

"Ah, good, then," Jocelyn answered easily, refusing to rise to her bait.

When they reached the saloon, they found the gentlemen had joined the women. The talk was all of charades, and Suzanne immediately left Jocelyn to go to Pierre's side.

Jocelyn watched their animated conversation, then turned as Peter joined her. She promptly led him to the nearby sofa and sat down so he would join her.

"Do I sense an undercurrent?"

"I chanced to spill tea on Suzanne's gown. Most regrettable of me, I know. However, when I insisted upon helping her to change, knowing her maid to be at dinner, I made an interesting discovery."

"And shall you tell me?"

"Of course, since you ask so nicely. The blue box is no longer in the bottom of her wardrobe. Now, what do you think of that!"

"The wandering clue," he said with resignation. "Why would anyone keep moving that box back and forth? Bloody stupid, if you ask me. Beg pardon, Jocelyn. Not myself this evening."

"Your language is excused, sir. You can be forgiven much this evening in view of all you have sustained."

Lora called for order, and suggested they do rather simple charades rather than ones that required elaborate staging. All agreed with a bit of laughter here and there.

When it came their turn, Jocelyn rose to toss a shawl over a reclining Peter. He, in turn, pretended to sleep, but kept one eye open.

It was Henri, not Maxim or Pierre as Jocelyn had anticipated, who guessed the answer. "He sleeps with one eye open," the cousin said with a certain relish.

"Indeed, I do," Peter replied with a steel-sheathed smile.

Chapter Ten

"I think it will be a pleasant day," Jocelyn said to Mrs. Hastings over the breakfast table. It was the first time the slightly older woman had joined the morning group. She looked a trifle shy, which was understandable given her elderly gown and lack of conversation.

Jocelyn soon gave up trying to instigate any discourse with her. Mrs. Hastings knew no Society gossip nor was she interested in the latest fashions. Considering her budget, Jocelyn could well understand why.

"Did you enjoy the charades last evening, Lady Jocelyn?" Pierre asked as he sauntered into the room.

"Well," she said, attempting to be honest, "I scarce can say I particularly enjoy doing them, but they were interesting to say the least. I believe I would rather watch than participate."

"Leigh had a bit of an unusual proverb—to sleep with one eye open. Is he that sort of chap?" Pierre ambled to the sideboard, selecting his morning meal with a discerning eye.

Suddenly alert, Jocelyn was offhand in her reply. "I should think he would be as cautious as the next person. I fear I have no firsthand knowledge, although his valet might. Surely you didn't take him seriously?" She contrived to sound as offended as she indeed might have been had she thought Pierre truly intended to insult her or imply that she was having a liaison with Peter Leigh.

"I did not mean to suggest anything improper, my lady," Pierre said with a haughty sneer in his tone.

"I feel certain you did not intend anything other than an ordinary comment," Peter said upon entering the breakfast room. "Good morning, all," he said to the room in general but with his gaze fastened upon Jocelyn.

"How are you this morning, Lord Leigh?" she said with a show of propriety. "I trust you are in good heart?"

He raised one elegant dark brow, but didn't tease her, as he might have otherwise. "Indeed, Lady Jocelyn," he replied with just sufficient emphasis so she suspected he was laughing at her behind that bland facade.

"The lady shows concern for you. Lucky chap. Why is it that the women fall all over a fellow once he has inherited a fortune?" Henri gibed as he paused in the doorway.

"We cannot all be handsome devils like you, Henri," Pierre shot back from his place at the table next to Mrs. Hastings.

She in turn appeared to be utterly fascinated with the repartee, apparently thinking this an unusual manner in which to begin the day. Jocelyn admitted it was a bit like watching a game of tennis.

"Does anyone know what is planned for the day?" Henri inquired of everyone in general.

"Tennis? Bowls? Angling?" Jocelyn tossed out in the hope of getting some response from Peter as to what he might intend for the day.

She wondered what he had thought of Henri's taunt regarding men who had inherited fortunes. Did he think of her in that manner? If he thought of her at all? She thought he might, given some of the comments he had made. But then, what did she know of the workings of his mind? She bestowed a guarded look at him when he selected the chair at her side, sliding onto it with that animal grace so much a part of him.

"I trust you slept well, Lady Jocelyn?" he said while carving his morning slice of gammon. He had taken toast and eggs along with an assortment of other items.

She took a glance at the nicely filled plate and grimaced. How could anyone in his condition eat so much so early in the day?

"You would join me in a game of tennis, my lady?" Peter asked quietly, yet so all might hear if they chose.

"If you like," she replied with the same sort of caution she had used earlier. She trusted Peter. She was quite sure she did not trust the others in the room—not one of them—not even Mrs. Hastings. She could feel his gaze rest on her briefly before he returned to his morning meal.

When she finished, she excused herself from the table, murmuring something about seeing baby Charles.

"The infant? A bit old for him, are you not?" Pierre said with what appeared to be teasing. Jocelyn suspected there was more behind his words.

"I do not think anyone is too old to offer love to an infant, Mr. Valletort," she said with a decided snap.

The nursery was above the master suite, with a little staircase so Lora might go up there without encountering anybody. When Jocelyn was bid to enter the room, she found her good friend seated with Charles on her lap.

"I trust I do not come at a bad time? I have had far too little time with this lad. Pierre thinks him a bit too young for me, mind you. I say he is just right!" Jocelyn laughed to show those words had not rankled, but they had. Had Pierre also been of the notion she might be interested in Uncle Maxim just to get a roof over her head? What utter rubbish.

"You look so fierce, Jocelyn. Is something troubling you—other than the missing necklace? Oh, I wish I had never seen it, or that Adrian had never entertained the notion of giving this costume party."

Jocelyn accepted the infant; cuddling the happy baby in her arms and relishing his baby scent while thankful for dry nappies and a full baby tummy.

"Did you know that Peter had been knocked unconscious yesterday afternoon while searching the storage room? He somewhat alluded to it during the charades last evening. Remember? He said something about sleeping with one eye open?"

"Adrian told me about it. It is so dreadful! To think of dear Peter suffering such a thing on our behalf cuts me deeply. I think we ought to issue a general accusation and be done with this skullduggery. It has become too dangerous."

From the doorway a rich baritone said, "Ah, but dear Lady Valletort, men live for danger. Is that not the right of it, my dear

Jocelyn?" Peter inquired as he sauntered across the room to study his soon-to-be godchild.

"I believe it," Jocelyn said, casting a puzzled look at him. "Why are you up here?"

"I cannot wish to see my godson?"

"I suspect more to it than that," she stated flatly.

"We need to talk, and where is there a better place? Who could lurk outside a nursery with the hope of hearing plans?"

"Do we have plans?" Jocelyn said with a glance at the nanny on the far side of the room. Rising with care, she crossed the room to hand Charles over to his adoring nanny.

"Why do we not go down to my sitting room?" Lora offered, gesturing to the private stairway. "We can chat over tea or whatever you please at this hour of the day."

Taking note of the direction of her gaze, Peter quickly agreed and followed the women down the stairs, closing the door behind him with care.

"Clever arrangement," he commented. "I must remember to have such installed at Leigh Court."

"Are you thinking of marrying at long last, Peter?" Lora inquired, asking the question Jocelyn had wished to ask but dare not. "I assume you would not think of a nursery stairs unless you were considering such. It is time and more that you set up your own nursery."

"Why is it that every woman who has just produced an infant wants to see every man a father?" he complained.

"Well," Jocelyn said with feigned diffidence, "I trust there are a good many others who take an interest as well."

"Do you, now?" he queried gently, lightly caressing her shoulder with his hand as he walked past the chair where she had seated herself in the hope that he would sit close by and she might watch him. She was worse than any schoolgirl with a passion for the dancing master. She was being consumed with her desire for Peter Leigh, and he appeared to toy with her. Poetic justice, perhaps?

"You suggested a game of tennis while at breakfast. Any particular reason for that? Or was it merely something to offer?" He leaned forward, resting his forearms on his thighs.

Jocelyn recalled sitting before him, her legs most improperly across those thighs on the wild ride back to the castle not so many days ago—yet seeming ages. He was a well-built man, yet at ease with that masculinity, not peacocking before others as some men did.

"Jocelyn," he prompted, his eyes gleaming with that silvery light again.

"Oh, of course, tennis," she gabbled, thinking she must be blushing from her head to her toes.

"What about angling?"

"I cannot see how we may solve the mystery of the missing necklace while hoping a fish might snap at our bait," Jocelyn objected.

"I confess I am stumped. I have examined this from every angle possible, and I cannot see who might be hiding the necklace. I was in and out of most bedrooms in this house, and there was no sign of the blasted thing." He sounded quite as discouraged as Jocelyn felt.

"I suppose we have no choice but to demand a search of all the rooms." Jocelyn glanced at Lora, who nodded.

"Adrian is the local justice of the peace, is he not?" Peter asked.

"As you say," she agreed. "He would be able to detain anyone he suspected, particularly if the necklace is actually located. I pray that whoever stole it has not had an opportunity to take it away from here."

"The ruins yesterday. Was there any time when any of the guests might have been able to secrete the necklace with someone else," Jocelyn asked Lora.

"No. Adrian and I watched closely. Since we were quite familiar with the area, we were able to devote our time to observation. Henri and Pierre returned to the house ahead of the rest of us. Do you think either of them could have been responsible for your bash on the head?" Lora inquired hesitantly.

"Suzanne was quite angry that Henri left her to return with the others," Jocelyn suddenly recalled. "I overheard him tell her he would devote the remainder of the day to pleasing her."

"Interesting," Peter said with a curious expression. He settled back on his chair, seeming to contemplate what she had said.

What conclusion he reached was not revealed, to Jocelyn's annoyance.

"I think we need to set a bit of bait for the culprit rather than angle for fish," Jocelyn said with a defiant look at him. "Although I'd not wish for another battered noggin."

"Jocelyn!" Peter exclaimed softly. "Dare I think you worry about me?"

"So I would have concern for anyone in danger."

"You believe there is more danger afoot?"

"Well, I doubt we shall merely stumble across the necklace, if you see what I mean. We—one of us—must face some manner of opposition to obtain that necklace. I doubt it was stolen on a mere whim."

"I doubt we shall find it sitting here, as pleasant as this room and the company may be," Peter said gallantly. He rose from the chair, offering a hand to Jocelyn. "Perhaps we might seek that game of tennis and talk as well?"

"I fear I have little talent for hitting the ball," Jocelyn admitted. She joined him, wondering if they ought to return to the nursery and exit from there, or perhaps leave from Lora's sitting room and raise an eyebrow or two if someone chanced to be in the hall.

"I suspect your talents lie elsewhere," Peter said with that silvery gleam in his eyes once more. Jocelyn was not certain what he meant, and too much the coward to ask.

"Try angling," she said instead. "I ought to have better luck with that."

"Are you good at hooking your catch, my dear?" He walked at her side to stand before the door to her rooms.

"We shall have to see, will we not? Allow me to change into something appropriate for a catch, whatever is in that stream." She gave him a saucy smile, then hurried to change, gently closing the door behind her.

Peter wandered across to his room, taking note that Henri and Suzanne were deep in conversation at the far end of the hall. Half the time she flaunted her charms for Henri, the other half, she attempted to lure him. Peter was not immune to her charms—she was a very beautiful woman—but he knew better than to get close to her. She was dangerous. Any man of sense could see that.

He collected the essentials for fishing, then awaited Jocelyn in the entry hall rather than tease her in her sitting room. He didn't want to overplay his hand.

"Going angling, Leigh?" Uncle Maxim said with forced heartiness. "Are you ready, then, for the costume ball that is to come in three more days?"

"That soon?" Peter said with dismay. When he realized he had revealed something of his fears, he amended his words. "The days have been so full, it is difficult to believe they have been so few."

Henri stepped from the library. "Busy? It seems to me you have been playing least in sight since you arrived. Or do you have games of which we know nothing?"

Peter gave a faint sigh of relief at the sight of Jocelyn skimming down the stairs, dressed in the same blue gown in which she had arrived.

"I have my most elderly garments on. I shall have you know I'll not ruin anything good just to impress you," she cried gaily, quite aware of the audience.

"Adrian said we can gather what we need in the room devoted to sporting gear. Shall we be off to the pond?"

"You do not attempt the stream? I understand it is well stocked," Uncle Maxim insisted.

"We shall see how it goes. I venture to say Lady Jocelyn does not care to tramp along a muddy stream bank."

"Good luck," called Henri. "I trust you shall hook what you want."

Once the door was shut behind them, Peter turned to assist Jocelyn down the steps. "This way." He guided her around the outside of the house to a side door. "I am sorry about all that back there. For some reason Henri takes a particular delight in baiting us. Uncle Maxim as well. Can you think why?"

"Not in the least," Jocelyn replied. "Henri might be envious of Suzanne's obvious preference for you, but I doubt that would bother Uncle Maxim one way or the other."

"She is lovely, but I'd not trust her an inch," Peter said, sending a ray of hope into Jocelyn's troubled heart.

They found the room where all the sporting equipment was kept, and Jocelyn gladly let Peter select the tackle, although she insisted upon carrying her own rod and reel.

"Where are you two off to now?" Suzanne cried from the terrace when Jocelyn and Peter came into view on their way to the pond beyond.

"We shall try a bit of angling. Do you fish?"

"Of course," Suzanne cried gaily.

"Tell me," Jocelyn said seriously, "do you prefer to use baby kitten meat or grasshoppers?"

"Eek!" Suzanne howled. "How could you!"

"I know some prefer puppies—the younger, the better. Personally, I prefer grasshoppers."

"You, you cannibal!" Suzanne screamed. "Have you no tender sensibilities?"

"Well, I do eat fish. It is difficult to catch one without bait. What do you use for bait, Suzanne?" Jocelyn asked sweetly.

"Suzanne has no need of bait," Uncle Maxim said, coming out to the terrace. "The fish takes one look at her and leaps into her net."

That bit of flattery obviously delighted the dark-haired beauty. She preened a little, then waved off the anglers to their fate.

"Good fishing, you two," she cried before sauntering over to a chaise longue that had been brought out for her use. She reclined with a grace any princess might envy.

"Remind me not to cross swords with you, my dear," Peter murmured as they slowly sauntered across the vast lawn in the general direction of the water.

"You would win in any event because I fear bloodshed, and I suspect a sword would be too heavy for me regardless." Jocelyn grinned at him.

The banks of the small lake were uneven, a ragged edge over which an occasional tree hung branches, a log offered a bit of sun for a venturesome frog, and little coves presented variation to the eye.

"This is definitely picturesque," Jocelyn observed. "That small cove suggests hidden delights for a fisherman. A deep pool, an overhanging bank, perhaps a sage old pike?" She pointed off to the distant curve of the lake.

"I believe you do know something of the sport," Peter said with surprise.

"Surely you do not think I intended to seduce you over my rod and reel?" Jocelyn said with a laugh. "I went fishing with my father years ago while he yet lived. I've always suspected he wanted me to be another boy, and so tried to encourage me in masculine interests."

"You do not fence, though?"

"Mother put a stop to that, I fear. I think it might have been a nice diversion." Jocelyn sank down on the bank, heedless of her old dress and ignoring the broad-brimmed hat she had taken in preference to a parasol.

"You make a pretty picture with rod in hand and the sun shining on you as it does."

"Thank you," she said demurely. "Pity it will rain again later on."

"What makes you say that? There are but a few scattered clouds in the sky." Peter baited his hook, then cast out into the water in the new style he had learned.

"I injured my knee as a child, and although it healed well, I am subject to twinges when the weather is about to change."

"Old before your time, are you?" he said lightly before dropping down beside her.

"You wished to talk over the theft if I rightly understood you earlier. There appears to be no one in sight. What can be said? We know little more than when we started."

"Pierre, Uncle Maxim, Henri, and Suzanne are chief suspects. I truly doubt if the shy Mrs. Hastings would be quite that desperate."

"Never underestimate the guile of a woman who has been deprived of what she wants. Think of not having the latest in cravats or waistcoats!" Jocelyn bravely baited her hook with the proffered grasshopper and rose to cast off as she had seen Peter do.

"I see what you mean. Still, I shall wager on one of the others as the guilty party."

"Much as I dislike Suzanne, I doubt she has the cleverness

required for all this shifting about of clues, not to mention the strength to conk you over the head." Jocelyn turned her head so to study him. "How is the wound, by the way? I've not dared ask while in the house, for fear I might compromise you. If it were known we spent a long time alone in that storage room, I fear some parson would be calling the banns."

Peter gingerly felt his skull. "The lump has subsided, thanks in part to the cold compresses and likely more to the brandy. I have a hard head—not to worry."

"Someone ought to worry about you. 'Tis obvious you have no care for yourself," she declared stoutly, refusing to look at him.

He had no reply to that, and Jocelyn fancied she had stepped out of line. It was not proper for a young lady, no matter how old an acquaintance, to make such observations.

"Let us move along the bank. The fish are not biting here," he observed after a half hour of silence.

Jocelyn nodded, helping to gather their things and walked along with him, happy to oblige.

There were artistically arranged banks of shrubbery here and there along the lake, no doubt the result of Capability Brown or someone like him of an improving nature. "It has been planned, but not, I think, obviously so," Jocelyn said when they paused farther away from the house."

"That is a clever little island over there, isn't it?" Peter gestured to the island at one end of the lake where a picturesque cottage had been built. "Wonder what it is like?"

"I have not the slightest idea," Jocelyn replied, not particularly caring of the place, no matter how charming it might be. "I think I have a nibble," she whispered.

Some time later she surveyed the good-sized trout that Peter had removed from her hook. "How nice. Now it is your turn. These fish have a proper sense of what is right, allowing the lady to catch one first."

"I doubt that enters into it."

"What are we going to do about the necklace, Peter? We have but three days until the costume ball."

"So Uncle Maxim pointed out to me while I waited for you in the entry," Peter said dryly.

"I wonder if that means he has the necklace? I mean," she offered diffidently, "would he be so pointed about the time unless he expected a brouhaha over the missing necklace when Lora goes to don her costume?"

Peter failed to reply to that suggestion as he was in the process of reeling in a trout that was of a size with the one Jocelyn had caught.

"Lovely!" she exclaimed. "Do you suppose they were twins?"

"Jocelyn," Peter cautioned with a laugh. "Let us move on, shall we?"

She agreed, and they meandered along the bank, pausing from time to time to examine a clump of flowers, planted by the gardener for effect, or to attempt another catch.

"Look, there is a dinghy. Shall we row out to explore that little house on the island?"

Jocelyn looked up to see clouds advancing across the sky. "Well," she said with doubt clear in her voice.

"Oh, come. It will not rain for ages—perhaps not until this evening."

Not wishing to be a prophet of doom, Jocelyn agreed. "So be it upon your head, in that case. I refuse to be responsible."

Peter plopped the fish into his creel lined with wet leaves, then nicely tucked it into a cool shadow.

It was pleasant out on the water, leaving the shore and all their problems behind for the moment. A small dock had been put in for the little boat. Peter tied the rope carefully to a pier, then assisted Jocelyn from her seat. They strolled to the center of the island, then on to look at the cottage.

"It is much smaller than one might think," Jocelyn observed.

"But not, I think, too small for us. I fear you were right when you said it would rain. Look at those clouds!"

Jocelyn picked up her skirt to run across the intervening space after she viewed the black clouds galloping across the sky. "It will be upon us in moments."

Torrents of rain fell, reminding Jocelyn of the day she had arrived at this benighted spot in the south of Derybyshire. "I wonder if it rains a lot up here?" she queried, stamping her feet once Peter had managed to open the door so they might enter.

"It's exceptionally green, so I would think you are right." He walked at her side, examining the room with a kind eye. A small table and two dusty chairs sat by the fireplace. Near the window stood a narrow daybed.

She looked up at the low ceiling, listening to the water pounding on the roof, then to the window where nothing could be seen beyond. "I believe we are in another world," she murmured. "We have been cut off and set adrift. I am whimsical, am I not?"

She turned to Peter, forgetting the damp skirts that clung to her when she saw that silvery light dancing in his eyes once again.

"Peter?"

He made no reply, drawing her—quite unresisting—into his arms.

Jocelyn felt as though she had come home when she felt those strong arms wrap about her. There would be no attempt to slap him. She knew him better now; perhaps she knew herself a bit better as well. She fearlessly met his gaze, thinking of nothing but the moment, certainly not beyond this time with him.

There was a great deal to be said for kissing. Unfortunately, her mind was not capable of a summation at that moment. If his earlier efforts had beguiled her, the present venture into the realm of passion was quite outside her experience. Could she melt and be afire all at once? She shivered with the notion that managed to make its way to the conscious part of her brain.

Peter broke away from her, looking at her with consternation. "You are freezing again. Just my luck to have you to myself only when it is raining."

Jocelyn gave him a guarded look, wondering if she had entrusted her heart to the wrong man again.

"Do not gaze at me like that, *ma chérie*. I have longed to have you like this ever since I captured you in the rain days ago. I think I shall never wish to let you go again." His smile melted her reserves.

"How lovely," she answered with a look of delight.

"I agree," he murmured, lowering his mouth to hers once again.

She ultimately regained her wits. Recalling that she was not engaged to this man, no matter he had asked her years ago and been rejected, she reluctantly pulled herself from his arms. She met the query in his eyes with a rueful smile.

"I fear we will not be able to stop ourselves do we not cease this now," she said with a sigh. "Oh, Peter, why does the world have to be so complicated?"

"And you, a proper lady?"

"Aye. A proper lady. What I feel for you will not be the less for waiting, however. I trust you, my dear. It is myself I do not trust." She turned away so not to be tempted by the warmth of his gaze. When she did, she immediately saw the rain had passed. "We may go now."

"You sound no more eager than I am, my sweet." Peter came up to pull her against him, resting his chin on her head.

"We must," she reminded.

"Aye, we must." He led the way from the little cottage down to the pier and the waiting dinghy. Only there was no small boat awaiting them.

"I know you tied that boat rope very carefully," cried Jocelyn in vexation.

"There it is—over there, drifting along the shore."

"What shall we do now?" Jocelyn turned to him to see with dismay he was removing his coat, waistcoat, cravat, and shirt. His boots, as well.

"Here, tend these until I return."

Stunned, Jocelyn watched as he waded into the lake, then swam across until he reached the boat.

The minutes dragged until he returned. It seemed an age had passed before he drew up to the dock.

"Get in," he ordered tersely.

Unwilling to comment on his brevity—after all, he must be half-frozen even if it was summer—Jocelyn obeyed.

He shrugged into his dry shirt, then waistcoat.

"The boat did not blow away because of the wind. It was deliberately let loose. Someone wanted us kept here."

"They did not count on your swimming to fetch this little craft," Jocelyn murmured in reply. "There must be other boats, then. But who would do such a thing?"

"We shall wait to see who it is, my dear. I fancy he or she will be evident soon enough."

Jocelyn said nothing to that, merely held his coat to her chest and thought. If it was what she suspected, someone wished them to be compromised. There could be no other reason! But who?

They reached the shore of the lake, Peter hopping out to pull the boat up so Jocelyn might not get wet again. Her shoes had not suffered before, and there was little sense in ruining them. She offered his articles of clothing, and he was in the process of donning his boots, when a sly, implicating voice came from behind him.

"Well, well, what have we here? Two lovebirds, I vow. You managed to weather the storm very well. Lady Jocelyn is not even wet. Did you find the cottage pleasant?"

Peter turned to see Pierre, Henri, and Uncle Maxim looking rather pleased about something. Behind them stood a cluster of other guests, all agog.

Chapter Eleven

"Well," Peter said dryly, "we have a charming group to welcome us. How, er, nice." He finished pulling on his boots, then rose to stand beside the silent and stricken Jocelyn. "I trust you will be pleased to know that Lady Jocelyn has done me the honor of accepting my proposal of marriage." He lightly placed his arm about her, presenting a united front as it were.

"Peter," Jocelyn began only to be silenced by a warning pressure on her shoulder. She was thankful for the comfort offered by his support, but what a dilemma! They could work this out. Things were too confused at the moment; she had no desire to discuss their predicament within the hearing of these three in particular.

"Strange," Uncle Maxim said, glaring at Jocelyn, "I had thought he was paying particular attention to Suzanne."

"I doubt there was sufficient for her to institute a breach of promise suit, if you think in that direction, Uncle," Henri said with a grin.

His uncle muttered something quite forceful in French and stalked away toward the house.

"This is a surprise, Lady Jocelyn," Mrs. Hastings said coyly. "Although I could sense something in the air at breakfast this morning. Indeed, I could. He looked at you so!" Mrs. Hastings chuckled, then followed Uncle Maxim to the house, no doubt to spread the word. She had so little chance to gossip; the betrothal must seem a heaven-sent opportunity to her.

The others who had been drawn to the scene began to drift away, no doubt to discuss this latest happening. Pierre and

Henri remained. Within minutes they were joined by a furious Suzanne.

"What is this I hear about a betrothal?" she demanded with a smile so patently false that Jocelyn almost laughed.

Peter gallantly drew Jocelyn closer, then began to move up the slope to the house. He turned to Suzanne, who perforce had to fall in beside them, to say, "I am surprised you did not guess my intention when Jocelyn and I went off by ourselves this morning. Surely, you did not believe we actually intended to fish?"

"Oh, Pierre brought your creel up to the house along with the rods. Adrian would no doubt forgive you if they were lost, but Cook welcomed the trout," Henri said.

"You fished and proposed? Bah!" Suzanne exclaimed. "That has no romance! Poor Lady Jocelyn."

"We were not precisely fishing at that moment, you know. Actually, we sought protection from the rainstorm. Providence provided the rest," Jocelyn replied sweetly, with an adoring look at Peter. If he could pretend, so could she. They would sort out details later. "I feel certain that Lord Leigh would like to change his clothes. Somehow the boat was released—providence again—and he had to swim to shore so to fetch the boat. We had gone out to explore the island, and that dear little cottage offered brief shelter from the rain—such as it was."

"You were in the cottage—alone?" Suzanne assumed the mien of a cat stalking her prey.

"What would you have done, dear? Stand out in the rain to become soaked and risk pneumonia?" Jocelyn said not so sweetly as before. She turned to Peter. "Come, we shall go up to the house so we both can change. I think we have a few things to discuss?"

"Aye," Henri inserted, "the wedding date, a ring, little things such as that." He laughed, and Jocelyn thought it a rather nasty sound.

"I do not understand this in the least," Pierre grumbled as he fell into step beside Jocelyn. "You would marry him to get a roof over your head, *ma chérie*? Stupid. It is clear there is no *grande passion*. There is no all-consuming love affair between you! That is plain to see."

"We do not flaunt our love for all to see and be amused, Pierre," Peter said quietly. "I believe quite enough has been spoken on this subject."

They gained the terrace, ignored those who wanted to discuss the surprise betrothal, and swept into the house and along to the stairs.

"My," Jocelyn whispered as they marched up the steps, "I have never appreciated a masterful man before this. I shall be sorry to see this end, if this is what I might expect from our alliance. You were quite, quite splendid."

"We shall discuss this when I am dry and in clean clothes. Twenty minutes in your sitting room."

"That sounds more like a threat than a promise," Jocelyn murmured before they parted.

It was amazing what one could accomplish given twenty minutes' time. Jocelyn whipped off the old blue gown. With the help of Mercy, who bustled in the moment she heard the door, Jocelyn donned her most becoming day gown, an almond-green jaconet with cream silk roses and knots of ribands at the single flounce and tiny roses at the front of the round neckline.

"You look flustered, milady," Mercy muttered while she worked on Jocelyn's hair, arranging it in a simple, yet sophisticated chignon. "Come from angling, I'll wager."

Jocelyn could not reprimand her longtime maid; they had been together far too long for that. "You may wish me happy, Mercy. Lord Leigh has done me the honor of offering for me."

"Again? And this time you had the sense to accept? I wish you happy, my lady!" Mercy followed this bit of outspokenness with silence. She stood back to survey her work and nodded that Jocelyn was free to leave.

A glance at the clock told her that Peter would be there any moment. Never had she been so nervous—not even the first time Peter had proposed to her. Then she had been a green girl, knowing nothing of passion or desire. Now she was far more aware of what was at stake. Could she manage to play her hand in this wild game?

She went in to the sitting room a moment before Peter entered. They stood staring at each other across the expanse of carpet. Silent. Tense. She thought he looked prepared to do battle.

"Won't you be seated?" Jocelyn said after clearing her throat. Awkwardness hung in the air.

"You must realize I had no choice," Peter began to her consternation. "We could not avoid the engagement. Your reputation would be shattered, and I would not have that on my conscience. Besides, it will give us more privacy. We can meet here to discuss clues and our search without censure."

There was no protestation of love, no words of assurance. He made it sound so purposeful, a part of their plan to regain the necklace, nothing more.

"Please, there is little need to explain. We were placed in a position that was impossible," she inserted, more flustered than before.

"Jocelyn, this is not how I wanted things to be for us," Peter continued as though she had not spoken. He crossed the room to her side, then drew her to the chaise longue. They sat, facing one another, each searching the other's expression.

"I have never seen your eyes so green. You need not worry. All will be well. You once said something about my having to find a parson were we to be found together," he reminded.

"Actually, I think it was something to do with a calling of the banns before you knew what was about," Jocelyn replied with an attempt at a smile.

He plucked a small object from his pocket. "A ring for your finger. We shall have to satisfy our audience. Can you continue to portray an adoring fiancée?"

"I was not aware I had done so," Jocelyn said, admiring the pretty sapphire on her finger. She liked its dainty size, and it fitted remarkably well. "You came prepared for any event, it would seem." She raised her gaze to meet his, wondering for whom this ring had been intended.

"I can hear you thinking again. You are speculating about the ring, curious as to how I happened to have it with me. Do I have the right of it?" He reached out to caress the sapphire. "It belonged to my grandmother, and I shall not tell you anything beyond that just yet."

"I am to be in the dark? How frustrating! In that event I shall leave all queries for you to answer," she said with rising ire. "It was not my idea to go to that dratted island. I warned you about the advancing rainstorm. But would you listen? No. So you must suffer the consequences."

"Please do not be angry with me. We shall build on this, I think." His smile cajoled, captivated.

"You do not make the slightest sense, you know," she retorted, unwilling to yield to him.

He laughed—a low, untamed sound. "Very well, Jocelyn, have it your way." He drew her into his arms and proceeded to kiss her as a newly betrothed gentleman ought. It was a very proper salute, brief and without passion.

Jocelyn thought it quite tame compared to the kiss shared while the rainstorm raged about them. Had she deliberately provoked him? Had she hoped for that passionate embrace once again?

"I apologize, Peter. I do not know what has muddled my brain."

"You said this was a maddening mull, as I recall."

"Indeed, it is." She relented to smile at him.

"Ah, now I see the rainbow after the storm," he murmured with satisfaction. He bestowed a second kiss, and this time it was one that matched the passion of the kiss at the little cottage, one that had Jocelyn reeling with its intensity.

"Now, my green-eyed girl, we shall go down to a late nuncheon and cope with the inevitable questions that will be sent our way. Can you manage?"

Jocelyn wanted to tell him that after such a kiss, she could manage anything from the wildest storm to a spitting, angry Suzanne. "I believe so."

She did not mention Suzanne, however. She rose from the chaise and crossed to the door to open it. Peering around and seeing nobody in sight, she left the room with Peter at her side.

They partook of a hasty nuncheon alone. The little breakfast room served as their retreat. Jocelyn found she had no appetite, while it seemed Peter was starved.

"Angling apparently makes you hungry," she said with annoyance.

"True," he agreed. He paused to study her, then grinned. "It has unexpected rewards, however. We must do it again some-day."

"Hmpf," Jocelyn replied, trying to sound angry but failing. Did he mean he was pleased with the outcome? She wasn't certain of anything at this point. The engagement had happened in such a rush. She was most confused.

"Eat something, or you will be fuddled when Adrian hands you a glass of champagne, as he is bound to do. Here, some bread and cheese at least."

She obeyed, realizing he was making sense of that, at least. "Do not think you will always have your way, my lord," she said around a bite of her food.

"We will deal together well, I believe." He polished off his meal, then led her down the hall.

When they entered the saloon all conversation ceased.

Lora danced over to greet them with affection. "Our two dearest friends, how pleased we are with the news, for you must know that good news travels quickly."

Adrian followed her, his eyes searching the newly engaged pair with care. "All is well?" he asked Peter.

"Indeed, it is, my friend. Couldn't be better."

"Champagne!" Lora cried. "We will celebrate so momentous an occasion. Now I know why you mentioned making changes at Leigh Court."

A glance from Jocelyn compelled Lora to cease her chatter. Fortunately, the assembled guests had begun to talk again, so her words were lost to most of them.

Not to Suzanne, however, who was standing close by, watching the toasted pair with narrow eyes.

"How lovely, Lady Jocelyn," Suzanne purred. "You will have a place to go when you leave here. Is that not so? A most fortunate circumstance. That Lord Leigh possesses a fortune is also to your advantage. Pity he did not five years ago."

Uncle Maxim moved closer to her, touching her arm. It must have been an effective reminder, for Suzanne clamped her mouth shut. She was about to turn away, then paused. Smiling slyly, she added, "You are not married yet, dear lady."

Slightly shaken by the intensity of that softly spoken threat—

for it could be only that—Jocelyn merely stared, fingering the lovely sapphire as she did.

Suzanne's gaze flicked to the ring, and she stiffened before whirling about. That she turned directly into Henri was likely an accident.

"*Chérie,*" he murmured, leading her away.

However, the good Saxby had been alerted and produced a round of champagne for all to toast the couple standing close together as though offering mutual support.

Lady Thynne came up to Jocelyn and smiled. "I am pleased to see you have put the past behind you, Lady Jocelyn. I predict you will have a good future. Lord Thynne says Leigh is a fine man. We have seen his estate, and can only admire all he has done to it these past few years. It has meant hard work, but my dear husband says it has paid off handsomely."

Jocelyn gave her a bewildered look. "I fear I do not know precisely when he inherited the Court. I have been quite out of touch with Society in general." She could have added Peter in particular, but didn't.

"These recent days have been full for you. Once the ball is past, you will have more time to visit, catch up on the past. We attended your brother's wedding, my dear. You made such a charming attendant. I trust you will plan such an affair?"

Apparently Peter had been eavesdropping as he turned at that point to say, "Not if I have my way. I have waited long enough for this lovely lady. We shall have a special license and a wedding as soon as may be."

Since this was news to Jocelyn, and she couldn't believe it anyway, she turned a suspicious pair of eyes on him. "My lord?" She had cautioned him that she would refer all unanswerable questions to him, and this certainly fit that category.

He bent over to whisper in her ear. "I can hear you thinking. I shall explain all later."

With those brief words she had to be content, it seemed. She smiled brilliantly at Lady Thynne, who drifted off to compare wedding memories with Mrs. Corsham and Mrs. Whyte.

The widowed Mrs. Murray discreetly flirted with Uncle Maxim. Jocelyn wondered if the widow thought to ensnare the older gentleman. Well, it might be possible if Mrs. Murray had received a sizable jointure that had not been depleted by her promotion of her daughter Cordelia.

This curiosity was not to be satisfied, for Lora murmured something about dressing for dinner to the women near her. They, in turn, with husbands or daughters in tow, drifted from the room in twos and threes until there was only Lora and Adrian to face Jocelyn and Peter.

"I should like to know what truly happened this afternoon— not but what I am pleased with the outcome, mind you," Adrian said quietly.

Lora said nothing, just watched Jocelyn's face.

She in turn left it up to Peter to answer the query.

"We went angling along the lake. I was curious about the little cottage on the island. Jocelyn warned me a rain was coming, and I thought she was being overly cautious. I convinced her to row out to the island. I would swear I tied up the boat with care. We made the cottage just as the rain hit us. Shelter was most welcome, I can tell you."

"And what then?" Lora wanted to know.

"When it ceased to rain, we returned to the dock to discover the boat no longer there. It drifted along the far shore, having mysteriously come untied during that short rain, which, I may add, did not have winds all that strong from a direction that would loosen it. Leaving a good bit of my clothes with Jocelyn, I swam to shore and returned with the boat. When we reached land again, we were met by Maxim, Pierre, and Henri—plus an assortment of other guests. You know the rest."

"You had no choice but to do the honorable thing, of course," Adrian said gravely. He looked at Jocelyn, knowing something of the past relationship between these two. "It could be far worse, you must know."

"I would never trap any man into marriage," Jocelyn said most fervently.

"This is one man who is most willing, my love," Peter said with a smile that would melt icicles.

Jocelyn felt breathlessly helpless, as though she was a passenger on a fast-moving coach without a driver and was tearing off to unknown territory at top speed. She met his gaze, wondering what he really felt.

"Well," Lora said with prosaic practicality, "we had best change for dinner. There will be dancing again afterward, so be prepared."

"That will spare Peter a roast from the men present," Adrian said with a grin.

"What might they do to you?" Jocelyn said to Peter as they walked up the stairs.

"Rather warm toasts, my dear. I should feel as though I were in an oven by the time they finished."

Jocelyn blushed at the thought of warm toasts. It seemed men enjoyed being crude to one another. But then, women could take their vengeance in a different way.

"What shall we do about Suzanne Fornier?" Jocelyn asked when they reached her sitting room doorway.

Peter reached around her to open the door, nudged her inside, and then led her across the room to stand by the window. "No sign of rain, I believe."

"Peter, all I asked was what we were to do about Suzanne— not for a discussion on the weather. She was openly hostile to me downstairs. I will not know how to handle her should she keep this up."

"Leave her to me in that event. Perhaps a word with Uncle Maxim?" Peter turned from his inspection of the view to study Jocelyn.

"Perhaps."

"You did magnificently well down there. I was very proud of you and how you sailed through what might have been an ordeal for a lesser woman."

She could feel her blush. "Thank you. I must say, you did rather well yourself. I could almost think you the besotted lover."

"I intend to continue in like vein, my dear girl. Become accustomed to it." That silvery gleam flashed in his eyes again, fascinating and intriguing her.

Delighted but not willing to reveal that pleasure, Jocelyn pretended to bristle. "It is not necessary."

"I rather think it is." He glanced at the door, likely wondering when Mercy would bustle in to prepare her mistress for the evening. "Wear something green and blue if you have it?"

"I have. May I ask why?"

"You shall know in good time." He bestowed a hasty kiss on her cheek, then left just as Mercy entered from the bedroom.

The chosen gown was a gossamer satin that had pale blue and green flowers splashed in a random design. It was trimmed with delicate lace, and Jocelyn thought it almost bride-like in looks. Once Mercy had dressed her hair, Jocelyn applied scent sparingly. She had always used lavender, but tonight called for something special.

When she entered the sitting room, she found Peter waiting for her.

"Do you know that most engaged couples are rarely permitted to be alone? It seems more is feared, then." Jocelyn eyed his subdued dress with appreciation. It did not explain why he had asked her to wear a blue and green gown, but she was not intending to quibble on that point.

"I know. I doubt that applies to us, however. We have an attachment of long-standing, do we not?"

"Is that what you wish me to say? That perhaps I never ceased caring for you and found myself swept away with passion when I saw you once again?" All of which was true, but she was not prepared to admit it.

"I can vouch for the passion part. I had no idea you were such an ardent creature, my dear."

"Stop that or I shall blush myself clear into next Tuesday."

"You never cease to delight me," he said with a laugh. Then he removed a slim box from inside his evening coat. From it he took a necklace with sapphires set in the same sort of style as the ring. "I want you to wear this. It was my grandmother's as well as the ring."

"How lovely," Jocelyn began, only to be cut off by Peter as he stepped close to put the necklace around her throat.

He sniffed and said, "What is that scent? It is as delicious as you, my dear."

"Fallen Angel. I bought it at a bespoke perfumery in Brighton when last there. It has musk and rose with a dash of frankincense, so I was told. Does it please you?" she asked with an artless lack of guile.

"It does tempt me to remain here with you instead of going

down to dinner. Since we are now engaged, perhaps it is permissible for me to claim all your dances? Especially today." He drew back to give her a roughish look.

"Fool! I believe that hit over the head affected you more than you admit. Come, we had best leave now. I'll not wish to be last this evening." She walked to the door, then paused. "The necklace is truly beautiful, and I shall take great care of it for you." She looked at him again and added, "Your head does not pain you, does it? You have not mentioned it all day, and I have been thoughtless not to inquire."

"I am fine, just a twinge now and again. I will not want to overdo this evening, so do not be surprised if I ask you to sit out once in a while."

Jocelyn thought that strange, considering all he had done that day, in particular swimming across the lake to retrieve the wayward boat. "I should like to know who it was that untied our boat this morning," she said as they walked down the stairs to the saloon where guests seemed to prefer gathering.

"I have a hunch, but it is too early to name a name," Peter murmured as they came to the elaborate door that led to the saloon.

Saxby opened it with a flourish, saying, "May I offer my sincere congratulations on your betrothal, Lady Jocelyn, Lord Leigh?"

"Thank you, Saxby," Jocelyn said for both of them. Peter nodded at the butler, then ushered Jocelyn into the room that once again fell silent upon their appearance.

"What do you suppose has happened now," Jocelyn wondered in quiet tones.

"Surprise," Lora said happily. She whisked a package from behind her to proffer it to Jocelyn.

Accepting the gift, Jocelyn felt the veriest fraud. She glanced at Peter to see him grinning at her; that devilish grin that did such crazy things to her heart.

"Open it, love."

"You must help me, or we shall have bad luck all our lives."

"Wherever did you hear that nonsense?"

"I made it up. But you will, nevertheless. Won't you?" Jocelyn laughed at him, and he helped rip the silver paper from what turned out to be a lovely silver bowl.

After both Peter and Jocelyn had said a gracious thank you, the assembled guests went in to dinner.

Jocelyn handed the silver bowl to Saxby before entering the dining room, then turned to Peter. In the noise of everyone settling at the table, she said, "How do we extricate ourselves from this, pray tell?"

"Do not worry about a thing, Jocelyn. I have all in hand."

She gave him a suspicious look. "I suppose you won't tell me a thing?"

The footman offered asparagus soup, and the conversation was at an end for the moment. Jocelyn resolved to tax Peter with the matter later on. She refused to compel him to a marriage he could not wish, although what she might do to stop it at this point she didn't know. He had been so blasted attentive to her, calling her precious names and not using her proper style. First names were reserved for family and exceedingly close friends. Period. It was the outside of enough for anyone else to presume such acquaintance. He had only himself to blame for that part—and the misguided trip to the island. The rest went to whoever set them up for discovery when they returned.

"Do let me know when you decide who took our boat. I shall think of a suitable reward for him." She smiled, but it was a thin smile and devoid of joy.

He raised his brows in query, which she ignored.

Jocelyn doubted if anyone else at the table was thankful when the meal was over beside herself. The food was delicious. Peter had been silent. On her other side Pierre had been the opposite, downright loquacious. She listened to a detailed description of his sadly encumbered estate, and wondered if he had thought he could replenish it at her expense.

The ballroom was brightly lit, the golden candlelight shedding soft illumination on all below.

Peter touched the necklace at her throat. "I like that on you, Jocelyn. I just wish we could find Adrian's."

"As do I," she replied with a frown. It seemed hopeless. Nearly all rooms had been searched and nothing found.

The music began, a lively reel, and Jocelyn soon forgot her troubles while concentrating on the various patterns of the dance.

"You are very good at this sort of thing," Peter said to her while crossing hands.

"We do dance in the country, you know. It is not only in London that people enjoy a bit of merriment."

"Why did you remain there so long?"

Jocelyn cast him a stricken glance. She could not tell him that. What would he say or think if he knew she had deliberately not gone to London so as to avoid seeing him, afraid of his reproach and possible rejection. One confrontation had been enough. She could not have endured another.

"I like the country," she said at last.

"That is not the correct answer, I think, but I can wait." He gave her that knowing look he often wore when with her.

"What makes you think it is a lie?" she challenged. "I am not given to prevarication."

"Only when it comes to our past association. I have watched you rather carefully, my love."

Jocelyn was frustrated when he danced away from her in the pattern of the dance. There was much to be said for the waltz, as scandalous as some thought it. Countess Lieven had danced it for years while in Russia, and she was anything but an example of rectitude, in spite of her embrace by Society. Yet it offered a chance to talk.

When next she saw Lora, she requested a waltz. "Surely you would not be thought provincial, dearest?"

Since no hostess wanted to be thought countrified, Lora hastily requested a waltz of the musicians.

Jocelyn placed herself before Peter just as the introductory strains were played. She flashed a guilty grin at him., "May I have this dance, sir?" she asked with a roughish lilt in her voice. In for a penny, in for a pound, she decided.

"Goodness!" he exclaimed with a laugh.

"Goodness has nothing to do with it. It is one place where we can talk without causing any scandal." She allowed him to place his arm about her and entrusted her hand to his.

"Outside your sitting room," he reminded.

"There probably has been gossip about that, and we simply have not heard it yet," she stated. "What are we to do about this engagement we have been coerced to assume? I should like to know."

How lovely it was to circle about the room in his arms, to be able to legitimately be close to him, and in public, no less.

"Why, my love, we shall marry as soon as I can obtain the license!"

Chapter Twelve

Jocelyn missed a step. "That is scarcely amusing, Lord Leigh," she scolded. "Be serious."

"I am. I ought to marry, and since I have already asked you once and you are still single, it made sense to me that we join in matrimony. I shall disregard your previous answer. I believe—and I think your response to me proves it—that you have suffered a change of heart these past years. You are not indifferent to me, regardless of what you may say. Besides, you like children," he concluded, quite as though that should end all discussion.

Jocelyn didn't know how to respond. She had just told him that she did not prevaricate. She had never been any good at telling lies. How could she look him in the eye and do so now?

"I might be tempted to persuade you." His baritone teased, taunted her.

She stared at him in disbelief, then nodded. "I will not doubt that for a moment. I have come to view you as the very dangerous Baron Leigh."

His bark of laughter brought curious glances from the other dancers. "Charming. I've never considered myself a dangerous man."

"Believe me, you are," she admitted rather unwisely. "That is, I should hate to cross you were I a villain." Drat her wayward tongue. He had the ability to totally rattle her brain. If she'd had any sense at all, the moment she realized he was at the castle, she should have turned around and gone away to somewhere else, even if it was pouring rain. She must have a cousin somewhere who needed a companion or would tolerate a guest for a brief stay? On the other hand, she wouldn't feel so alive!

"Let us hope that the person who did us that favor this morning appreciates your view. Jocelyn, you must realize that we truly have no option. In our restricted Society, word passes quickly. There are many who know our past association. Can you imagine what would be the gossip should we *not* wed? Particularly after the time we have spent together? We have been as close as inkle-weavers. Only Adrian and Lora know we have joined in an attempt to find the missing jewels—something I must add that we have failed to do so far."

Jocelyn made no comment to that bit of wisdom. "What can I say? Although I *told* you it was not a good idea for you to spend so much time in my sitting room. You cannot say that you were not warned!"

"Most effectively," he said, gazing down into her eyes with that silvery gleam again.

Jocelyn wished she knew what was in his mind when that occurred. On the other hand, maybe it was just as well she didn't. Peter spun her about rather deftly, and she clung to him, noting he retained that mischievous glimmer in his eyes. Oh, any woman who didn't think this man was dangerous needed her head examined.

She gazed around the ballroom to note the absence of the spectacular Suzanne. "Miss Fornier is missing."

"I had not noticed," Peter replied, a most satisfactory answer as far as Jocelyn was concerned.

"Well, she does add a touch of style to the room," Jocelyn said in defense of the young woman she could not like.

Adam Tremayne waltzed past with Miss Murray triumphant in his arms. Hugh Fordyce and the shy Alisha Osmond seemed to manage a great deal of discussion as they made a sedate circle of the floor. Pierre stood against the wall and appeared to search the room.

"I think Pierre is looking for her."

"Why are you spoiling our waltz with talk of that predatory female?" Peter complained.

"She is, is she not?" Jocelyn murmured, content to agree on that score.

All good things come to an end eventually as did this waltz. Peter led Jocelyn from the room to where Saxby and Cook had arranged a delectable buffet.

"I might have wished to dance again," Jocelyn observed casually.

"I was hungry, and if I'm so dangerous, I must be fed. Or are you offering yourself as supper?"

"I do not trust that gleam in your eyes, Lord Leigh," she said in lofty accents.

"Rubbish, since you put it there. Here, have something to eat and we can discuss wedding plans."

She frowned, accepting the plate he had loaded with a nice variety of victuals. She especially liked lobster salad and the crunchy little rolls Cook made. Plunking the plate down on a small table, she turned to study him. "Are you *really* serious? You are certain this isn't something you want to let slide for a bit, then decide we do not suit, or something like that?"

"No, my dear Jocelyn. I have actually sent off for a special license from Doctor's Commons. Adrian helped. The letter and all should be arriving there tomorrow. When the license comes, we can find a parson. I trust you prefer a wedding in church?"

"Naturally. It would not seem right elsewhere. Not that Adrian's saloon isn't lovely." Then she realized what he was doing to her, and she stamped her foot. "I did not accept your proposal."

"I shall have to persuade you."

He sounded so satisfied at that notion that Jocelyn began to back away from him.

"Now, love," he admonished. "Come here."

She would never understand why her feet refused to obey her and listened to him instead.

He barely touched her, merely lips to lips. Jocelyn decided he was part magician, he had to be. Any sanity she had left departed. Her willful feet took steps so she might be closer to the source of such delight. Thankful she had placed that plate on the table, she gingerly put her hands on those broad shoulders and sighed blissfully when he eventually released her.

"Say yes, Jocelyn," he instructed.

"Yes, Jocelyn," she repeated foolishly. "I mean, you cannot do this to me!"

"Ah, but you did say yes, my dear. Now, shall you want to order a dress? Lora says there is a rather good mantua-maker in Derby who will be glad to make the trip out here with a collection of suitable fabrics. She could also bring a proper hat if you give her an idea of what you prefer. Adrian has a glasshouse full of assorted blooms, or you may like those roses we viewed the other night. That scent was rather appealing, I thought. Mercy said you have some elegant cream slippers that are, she claims, just perfect for a wedding. Have I missed anything?" He gave her a look of pure innocence. She had seen children with that expression when asked if they had eaten the cherry pie while sporting red-smeared mouths.

"You truly are serious," she said, wonder making her fumble for a chair. This was not a moment to depend on shaky knees.

"I am," he replied. What else he might have added to this revelation was not to be known.

Lora came rushing up to them, a look of apology on her face as she interrupted what was obviously a *tête-à-tête*. "Suzanne seems to have disappeared. Have either of you paid the slightest attention to anyone else this evening?"

"Jocelyn observed during the waltz that Miss Fornier was absent. I can't say I noticed her."

"Amazing," Jocelyn muttered under her breath.

The others looked at her with brows raised.

"It's amazing she would miss a ball when she seems to love dancing so much," Jocelyn hurried to say. "Pierre seemed to be searching over the room before we left there for the buffet.

"I wonder if Henri is about. They always seem to have much to discuss," Peter observed.

"So I have noticed," Jocelyn agreed. "He seemed inordinately pleased this morning that you were compelled to offer for me because of our seclusion on the island."

"I heard you gave Suzanne a proper set-down when she quizzed you about it," Lora said.

"Never cross words with Jocelyn, Lora. She can be fierce

when riled." Peter's expression was bland, but for some reason Jocelyn suspected he was laughing at her behind that facade.

"Do you want us to help you look for her?" Jocelyn asked, ignoring the impossible remark Peter had made.

"Please. Uncle Maxim will be furious if he discovers she has slipped away."

"We shall be a team," Peter offered.

"I do not think so," Lora said with a glance at him. "Somehow I doubt if you would get past the first secluded spot. It is not so long since Adrian wooed me, you know."

Jocelyn suspected she was blushing, and to cover that, she rose, turning away from them as she said, "I shall search on the terrace."

"Jocelyn," Peter began. She paid him no heed.

The cool night air felt wonderful on her heated cheeks. How in the world could she cope with Peter and his wicked ways? Dangerous? He was hazardous to her sanity.

Recalling what she was to do, she made a systematic search of the terrace. Since there were columns and enormous pots of flowers and ivy, not to mention a statue here and there, this was not a simple task as one might first think. Besides, there were people drifting out to enjoy the stars and scents from the garden. Feeling foolish, Jocelyn wandered about, peering at the various couples to see if Suzanne had perchance lured Adam Tremayne or Hugh Fordyce into an indiscretion. The gentlemen were there, but with Miss Murray and Miss Osmond.

Lady Thynne paused in her conversation with Mrs. Whyte to query Jocelyn. "Are you looking for someone, my dear?"

"Miss Fornier." Jocelyn couldn't think of a reason why she might be searching for the girl, so she did not give one.

"It has been some time since I saw her. Mary? Have you seen her?" she asked of Mrs. Whyte.

Another negative answer, and Jocelyn set off again. In a short time it was obvious that wherever Suzanne Fornier was, it wasn't on the terrace.

Jocelyn sought out Lora, who had been quizzing Saxby.

"Now what? Are you truly worried?"

"I think one swiftly accepted proposal is sufficient for a house party," Lora said obliquely.

"It was not so swift," Jocelyn objected. "He had to persuade me. Besides, who would be after Suzanne that is not around here? I saw Mr. Tremayne and Mr. Fordyce on the terrace just now. The only other single men of interest are Pierre and Henri. She fights with both of them."

"But most often with Henri," Lora added.

Jocelyn exchanged a look with her cousin. "I shall go upstairs to nose about there. Where did Peter go?"

"He muttered something about it being a good time to search, whatever he meant by that."

"Oh," Jocelyn replied, her mind working furiously on that puzzle.

Leaving her cousin to pretend nothing was amiss, Jocelyn hurried along the hall until she reached the stairs. At the top she paused, wondering which way to go. She heard the sound of a door opening at the far end of the hall, so flattened herself into the shadows, far from the wall scone, where a lone candle shed dim light.

She saw a man exit what Jocelyn knew to be Suzanne Fornier's room. Had Henri made an assignation with the beautiful young woman? If Uncle Maxim learned of this, he would be more than furious. Henri and Suzanne would be marched to the parson in double time.

However, this gentleman was taller than Henri. His shoulders looked to be a bit broader as well. Henri was inclined to stockiness. You could never say that about this man.

Deciding he was about to see her if she didn't do something, she retreated to the door of her sitting room and entered, peeking out to see if she could identify the man who had sought the gorgeous Suzanne. She wasn't anywhere else around here—she must be in her room.

Jocelyn stiffened when the man drew near a wall sconce and the light fell upon his face. Peter!

Quickly shutting the door, Jocelyn leaned against it, her heart beating madly. It couldn't be! Surely not! But Suzanne was incredibly beautiful, and had noticeably flirted with Peter Leigh. She would be tempting, Jocelyn supposed. It would be difficult to turn away from that proffered beauty. She didn't think Peter sought the liaison. But if Suzanne summoned him to her room, could he resist?

A tap on her door drove Jocelyn across the room to stand by the window. "Enter," she said after taking a deep breath.

"What are you doing standing in the dark, love?" Peter gently queried.

"I have been hunting for the missing Suzanne," Jocelyn admitted.

"When did you come upstairs? I thought you went to the terrace?"

Jocelyn felt chilled. "Just now. I wanted to fetch a shawl from my room." That was a silly excuse. She ought to have thought of a better reason, but she was wretched at prevarication.

"I gather she wasn't there in that case?" He moved away from the door, then crossed the room to the fireplace, taking a candle to light it in the glowing coals in the hearth. From it he lit an entire branch of candles, then turned to face Jocelyn.

"Do you know where she is?" Jocelyn asked, hating the tremor in her voice.

"No."

"I saw you just now. You came out of her room."

"If I say that I did not see her, that she wasn't in that room, would you believe me?"

Jocelyn quickly recalled all he had said of the woman as well as his insistence of marriage to herself. Peter was an honorable man. He'd not do something so sneaky and reprehensible. "I believe you," she replied, knowing that she truly did. It felt good, to have this trust in someone. She had not felt that toward Simon. Not anyone, other than her father, come to think of it.

"My Jocelyn, so brave and honest. I was afraid for a moment that you would tear into me for having an assignation with the gorgeous Suzanne. You must know that I vastly prefer girls with green eyes. You, my love."

As an explanation it was more than satisfactory, as was what followed.

At last she murmured, "We are not making much headway at locating the luscious Suzanne Fornier, are we?"

"I had forgotten all about her. Dratted woman, why cannot

Henri or Pierre make her a wife so we need not worry about her ever again?" he complained, resting his head atop of Jocelyn's.

"I suspect one or both of them would like that. I did not say that well, I mean both Henri and Pierre wish to marry her, I think. She appears to delight in toying with them, not to mention flirting with you and any other eligible male within her sights."

"Thank you, I think. At least you consider me eligible," he said with a low laugh.

"Peter Leigh, you must know you have the qualities matchmaking mamas dream of! You are handsome, have a lovely home—from what Lady Thynne says—and a fortune to boot. Not only that, you are a charming gentleman and dance divinely."

"I am beginning to think I do not deserve you. I cannot possibly live up to your words."

"You mean your fortune is all a hum? Or did the house fall down after Lord and Lady Thynne departed?"

"None of the above. Come, my love, we had better leave this pleasant room before I totally forget my breeding and do what I would like."

Feeling quite daring, Jocelyn grinned at him and asked, "And what might that be?"

"I will not tell you now. When the moment is right."

With that, she had to be satisfied. Peter checked the hallway before they left. "I should like to know if that wretched girl has returned. *Or* if someone else wants to meet her in her room."

"What do you mean, someone else?"

"Pierre stuck his head around the door while I was in there."

"Without knocking?" Jocelyn wondered.

"A rattle of the doorknob was all the warning I had. Good thing the box is gone from her wardrobe, or I would have stepped on it."

Jocelyn giggled at the thought of Peter hiding in that wardrobe. "However did you manage to stuff yourself in among all those clothes?"

They reached the main floor, and Peter took Jocelyn's hand to drag her along the hall and out the front door.

"I thought I would suffocate. Good thing he left right away. Now, where could she be?"

Jocelyn gazed about searching shadows, uneasy at the rustle of trees and the bark of a dog. "Everything seems suspicious in the dark—had you noticed?"

"The only thing I notice in the dark is you." He tugged at her hand. "Come along. Perhaps she is by the archery range."

"What on earth would she be doing there at night?" Jocelyn, pleased at his words, stumbled as she attempted to keep pace with him.

"Who knows? She might find it a good spot to meet her lover."

"I wonder who he would be?" Jocelyn mused, glad when Peter slowed to a stealthy prowl.

"Shh," Peter cautioned. "There appears to be someone at the archery target."

"Who?" she whispered, wishing she could see better. Peter must have eyes like a cat if he could detect people in this dark. Her answer came from an unexpected source—the trio by the target.

"What are you two doing out here, eh, Henri?" Pierre demanded.

"Do not be so stuffy, Pierre," Suzanne cried, her manner coy. "How else can Henri and I have a bit of, ah, conversation?"

"You were not talking when I found you."

"Bah," Suzanne said with obvious disgust. "I want a bit of fun in my life. To be always proper and stuffy like you is dull. I loathe being dull."

Peter took Jocelyn's hand, and together they crept back to the front of the house.

"I believe we can report to Lora that her ewe lamb can well take care of herself. If Uncle Maxim cares, he can jolly well interfere. I am not about to enter the fray. Not when there are more interesting things to do."

"I suppose we had better find Lora now?" Jocelyn said, adopting the same coy tone in her voice she had heard Suzanne use so effectively.

"Jocelyn, you play with fire," Peter cautioned.

He tugged her hand, and she obediently followed him into the house, seeking Lora or Adrian.

They found Adrian, explained about the trio in the garden, and then announced they were going to join the next set for the quadrille.

Peter kept her in the ballroom from then on, dancing every dance with her, keeping her very much in view, although she doubted if one person there cared a fig what she did. She was becoming reckless in her old age. Did Peter mind marrying a spinster? She ought to ask him, but on the other hand, why?

Rather late, but in perfect demeanor, Suzanne made an appearance looking as cool as an iced melon. Jocelyn was tempted to ask her how the archery was, then recalled she wasn't supposed to know about that. But it was tempting to vex the saucy beauty who thought she could get by with anything.

It was after midnight when the guests straggled up the stairs and to their rooms.

Jocelyn bid Peter a sleepy good night at the outer door to her sitting room, then joined Mercy, who persisted in waiting up for her no matter what Jocelyn told her.

"You told Lord Leigh about my cream slippers," she remembered.

"Indeed, I did, milady. They are like new and most suitable for wedding attire. I trust you will be ordering cream satin and lace from Derby?"

"I rather like taffeta, Mercy. At my age it would be nice to make a bit of noise, if you see what I mean."

Jocelyn faced the reflection in the looking glass. Coward. You ought not to yield so easily. Although he seemed remarkably intent upon this wedding.

"Lord Leigh has sent to Doctor's Commons for a special license, Mercy," Jocelyn said with a narrow look at her traitorous maid.

"You shall be wed here in Derbyshire, then? 'Tis well enough. You will have your cousin to attend you."

"Mercy, do you not think it strange that I am going to marry the man I refused five years ago?" Jocelyn asked softly, a few of her doubts creeping up to bother her.

"Goodness, no, not at all. Plain as the nose on your face that you have pined for him all these years. I knew you didn't care a pin for that other, Simon Oliver. Tried to please your brother, that's what you did. 'Tis no good in doing that. What does a brother know, after all?"

Jocelyn allowed Mercy to plait her hair, then crawled into bed. Her dreams centered around a taffeta gown that swished.

"It appears you slept well, Jocelyn," Peter said when she entered the breakfast room.

Mrs. Hastings looked up, her face assuming the mien of a bird dog on the scent of a partridge.

"Thank you. I had pleasant dreams," she added before she considered how it might sound.

Peter choked slightly but said nothing.

Mrs. Hastings nattered on about dreams versus nightmares for a time before her voice faded into nothing. The silence might have been unnerving to most. She tenaciously remained, picking at her food, watching the pair at the table with her.

"I was hoping you might join me for a bit of archery," Peter said to Jocelyn in a low voice with a glance at Mrs. Hastings. If he hoped she didn't hear, he was mistaken.

"It rained a bit last night, but the sun has come out now. I should venture to say the target must be dry by now."

"Thank you, Mrs. Hastings," Peter said with perfect courtesy and nice formality.

She became so flustered that she rose and left the room without having finished her breakfast.

Jocelyn giggled. It had been so long since she had felt like this. Doing worthy deeds and serving on the parish church committee for the poor somehow did not match being courted by a dangerous man—although he looked quite harmless this morning.

"You slept well, Lord Leigh?" Jocelyn said primly, quite aware that someone might come around the corner at any moment.

"Indeed, Lady Jocelyn," he replied, his lips twitching with amusement. "And now that we have covered the weather for the morning and our night's rest, I trust we may leave here confident we face the archery target unchallenged?"

"If you wish," Jocelyn said, relenting in her teasing.

Not very hungry, she pushed her half-empty plate away and joined him to head for the archery area of the garden.

"We are going to pick up some bows and arrows, are we not?" she inquired hesitantly.

"The equipment room is around to the side, remember? We went there for our tackle."

"How could I forget? I do hope one of the servants put everything away for us," she added with a trace of guilt.

"Adrian has a well-trained staff. They were stowed where they belong." He took her hand and pulled her along with him to the room where all the game equipment was stored. Bowls, tennis rackets, bows and arrows, rods and reels, oars for the rowboats, everything neatly kept in order.

"I would like to know who took our boat," she mused while selecting a bow.

"Come, I have the arrows. I don't care what bow you grab, I just want to get there before anyone else."

"Why did you not say so, then," Jocelyn complained. She took the first bow to hand, then followed him out, nodding to the servant who entered as they left.

"Actually, I am rather good at this, you know," Jocelyn said to make a bit of conversation as she tried to keep up with Peter's long-legged stride.

"Good. You can help me once we get there."

She gave his back a puzzled look, but said nothing. He must have had a bad night. Or second thoughts. Well, she was not going to stick her neck out on that. He had insisted, so he could jolly well suffer.

"Here we are. Now, help me look."

"Look? For what?" Jocelyn knew she was not brilliant, but this was a bit beyond her.

"For clues. Recall those three were all here last evening. It is possible a clue to the missing necklace is around here."

"Not likely," Jocelyn protested. "I mean, after all, why would whoever stole the necklace bring it out here?"

"To brag? To show off? Remember that Suzanne complained that Pierre was such a dull dog? It is also possible that Henri wished to show Suzanne he would have the means to support her. That necklace would take care of her wants for a long time."

"I'd not thought of that." Jocelyn propped the bows up against a stand made to hold arrows for an archer, then knelt on the grass with Peter. "I do not see the necklace. It's rather large, you know."

"You know, Suzanne might have stolen the necklace to be independent and have an adequate dowry," Peter mused while separating blades of damp grass.

"You are getting grass stains on your breeches," Jocelyn said absently while she also examined the lawn blade by blade. If that was what Peter wanted, she would go along with him, no matter how crazy it seemed to her.

"Jocelyn," he muttered in a sorely tried manner.

"Well, you are. I trust Dickman is as good as Mercy about things like that."

"He is."

Silence prevailed for a time while the hunt continued.

Jocelyn was about to give up—in fact, she had sat back on her heels, ready to rise—when he gave an exclamation of satisfaction.

"You found something? You actually found something? I cannot believe it," Jocelyn said quietly with a look around to see if anyone was creeping up on them.

"Look, a gemstone. I doubt if the gardener or the workmen have anything like this!"

"A ruby! It would appear the proper size for the necklace, as I recall it." Jocelyn touched the stone, then raised her gaze to meet Peter's. "This confines the suspicion to one of those three without a doubt."

"As I figured. Adrian was correct to suspect one of his cousins."

"So . . . now what do we do? We do not know which of those three is the culprit."

"See if you can hit the target, of course. Most women I have observed are terrible. They cannot even manage the outer circle."

Jocelyn gave him a hard look, then picked up the smaller of

the two bows, nocked an arrow with accustomed ease, took aim, and let fly. She hit the red circle.

"Not bad, not bad." He grinned, insufferable in his smugness.

She took another, glanced at him once again, nocked the arrow, aimed, this time hitting the gold center.

"Remind me never to take you for granted, love."

"Do that," she quipped, and felt enormously pleased.

Chapter Thirteen

Adrian looked rather grim when Peter showed him the ruby found in the grass by the archery target.

"This proves beyond a doubt that one of those three is guilty."

"I'd put my money on Henri," Jocelyn said, lips pursed and eyes narrowed.

"I don't know," Peter mused, "Suzanne wants money rather badly, you know. *Cherchez la femme,* isn't that what they say?"

"Well, I wouldn't know, *chéri*," Jocelyn said. "I have not been all that close to her, nor to the others." She looked away for a moment, then screwed up her courage to add, "I must say, Adrian, I cannot be fond of your relatives."

He shook his head. "Nor can I. One may choose one's friends, as 'tis said, but relatives are yours come what may."

"What about Pierre?" Jocelyn asked, wondering if he might not have more than an abundant motive.

"Uncle Maxim seems willing to help him out with some funds, not that the fellow has much to spare. The thing is," Adrian confided, "if I assist them financially, they will be leeches for life. I strongly feel I would not be doing them a favor in the long run. Better to face up to responsibilities and cut spending. Surely Henri does not require two of everything in the latest style? Particularly in such repellent colors?"

"Indeed," Jocelyn murmured, thinking of the utterly distasteful waistcoat in pea-green with embroidery done in naccarat and lilac. The tangerine color with the lilac on the pea-green was enough to make one ill. Although she had to admit that when combined with his primrose coat and celestial-blue breeches, he made a colorful sight.

"I do not think he would agree with Brummell on the niceties of dress," Peter added dryly.

"So—you do not think I am cruel to them?" Adrian asked with a wry smile. "Lora, bless her generous heart, would have me rescue them, not understanding that then they would become spongers forever after."

"She is very good," Jocelyn said with her fondness evident in her voice and smile. "*I* am most fortunate in my relatives."

"Even your brother?" Peter muttered.

Jocelyn's smile faded, recollecting that her brother had advised her not to marry Peter. "Most of the time he is a dear, and he meant well, you know."

Peter glanced at her, then back to his good friend. "Allow me to differ." Then he looked out at the morning sun shining on the gardens and took Jocelyn's arm in an urgent clasp. "Come, I believe we had best get to the archery target immediately."

Jocelyn sent Adrian a bewildered look, but did not argue. Peter had something in mind, and she would wager it had to do with solving the mystery.

They hurried out the side door that was close to the equipment room. Peter dashed inside to grab a couple of bows and a case of arrows kept at the ready.

Jocelyn nearly ran to keep up with him as they headed along the grassy path to where the target was always left standing. In the event that weather improved, one might find the target ready and waiting to take advantage of sunshine. She reminded herself that there was a reason this countryside was so green. It rained a lot.

They rounded the path to discover Suzanne on her hands and knees searching over the ground where she had stood the night before while with Henri and Pierre.

"Have you lost something?" Peter asked courteously.

Taking a cue from Peter, Jocelyn added, "May we help?" She dropped down on the lawn, thankful she had a day gown of mulberry with narrow white stripes. Mercy might complain, but it wouldn't be as though Jocelyn wore pale yellow as Suzanne did. "What is it? Something tiny? An ear bob, perhaps? Is it gold? The glitter would show."

"Oh, do go away," Suzanne snapped. "I prefer to hunt alone."

"We would be sorry friends were we to permit that!" Jocelyn declared. "What are friends for, if not to lend a helping hand? Am I not right, Lord Leigh?" She beamed an angelic smile up at him.

"By Jove, you are right, Jocelyn." He placed the bows and case of arrows aside,and joined Jocelyn on the grass, a query on his brow. "Now, if you would be so kind as to tell us for what we search . . ."

Suzanne sighed, giving them an angry look. "A stone. It fell out of my, er, necklace."

"Diamond? Emerald? What?" Jocelyn said, parting the grass as though to find the elusive gem. It occurred to her that it might be possible more than one stone had been lost, in which case there could still be one hiding among the blades of grass.

"I say," Peter began, then sighed with regret. "No, merely a pebble of a rather pretty greenish hue. Perhaps it is red we seek?"

"A ruby," Suzanne replied, sounding sorely tried.

Jocelyn exchanged darted glances with Peter and kept searching. Although Suzanne had given but one stone, it was still possible there was another. Suzanne crawled about, turning so her back was to Jocelyn and her side to Peter.

The sun peeked through the leaves of the overhanging birch, and Jocelyn just refrained from gasping when she found a tiny cameo face on the ground. Didn't the necklace have such a thing at the top of the pendant? She palmed the tiny thing and continued to hunt. If the ruby and cameo had fallen out—or been dropped—there could be an emerald and sapphire in the area as well.

Peter paused, looking at Jocelyn. "Perhaps we ought to do as Suzanne asks, love? The ground is a bit damp. I had thought we could shoot a bit, but one of us might hit Suzanne instead of the target."

Jocelyn bit back a grin. "Are you implying that I am not a good shot? Well, let me tell you, I can hit that target every time.

Well, most of the time," she amended, trying to sound silly and thinking she had succeeded too well, judging by his expression. "Let me demonstrate!"

Peter rose and assisted her to her feet. She picked up the smaller of the two bows, pulled out an arrow, nocked it, then took aim. The arrow landed just short of Suzanne.

"Heavens above, I shall be murdered!" Suzanne cried. "I must have been mistaken, there is no stone here. You may have your archery." She rose and stomped off in high dudgeon.

"That was not very well-done of me, was it?" Jocelyn said with a repentant look at Peter. Then she giggled, unable to help herself.

Peter shook his head and grinned. "You may as well hit the target. I know you can."

The arrow went to the center of the gold, and Jocelyn permitted herself a brief smirk. Then she recalled the cameo. Dropping the bow, she revealed where she had hastily concealed it in the bodice of her gown. "See what I found?" She held out the dainty cameo for his inspection. "I am certain this is from the center piece that hangs down, a sort of pendant from the circlet of stones. There must be nearly a half dozen in the matching bracelet as well. I do not know what he or she is about, but stupidity is high on the list of attributes. What about you? I suspect you picked up something as well."

"It's a trifle muddy, but it appears to be an emerald." He proffered the gem, and Jocelyn nodded.

"If we rinse these off, we shall take them to Adrian looking their best. Do you suppose there might be a sapphire around here as well? It would be logical. The stones are in a specific order, and as I remember, a sapphire comes between the ruby and the emerald."

"Clever girl," Peter said with admiration in his look.

It was Peter who found the sapphire. He pointed out the location of the three gems found, then hunted a bit, coming up with the blue gem in a short time.

"I doubt there are more than these stones. But they are enough to convince Adrian that whoever took the necklace intends to break it up to sell the stones separately," he said quietly.

"Which is a stupid thing to do. The necklace must be worth a fortune in its entirety." Jocelyn shook her head at the mere thought of such folly.

Peter gathered the bows while Jocelyn picked up the case of arrows. The walk to the house had none of the rush coming down. Pity they had a mystery to try and solve. The day was gorgeous with the promise of full sun and little wind.

"Someday I should like to just please myself and shoot at that target, perhaps laze on the lake in one of the little boats." Jocelyn swung the case gently to and fro, tilting her head back to feel the warmth of the morning sun on her face. "Umm, I shall probably get freckles, but this is delightful, you must admit."

"I predict we shall become wanderers in search of endless sunny days and starlit nights," Peter said with a laugh.

"That does sound appealing, but you know that life is not like that. There is rain and mud and pain and days that end all too soon," Jocelyn said with a sigh.

They shortly found Adrian on the terrace. If he took note of Jocelyn's soiled gown, muddied a bit when she crawled about on the damp grass, or Peter's breeches, smeared with grass stains, he said nothing within the hearing of the guests strolling about enjoying the flowers and sun.

However, he did join them in admiring a particular rose to which Jocelyn called his attention.

"I presume you have an explanation for your appearance?" Adrian queried with a gentle smile. "You two have been up to something? You usually look quite up to snuff."

"See what we found by the archery target?" Peter asked rather offhand, offering the cameo, emerald, and sapphire to Adrian.

"We went to shoot a few arrows and discovered Suzanne crawling around on the ground—in a pale yellow gown—wishing us far away while she hunted for something she lost. Claimed it was a ruby, a single gem from her necklace." Jocelyn studied the now-clean gems in Adrian's hand.

"Naturally, we said nothing about our finds to her." Peter looked about him, then added, "I do not believe there are any more gems there. From the way Jocelyn described the necklace to me, I agree with her that it is logical that no more would have fallen—"

"Or been removed," Jocelyn inserted and Peter nodded.

"—from the necklace," he finished.

"Thank you, both of you, for I suspect this is quite a joint effort on your part." Adrian glanced about him. "We had best saunter into the house so I can tuck away these gems until we obtain the entire lot."

Jocelyn brushed down her skirt, exclaiming over the dirt in a manner bound to earn sympathy from any of the women. Peter ushered her into the house with a sensitive attitude.

"I can see where you might make an excellent husband," Jocelyn remarked casually. "You are able to enter into the spirit of things so well."

He laughed. "I believe you will find other, more desirable traits before long, my love."

"I wish you would not call me that," Jocelyn said quietly. "I feel that endearment ought to mean something, not be a merely casual term that might apply to anyone reasonably close."

"Believe me when I tell you there is nothing casual in the way I feel about you, Jocelyn." Peter flung an arm around her shoulders as they entered the library, closing the door firmly behind them.

"The room is empty?" Jocelyn whispered. It was such a large room, it would be possible for someone to hide in the far recesses of a wingback chair and not be noticed.

Peter strolled about, leaving Jocelyn standing by the desk. "Nary a soul, my dear." He put a slight emphasis on the last word, with a significant look at her.

Jocelyn felt a glow of warmth seep through her. Perhaps this all would work out for the best.

"I imagine the other guests think Jocelyn and I are off cuddling or something of the sort," Peter murmured to Adrian. "We certainly have not been around much during these past days."

"True," Jocelyn added. "But does it make much difference? As Peter once remarked to me, a lord can get away with anything, and I am a spinster of renown, old enough to know better, too old to care, perhaps?"

"You are always scolding me about coming into your sitting room," Peter objected.

"I do not want to know what you two are up to around the house," Adrian chastised with a grin. He removed a small chamois bag from his desk, dropped the gems Peter and Jocelyn had found into it, then replaced the bag, locking the drawer with a dainty key kept on his watch chain.

"Not the vault?" Jocelyn queried.

"Remember, they do not know we have found them," Adrian reminded. "They will look anywhere but here."

Peter agreed. "Now to discover who has the rest of them. I should wager they will not hunt at the archery target anymore. However, perhaps we ought to linger in that area, just in case?" He looked at Jocelyn.

"You are seeking my approval? Fine! I shall go with you, utterly delighted to be out on this lovely day. A rare day in June, I vow." Jocelyn smiled at both men. "I need not bother to change, for I have a suspicion I shall be required to crawl around doing something underhanded." She grinned at Peter, then walked to the door.

"Wait for me by the terrace, or perhaps in the equipment room. You can cull through the bows to find the best weight."

Seeing the men wanted to talk, Jocelyn left with a good-natured smile. She could nose about on her own.

Peter watched the door close, then turned back to his good friend. "There isn't any danger, is there? I mean, there is no chance Jocelyn might be harmed? That episode with the rowboat was annoying, but she wasn't hurt—other than to be required to marry me. People are dashed peculiar when it comes to a fortune in gems."

"I should not think it would come to violence," Adrian said with confidence Peter did not share. "I hope they do not remove the rest of the stones. They could do serious damage to the setting," Adrian said with a worried frown.

"It's to be hoped we find it before that happens. Can we bring everyone together so that Pierre, Henri, or Suzanne—whoever it may be—has no time to work on the necklace?"

"We can try. Anything in mind?"

"How about an archery contest? Jocelyn ought to surprise

everyone. Amazed me. You know most women cannot hit the edge of the thing, let alone the center. She, well, you will have to watch to believe her."

"What for a prize?"

"How about a pretty hat? I suspect she wants one for the wedding."

"You are so sure? Suzanne is not bad with her bow."

"I am certain." Peter grinned, a masculine and very confident aura about him.

"And the wedding? Are you as sure about that? The special license ought to be here within a few days."

"I have never been more certain about anything. She is one in a million. If I ever get hold of her brother, he might not be too happy with me. He cost me five years with Jocelyn, from what I've deduced."

"You can scarcely blame him, Peter. At that time you were but a baronet without a home or fortune. Would you allow your sister in such a match? Or your daughter? Just wait until you have a daughter, my friend. You may find things are different when the shoe is on your foot."

"I suppose you have the right of it." The confidence was lacking in this statement, however.

"Come along, we shall challenge the ladies to a contest in archery. I'll wager Jocelyn may not find it such a snap as you seem to think."

Peter laughed as Adrian intended, but he looked thoughtful as they left the room to join the others on the terrace.

Suzanne drifted across the lawn to join Peter and Adrian as they left the terrace. "The roses are so lovely. How I wish Uncle Maxim would grow roses."

"You live with him now, why do you not plant some?" Peter inquired. "It ought to be a simple matter of having the gardener put what you want where you want it."

"Ah, *chérie,* if only life were that simple," she said, not smiling. "Where is your Lady Jocelyn?"

"I believe she went to the equipment room to find a proper bow," Peter replied, exchanging a glance with Adrian.

"Ladies," Adrian called to all assembled, "there is to be an archery contest this afternoon. You have an hour to practice before nuncheon."

"Well," Peter murmured, "that brought an instant reaction."

Lady Thynne and Mrs. Corsham, followed by Mrs. Hastings and Mrs. Murray hastened around the terrace to where all the bows were kept. Alisha Osmond and Cordelia Murray gaily sailed along ahead of all, chattering about how charming a pastime they found archery and wasn't it delightful and what a clever idea to have a contest.

"I shall win," Cordelia Murray said confidently. "I am very good." Alisha Osmond looked doubtful at that.

Peter turned away at that, unable to stifle his laughter. If Cordelia could hit the target, he would be very much surprised.

Suzanne stared at him a moment. "What is the prize to be?"

"A very pretty hat from a shop in Derby." Peter sobered and considered the woman who looked at him with such a calculating expression.

"I could use a new hat," she mused. "I shall partake of the contest. Perhaps I shall even practice a little. Does Lady Jocelyn enter?"

"Of course. And all the gentlemen are bound to watch. Tomorrow we shall have a contest for them."

"Ah, *chérie,* what sort of contest? Henri and Pierre are not skilled with the bow."

"Angling," Peter responded, thinking of the remarks Henri had made following the fateful fishing expedition made with Jocelyn.

"Well, I think you make a mistake there. Henri is very good at that. So are Uncle Maxim and Pierre. I do not think you can best one of them." She gave him a saucy smile and sailed forth down the lawn and around the house to the equipment room.

Peter slowly followed, wondering how long he had to remain with the group before he could slip away to search those rooms. With a start, he recalled that Henri and Pierre shared a room. They were either skilled at concealing something like that necklace, or they were in it together. He hadn't considered that before, and he should have. His mind must have scrambled while chasing the delicious Jocelyn. Once this week was over, he could devote all his time to her. The thought gave him a great deal of pleasure. And she was so biddable!

Jocelyn tested her bow, thinking she had found the best weight for her skill. She ought to do Peter proud this afternoon.

The door opened to permit all the women, other than Lora, to enter. Jocelyn gave them a confused look.

"We are joining the contest," Cordelia announced. "We all want the promised new hat from Derby!"

Figuring that she would learn all the details before long, Jocelyn merely nodded.

Suzanne came in last and cast an unfriendly look at Jocelyn. "You did not stay at the target long earlier."

"No, my gown became damp after crawling around, and I wanted to dry it out." As an excuse it was pretty lame, but Jocelyn wasn't at her best form at the moment.

"I see you did not bother to change," Suzanne commented with a disparaging look at the simple mulberry-striped gown Jocelyn wore.

"There is time enough before nuncheon. I will not worry about a little thing like a gown when I am shooting."

"Lord Leigh seems to think you are very good."

"I live in the country. Without the diversions one has in London, it is necessary to find something pleasing to do. Archery is agreeable."

"I practice in London. There are splendid grounds where one may enjoy it."

Jocelyn raised her brows in seeming surprise. "Delightful, I'm sure."

She collected a quiver of arrows, slung it over her shoulder, then took her bow and marched from the room, followed closely by Suzanne. She had picked up a similar bow plus a case of arrows.

"A quiver of arrows looks rather masculine on a woman," she observed.

"But convenient. I do not allow things like that to bother me," Jocelyn said at her most lofty best. She was not the daughter of a marquess for nothing.

The gentlemen were standing and, in some cases, seated in

wooden chairs fetched for them. Uncle Maxim sat on one of these, giving Suzanne a cautioning look as she entered the archery area.

Jocelyn decided it would be best to permit all the others to play ahead of her. It was good strategy, for it gave her a chance to see what the quality of the competition was.

Cordelia was not a bad little archer. She had the proper stance and nocked her arrow with care. She overshot, however, and did not seem to know how to correct her aim. Jocelyn did not instruct her.

The older ladies were also better than expected. Perhaps it was the promise of an elegant new hat that inspired them?

"Was that your idea?" she asked Peter when he joined her.

"It was. And I trust you to win so you can have a very fetching wedding hat as a gift from Adrian."

Jocelyn gave him a thoughtful look before turning her attention to the target once again. Bits of straw flew outward when the servant, detailed to attend the archers, pulled out the ones that had penetrated the target. Most were in the white and black bands.

Suzanne took a stance—right-angled to the target with the arrow properly nocked. Her aim was true, and she hit the red band on her first try.

"There is your competition, my love."

"I thought the idea was to keep everyone busy so you could snoop?" she said lightly.

"I count on you to make it good. Lead them on, keep it going from the time I leave until I return. Adrian will help. If necessary, he can persuade the men to give demonstrations. Just make certain that Henri and Pierre remain here, along with Uncle Maxim, of course."

"Suzanne means to defeat me."

Peter looked annoyed. "She does, and she is good. You have an enemy. Whether it is because we interrupted her hunt this morning or other, I cannot say."

"I think she rather fancied you for herself and is resentful that you appear to prefer me." Jocelyn gave Peter a warm look.

He smiled back. "I do."

Jocelyn absorbed the fervency of those spoken words with

joy, and when she took her place, managed to hit the red every time. She had not intended to hit the center gold, it would be tipping Suzanne off a little too much.

She slipped up to her room to change before nuncheon, then wearing one of her favorite gowns, an almond-green muslin, she joined the others in the saloon. Peter led her in to the dining room, sitting her close to his side and giving Pierre a cautioning look when he seemed to want to sit a trifle close on the other.

"Peter, I do not think he intends to eat me," Jocelyn murmured with a quickly hidden grin behind a convenient napkin.

"Better not," Peter mumbled in reply. He made short work of his meal, excusing himself to check the targets and the bows— a few of which would have to be shared. The arrows had all been looked over by the gardener's helper, whose job it was to tend these sort of things.

Left to fend for herself, Jocelyn made polite conversation with Pierre, trying to figure out a way of bringing the costume ball into the discussion.

"Do you all know what you will wear to the costume ball?" she said at last, deciding to be direct. "What about you, Pierre?"

"I will wear the attire of a monk."

"Figures," murmured Uncle Maxim. "And I shall be a cavalier complete with lace and one of those huge hats."

"I will be a shepherdess," Cordelia Murray said with breathless delight in her originality.

"Perhaps I will surprise everyone with my costume," Suzanne said quietly. "And you, cousin? Will you wear the gown designed to look like Adrian's ancestor—complete with the necklace?"

"I plan to wear it, yes," Lora said, casting a glance at Jocelyn.

"I fancy Lady Jocelyn will appear as a bride," Cordelia said with a giggle.

"Actually, I have a pretty costume, borrowed from Adrian. I will not tell you what it is, but I like it."

Adrian looked at the mantel clock, then signaled to Jocelyn. "Perhaps you wish to go meet Peter. Tell him we will all be down there momentarily."

She thankfully left the room in a demure rush, if you could call her hurried exit that. She found Peter standing by the target, checking over the area once again.

"Welcome," he said, returning to his feet and brushing down his breeches. "I looked but didn't find anything more. It is as we suspected, those were the only jewels to be found here."

"The others will be here in minutes. Any advice for me?"

"Try to play last. Then you know who it is that you will play in the final round. Adrian suggested we have eliminations so it will take longer. I'll disappear now. Say nothing if anyone asks where I am. You know nothing."

"Indeed, I know nothing. I shall concentrate on my target. Hush. Here they come now."

Peter gave her a smile, saluted, and was gone.

Jocelyn looked at the sundial. High noon. She would try to give him two hours. If possible.

"Well, Lady Jocelyn, do you think you can beat me?" Suzanne cried.

"Shall the first round begin?" Jocelyn asked in reply.

Cordelia did better than expected. With a concerned eye on the sundial, Jocelyn timed each round. At last it was down to the three of them. Cordelia went first. She missed the target completely with her first shot and was out. Suzanne hit two golds and a red.

Jocelyn glanced at the sundial. Two hours gone, if that was remotely reliable. She decided to end the contest. With care she nocked the first arrow, took aim, and got gold, a second try won her gold as well. She was about to do her third shot when she saw Peter slip behind the last row of gentlemen. He smiled and nodded.

Relieved, Jocelyn shot again to win a third gold. Peter had completed the search, and he looked satisfied. Pray he had found the necklace.

"Lady Jocelyn, well-done," Adrian said with a big smile. "You shall have your hat as soon as may be. A wedding hat, I vow!"

"Sounds as though it was all arranged beforehand," Cordelia muttered to Miss Osmond.

"I heard that," Jocelyn said quietly to Cordelia. "The only

reason they picked a hat as an award was they knew we all liked hats. That is all." She left the girls to join Peter.

"Did you find what you were looking for?"

"More or less. When you can get away from all this, I shall tell you all about it, my love."

Chapter Fourteen

As soon as Jocelyn reached her sitting room, she found Peter entering right behind her.

"Did you lurk in the hall, waiting for me to come?" she said lightly, hoping that no one else saw him. She disliked being gossiped about, and surely his presence in her sitting room was a juicy tidbit.

"Indeed, I did." He strolled across the room, hands in his pockets, studying Jocelyn intently.

"Well, do not keep me in suspense. What did you learn? I gather you did not find the jewels." She dropped her shawl on the chaise, then sat beside it.

"The blue cover is now back in the wardrobe where I first found it. There was nothing in Suzanne's room, or Maxim's room. However, inside the blue box I did discover a small tool that would be useful for prying gems from a setting. You realize what this means?"

"Either Henri or Pierre is guilty. How do we find out which one did it? I am for accusing them directly, now that we have it limited to two people."

He grinned at her and shook his head. "I like games. I would rather bait them, try first one, then the other, to see who has the necklace. But . . . where do they hide it? That is the question."

Jocelyn shrugged, thinking she would rather forget all about the necklace, the Valletorts in general, and concentrate on Peter Leigh. "I cannot imagine."

"Mull it over, and we can discuss it later."

"Well"—she glanced at the clock—"I had best dress for dinner and the evening ahead. I trust you will think of some means of exposing the true thief?"

"I shall," he said with confidence. "Give me a bit of time, and I shall think of something quite diabolical."

"That I can believe," Jocelyn declared while ushering him from the sitting room.

She found Mercy in the bedroom, placing an elegant lavender gown on the bed. Silver lace trimmed the low neckline, and delicate lace appliqués decorated the flounce at the hem. Jocelyn raised her brows in inquiry. "For a simple evening doing little?"

"I believe it is important for you to look your best, milady. You are not married to Lord Leigh yet."

"True," Jocelyn muttered, slipping off her day gown while considering the ways and means that Peter Leigh might call off the wedding. Never had she been so uncertain of herself, nor others, for that matter. Peter Leigh confused her terribly. Mercy was right. Jocelyn had best arm herself for battle! She recalled how she had hated Peter before coming here, or convinced herself that it was so. He had alarmed her with that charm he employed too well. But had it been trepidation on her part, or had she not known how to cope with that attraction that positively oozed from him? The thought gave her pause.

That evening was reserved for games. Whist occupied the over-thirty guests. The younger people played at silly things like jackstraws and lotto for a time until they palled.

Suzanne cried, "What about a game of blindman's bluff? We could go out to the terrace. I think it would be very romantic." She cast a flirtatious look at Peter that instantly put Jocelyn on her guard.

Soon they were all outside with the pretty lanterns Lora had ordered lit, offering a romantic setting. Miss Murray and Miss Osmond giggled nervously while eyeing the uneasy faces belonging to Mr. Tremayne and Mr. Fordyce. If Jocelyn was a betting woman, she would wager that somehow or another those girls would catch the man they wanted.

Peter, deciding he would far rather be out with Jocelyn than playing a game of whist, proffered a large handkerchief to be used to conceal the eyes of the person playing *it,* but only if he did the honors.

Volunteering to be first, Jocelyn inhaled that familiar scent as he adjusted the square of cambric over her face.

"Can you see me?" he asked when done.

"Not a bit. The twilight helps *you,* I am certain. *I* cannot see a thing. Everyone must stay on the terrace, and no hiding behind a statue," Jocelyn stated, hoping to avoid a silly situation. She could imagine the indelicate remarks from Henri were she to embrace that statue of Hermes that stood off to one side. "In fact, I suggest that if anyone is in danger of enfolding one of Adrian's works of art that someone should call them away from it."

At first it seemed hopeless. She turned here and there, truly frustrated with the elusiveness of the others. Then she detected the scent Suzanne liked to pour over herself before she dressed. A few moments' calculation and Jocelyn had tabbed the lovely young woman as the next one to be the hunter.

Suzanne caught a blushing Hugh Fordyce in incredibly short time, making Jocelyn think that the handkerchief had not been tied well.

"I thought she would have captured you," Jocelyn murmured to Peter. "She certainly makes her preference for you clear otherwise."

"I am coming to believe she merely likes to tease Henri," Peter observed, while backing away from the searching Hugh.

"Does she care so much for him, then?" Jocelyn wondered in a whisper.

"With Suzanne, it is hard to tell. I am still curious as to the matter of the moving clue. Why would either Henri or Pierre put the blue case first in that wardrobe, then in Suzanne's, then back to the other? It makes not the slightest sense."

"I agree. Peter, what are you doing?" Jocelyn murmured as she was drawn away from the area lit by the lanterns. "We are supposed to be partaking in the game."

"I have a game of my own, and it does not involve the other guests, my love."

Jocelyn smiled, but wondered if that wasn't truly what he played at? A game—using her as his goal? Earlier he had said he liked to play games. Did that include her? Was a woman ever certain that a man really cared for her? She was to marry Peter, but in spite of his words, what did he truly feel for her? Uncertain, she set aside her doubts for the moment and allowed Peter to kiss her.

Actually, it would have been impossible to refuse something she wanted so much. It was like being a child in a sweet shop and offered everything in view. Irresistible.

"I can think of nothing I want more than to have you all to myself," Peter said in an undertone guaranteed not to be heard beyond her ear.

"Thanks to Henri and his accusations when we returned from the island, you will undoubtedly have that pleasure before too long." That it would be a pleasure, Jocelyn did not doubt. Peter Leigh was the most devastatingly attractive man she had ever met. She had been most correct when she termed him dangerous. He exuded a masculine appeal that caused female eyes to linger on his form, desire his company, and try everything in the book to attract his interest.

So, what about *her* appealed to *him*?

"Come, although I prefer to remain here with you in my arms, we had best return to the others. I'd not have them cast aspersions on your character." He offered his hand to lead her to where the others shifted about, eluding Hugh.

Jocelyn willingly joined him, wondering what had prompted that remark. Had someone, some gentleman, made a nasty inference regarding her? She had warned Peter about his coming to her sitting room. It wasn't the slightest bit proper. How ironic for her to be admonishing him for a lack of propriety in which she had willingly joined. She had been so very proper all her life. And now, it was as she said—she was old enough to know better and simply too old to care anymore. Or so she pretended.

Hugh Fordyce captured a willing Miss Murray. She in turn snabbled Mr. Tremayne.

"I'll wager he catches Miss Osmond," Jocelyn murmured, quite safe behind Peter.

"The question remains, who will she capture?" Peter murmured.

"Not you, I think."

It went as Jocelyn guessed it would. Henri submitted with good grace when caught by Miss Osmond. Surprisingly he seized the luscious Suzanne, who hadn't tried hard to evade him. Since Pierre had not joined in the youthful pursuit, all had known a turn except Peter Leigh.

"I crown Lord Leigh the winner as he managed to avert capture," Suzanne declared, her eyes dancing with mischief.

"But my heart is already captured by the beautiful Lady Jocelyn. In a sense I am captured far better than the rest of you— more permanent, if you see what I mean," he said with a light chuckle.

Jocelyn was touched by that remark until she had a chance to think it over. He was merely being gallant. Only time would tell if he meant all those fulsome words.

Saxby marched onto the terrace to announce a supper served in the dining room for any who so pleased. It broke up the entertainment for the evening, Jocelyn was pleased to note. She was tired after a long day of activity.

"You look ready for bed," Peter said quietly as they returned to the house.

Jocelyn wondered how he managed to give the simplest words an inflection of roguishness.

"I shall welcome my sleep. Tomorrow will be another busy day. You do realize that it is our last day to search. The day after is the ball, and we must have the necklace restored to Lora and Adrian by then."

"Jolly good of them to allow us the hunt," Peter said while helping himself to a large portion of asparagus and mushroom fritters.

"I imagine Adrian has had a lot on his mind, but I also believe he will not permit this to go on much longer. He wants that necklace undamaged—and soon."

Peter agreed, and they settled with the others to consume far too much delicious food.

"I trust the gentlemen are thinking of the morrow's contest," Adrian said, rising at the foot of the table. "I have a particularly fine bottle of old French brandy to offer as a prize."

"Here, here," Lord Thynne declared. "I believe we shall all do our best to obtain such a reward."

"I wonder how it will go?" Peter mused as he later escorted Jocelyn to her sitting room door.

"Have you thought of anything regarding the necklace?"

His eyes lit up with that delightful gleam. "I believe whoever it is keeps it on him, perhaps wears it."

"Good grief!" Jocelyn murmured. "A man wearing that necklace? I cannot accept that."

"Long ago the gentlemen wore elaborate necklaces—in Tudor times, for example. Think of the portraits in the long gallery."

"Perhaps," she said dubiously. "Now, to think of some manner in which we can reveal the true thief! Put that fruitful mind of yours to work on that!" With those words, Jocelyn whisked around the door and away from the most disturbing man she had ever met.

The contest for the largest fish, whether it be a trout or other, had truly captured the attention of all the guests. Jocelyn suspected that while they might not exhibit such enthusiasm at home, the prospect of a fine bottle of brandy plus besting the other men prompted their eagerness.

"What do you plan to do next, besides fish?" Jocelyn asked Peter while she strolled from the breakfast room to the terrace. They had left the others consuming a substantial breakfast as though fishing was a demanding sport.

"When I searched Henri and Pierre's room, I was so certain I would discover what we sought," he complained.

"But the necklace *wasn't* there. That is strange, is it not? I have thought and thought all night, and cannot think where he could hide it. It should have been in the bedroom." Jocelyn stared off across the lake, glimpsing the little island cottage through the branches of a spreading oak. Had she been here less than a week? It seemed more like a month. "I cannot accept either man would actually wear it."

"But he *must* have it on his person." He paused in their perambulation of the terrace, so it appeared he was admiring a particularly fine specimen of petunia.

A number of creels, their willow twigs neatly woven and lined with newly inserted damp rush, were stacked just off the terrace. Peter picked one up to examine it while he murmured. "Consider this—if Henri has the necklace on his person, he could not possibly stick it in a pocket—his breeches fit him too tightly, and I doubt the pockets of his coat allow for anything that size."

"Then, he could not carry it with him," Jocelyn stated quietly in agreement.

"But he *could* wear it around his neck, under his shirt."

"What makes you think it is definitely Henri? Why not Pierre? And how could we find out if he is doing something so outrageous?" She bent over to sniff the petunia, inhaling with pleasure before glancing up to Peter.

"Well, we must take one at a time, and I think Henri is the most logical, so we shall try him first. Were he to fall into the lake and become soaked to the skin, we should soon see, would we not?"

"That truly is diabolical. I will not ask how you intend to accomplish that feat. Your inventive mind shall surprise me."

"Sometimes things must be left to fortuitous accidents."

The way he looked at her, Jocelyn wondered if he was thinking of that day he rode from the castle to rescue her from pneumonia or worse. No more was said, for Miss Osmond and Mr. Fordyce came to join them.

All the guests were to gather on the terrace before the men marched down to the edge of the lake where the boats had all been assembled by the little wood dock.

Clusters of fishermen soon formed, debating the type of bait, arguing over the sort of line that was best. They began to saunter to the lake, and the boats that awaited all who wanted one.

"Will those swans on the far side of the lake take exception to the gentlemen who wish to enter the angling contest?" Jocelyn asked Adrian while they watched the various fishermen prepare for the day's activity.

"I shouldn't think so as long as they keep away from the nest. See that pile of what looks like sticks and brush that barely shows near that willow tree? That is the nest, and they take turns sitting on it. I hope we will have some cygnets swimming about before too long."

"Do they not become rather nasty if disturbed? Perhaps we had better warn the men?" Jocelyn mused, watching as Henri entered a rowboat to head in the very direction of the willow tree.

"You can if you like. I think most people know to keep away from a nesting swan," Adrian replied before turning aside to assist Lord Thynne with his tackle. Mr. Whyte was being admonished by his wife to take extreme care not to take a wetting.

Mrs. Hastings had retired to the terrace to watch from a comfortable distance, most likely thinking her husband would not take kindly to any words from her. Mrs. Osmond and Mrs. Murray both urged Uncle Maxim to try his best, while their daughters prettily begged Mr. Tremayne and Mr. Fordyce to catch the largest fish.

The morning was not far advanced before every gentleman at the castle from Mr. Corsham to all the Valletorts, were out on the lake. Some men preferred to use a rod and reel, others just an old-fashioned casting rod.

Jocelyn had listened with amusement to the heated debate regarding the merits of horsehair as opposed to silkworm gut. Did women ever become so fervent in comparing the sorts of needles used in their fancywork? She doubted it.

"I still say," Peter remarked to Adrian, "a good horsehair stained with soot, alum, and walnut juice is the best line available. Practically invisible to trout—although I know you like the silkworm gut best."

"Good luck with the trout," Adrian said. "My keeper has stocked the pond with trout, bream, and a few tench. He's rather clever with them and manages to keep the birds away from the hatching pools. He is trying graylings this year, but I fear the water is not sufficiently cold for them. I think they do better up in Scotland."

"What? No carp? What about pike?" Peter inquired as he took his tackle from the dock while standing in the little boat he had selected. Jocelyn observed it seemed to be the same one they had taken to the island that fateful day.

"Pike are only useful if you want to hold down the number of trout. We decided it was not necessary here, and they are a dreadful nuisance."

"They can be excellent fighters, though," Peter observed as he pushed away from the dock.

"That fool Henri is definitely headed straight for that willow and the nest," Jocelyn murmured to Adrian.

"That is his problem," Adrian replied testily. "I have little patience with the man I strongly suspect of having stolen the family necklace."

"It will be interesting to see what happens. I do hope he falls in the water," Jocelyn said with great relish.

"You want him to get wet?" Adrian asked, almost forgetting to speak in an undertone, so great was his astonishment.

"Peter thinks the necklace is worn by one of them, as it isn't anywhere in the room. If Henri were to fall in the lake, it would soon be evident to you whether or not he is wearing that necklace under his shirt."

"Good heavens!" Adrian whispered, staring after Henri.

"We decided it was the best way to find out. Time is running out for us. I suspect you do not relish having to make an accusation unless you are certain of the culprit."

"By this time I could easily accuse anyone," Adrian retorted. He turned to seek out Lora and consult with her.

Miss Osmond and Miss Murray quickly lost interest in so dull a sport as fishing. In a short time they were playing at battledore and shuttlecock, with Miss Osmond a surprisingly strong contender.

Leaving the rest to watch the fishermen, Suzanne wandered into the house and found solace at the pianoforte, offering a delightful selection from Mozart. Mrs. Hastings also abandoned the terrace for the drawing room and the sound of Suzanne's music.

Jocelyn decided she would stroll along the perimeter of the lake. One never knew about these things. She might be called to offer assistance of a sort. Pausing to gather a shawl that could be used as emergency wrapping, she signaled her intent to Lora.

Lora shrugged and returned to her duties as hostess to such a large party. She had brought the baby out for an airing, and he was basking in the delighted attention of the more motherly women.

From his position in the center of the lake, Peter watched as

Jocelyn began to walk slowly along the edge of the lake. That vast shawl she carried might prove helpful. Not a bad idea, he mused. Then he shifted his attention to where Henri drifted closer to the willow and that tumbled mixture of sticks and rush.

The swans had taken note of the intruder. The pen on the nest arched her neck, eyeing him with a malevolent eye. The cob paddled in a slow circle, as though determining precisely what sort of menace that boat and man offered.

Henri paid not the slightest attention to such a thing as a mere pair of birds, nest or no. He was a clever man and intent on that fine brandy. If he also sought to impress the desirable Suzanne, it would be understandable.

Baiting his hook, Peter cast out, allowing his line to play out until he felt it go slack. Perhaps the trout would fancy a bit of wiggly worm for a snack. He hoped so. Adrian said that some of the trout must be ones planted by his father's keeper, and thus of considerable weight. Peter relished the thought of winning the contest—not that he was particularly a show-off. He enjoyed games of all type and this sort in particular.

Mr. Whyte was the first to bring in a fine-sized trout. Peter took note of it when it was netted and brought into the small boat. Whyte had no help. It had been agreed that each man would be alone, no valet or groom to assist in selecting flies, baiting hooks, much less in netting the fish one caught.

Shortly after Lord Thynne brought in a fine bream, not the weight of the one Whyte had caught, but good size nonetheless. Mr. Corsham and Mr. Hastings each rowed to the other end of the lake, presumably to hope for a better spot.

A slight breeze ruffled the water. Peter studied Henri, who drifted nearer and nearer the willow tree. It was difficult to pay attention to the fellow when trying to attend to his own rod. He felt a nibble and forgot about Henri for a moment.

On the shore Jocelyn watched Peter. He looked on the verge of pulling in a fish—she thought. All she knew about the art of angling was that it took patience and a willingness to handle slimy worms and wriggly grasshoppers.

Transferring her attention to where Henri sought to bring a fish to his net, she held her breath. He had risen from his seat to better reel in his fish, and the little boat looked a precarious thing. He bent to pick up his net when it happened.

The cob apparently decided him to be a menace, floating too close to his nest, that must be repelled. Hissing furiously, he attacked.

Henri, caught completely off guard, waved his arms about—trying to hang on to his rod, the fish he had nearly netted, and his balance. He lost.

The splash, Jocelyn considered from where she stood on the bank, was spectacular. Henri landed in the water on his back, arms out, his rod flying in an arc and disappearing when the fish decided to try for his freedom. The boat wobbled a bit, then overturned—another splash of notable proportion. The pen closed in on Henri, continuing to hiss, circling about the helpless man with hostile intent.

Henri in turn thrashed about, surely frightening any fish that chanced to be in that area, sending them off to another part of the lake.

"Henri," Jocelyn called, "can you swim? Come toward shore but away from the willow."

At first she thought he had not heard her. Then her words seemed to penetrate his head, and he turned toward shore, floundering somewhat before getting himself in hand and striking out for land.

It took him a while to reach the bank where she waited. None of the other men, after a first look, had bothered to come to his aid. Why should they risk their win for a fellow stupid enough to drift too close to a pair of nesting swans?

He reached the bank after paddling dog fashion in a truly ungainly manner. Jocelyn offered the shawl she had brought with her while searching his upper person for a sign of the necklace. She saw nothing more than a wet shirt that somewhat concealed a mat of dark hair on his chest. There was no sparkle of gold to be seen. The most colorful bit of his attire was the blue-and-white-spotted Belcher neckerchief he sported above his shirt. That was too small to conceal the necklace.

Politely averting her face when he waded up on the pebbled shore, she held out the shawl. "Here, wrap this around you—for modesty if not warmth."

"Bloody birds," he muttered, rising to his feet and wrapping the shawl about his shoulders. Since it was a vast size, it covered his person tolerably well. "Sorry," he muttered to Jocelyn when he realized he had sworn before a lady.

"Understandable, I am sure," she said graciously. "Here comes one of the footmen. I fancy he will offer some assistance. I shall be away." Without waiting for a reply, Jocelyn walked rapidly along the bank, taking care to avoid the proximity of the willow and the nest. Henri would not thank her for waiting.

Looking out to the center of the lake, where Peter was, she took note he was in the act of netting a very large fish. Good. Perhaps he might succeed; he seemed to enjoy winning, but then she supposed most men did. Why else were they always betting on the most unlikely things, like falling raindrops and geese crossing the road, not to mention horses and dogs racing? Perhaps it came with being a male?

She had rounded the far end of the lake when she looked up to see Peter coming toward her. She waited patiently, for his rowing was good, but he was far out.

When he at last reached the shore where she stood, he said, "Well, did you see anything of note?"

She shook her head. "A very wet shirt and Belcher 'kerchief as well as an extremely angry man."

Too disappointed to say anything at first, Peter finally smiled at her. "Well, we tried. That was good of you to carry a shawl. I would not have suspected Pierre," he concluded with a look at the far shore where the man in question now fished from the bank, casting his line far out into the lake with modest success.

"The problem now is how to trap him into revealing the necklace. I do not think we can cause him to fall into the water. I must say, I was surprised that no one came to assist Henri other than myself and the footman."

"This is a contest, Jocelyn. It is every man for himself," Peter explained.

"That bottle of brandy must be quite something."

"Not merely the brandy. It is winning."

"That is what I suspected. So, go back to your contest and the fish. How have you done so far?"

Peter showed her the large trout he had caught, smiling at her generous compliments. When she stepped back from the bank, he turned his boat about and headed back to where he had been—after making certain that the cob was nowhere near.

Chuckling, Jocelyn continued her walk. She passed the island, then went on. It was longer than she had anticipated, and she was thankful to rest in the shade offered by a fine wild cherry tree.

From there she could see all the fishermen. Every now and again one of them would pull in a fish. It was a tranquil scene, and she could almost have fallen asleep. She was startled to alertness when she saw Henri come from the house down to where Pierre sat at the lake's edge. There ensued an argument of some sort. Rising, Jocelyn decided she would complete her walk and see if perhaps she could learn anything when she neared Pierre.

It did not take her long to finish the last lap of her circle of the lake.

When she neared Pierre, she noted his creel was overflowing with trout. Evidently he had enjoyed a good day. "How does it look?" she inquired.

"So so," he admitted. "They seem to be small. Henri was certain he had caught the winner when that stupid bird attacked him." Pierre chuckled, an unkind sound.

Adrian went out to the end of the dock to wave a red banner, a signal that the contest was at an end.

Jocelyn watched the men come to shore, wondering how Peter planned to retrieve that necklace from Pierre. As far as she could see, there was no flash of gold from under his shirt, either.

Chapter Fifteen

There could be little doubt as to the winner of the angling contest. Once the catch had been laid out on the grassy bank it was quite plain, even before the careful weighing on the scale brought out by Adrian's gamekeeper.

"Peter, you old dog, you must have used magic to make such a catch," Adrian said with admiration.

Peter, Lord Leigh, stood modestly by the eight-pound trout he had reeled in.

The other men, with Henri standing sullenly by in dry clothing, exclaimed about the very nice trout. They again compared notes about the type of line, the sort of bait, and the other niceties of angling. All avoided mention of Henri's spectacular plunge in the lake.

Suzanne came dancing up to Henri. "Poor man, to be so utterly soaked by that nasty bird. I cannot see why anyone would keep such fowl on their property." She darted a sly glance at Adrian.

"I'd vow my fish was larger than Leigh's," Henri said loud enough to be heard by Jocelyn.

She gave the man a withering look before turning away to join Peter on his way to the terrace.

"Well, you won that little game," she began. "Now to the other. Any ideas in that diabolical mind of yours? Did you know that the cob would chase Henri, by the way?"

"It was very likely. I admit I merely hoped he would do something stupid and relieve me of the necessity of thinking of a way to trick him into the water."

"An accidental happening, in other words?" Jocelyn chuckled. "I know I ought not be amused, but it was a glorious sight."

"It is a lesson for all. Never rile swans while nesting."

Jocelyn glanced behind her. "Suzanne seems intent upon consoling him—whether for the loss of the contest or his fall into the lake, it is hard to say."

"Those two are becoming thick as inkle-weavers. Neither Maxim nor Pierre seem pleased with the connection."

"I wonder why? Pierre, I can understand, but Uncle Maxim?" Jocelyn glanced back a second time to observe Pierre glaring at his cousin with undisguised hostility.

"You mean that Pierre is jealous but that Uncle Maxim has no motive? True. Perhaps Maxim wants Suzanne to look elsewhere?"

"I gather you mean he would prefer her to look in your direction? But you are supposed to be engaged to me—although she looked pointedly at my finger to see if I wear your ring. She was not best-pleased to see the sapphire." Jocelyn swallowed the words she would have liked to utter. Did Peter intend to see through this forced betrothal? His words to her indicated he was sincere. Yet she knew uncertainty. Perhaps if Peter were not quite so handsome? Maybe if he did not have the effect of melting her very bones?

"To her contorted thinking, we are not yet married so that makes me still fair game," Peter admitted.

"Games!" Jocelyn exclaimed with wrath. She gave Peter an irate look, then strode off to the drawing room to collect her composure.

"Jocelyn," he said from the doorway, having followed her but unwilling to enter the blue drawing room in his fishing clothes. "What I feel for you is not a game, nor is our approaching marriage. It is very real, my love."

Jocelyn slowly turned to face him, feeling foolish. "It is I who must beg your forgiveness and forbearance. I simply do not understand what has happened to my common sense." She threw up her hands in dismay.

"I dare say there is nothing common about your sense, dear Jocelyn. I find everything about you far above the ordinary." He smiled at her, that wicked gleam creeping into his eyes.

Jocelyn returned his smile, thinking that when he looked at her like that she was putty in his hands to be molded at will. How glad she would be when he solved his "game" and life might return to a more normal pattern. But could life with Peter ever be considered normal? The mere thought of his kisses brought heat to her cheeks.

About to depart, Peter paused to take note of her flushed face. "I'd give a monkey to know what you are thinking." With that he walked down the hall and up to his room.

Jocelyn was still in the drawing room staring out of the window at the gardens below when Lora entered. Turning, Jocelyn took note she was alone.

"Has Peter learned anything of help?" Lora inquired softly.

Jocelyn explained, "Nothing much that is new. You must know that apparently Henri is innocent. There was no evidence he wore the necklace beneath his shirt when he came out of the lake." She recalled the skin and dark hair on his chest that had been visible and felt her cheeks warm. "I truly believed it was Henri, you know. Pierre does not seem the sort to steal that necklace. He is so proper and unassuming—for a Valletort, that is. Your husband's relatives are far from ordinary, you must admit."

"*I* would have wagered that it was Suzanne who snatched the necklace," Lora declared. "She came to see me while I was being fitted for my costume and looked long and covetously at that necklace, admiring the jewels." Lora glanced at the clock. "It will not be long before dinner. Do you keep the early country hours? Or do you dine as Londoners?"

"I have done both, depending on circumstances. I do not know what the future holds regarding meals," Jocelyn said with a forlorn note in her voice before she took herself in hand. "But then, I must not repine. I shall be taken with the green melancholy and not fit to have around." She made a silly face at her cousin.

"Oh, Jocelyn, you are so funny," Lora said shaking her head. "You must know that Peter is serious in his intent to wed you. I think your fate was sealed the moment he found you on the road to the castle. I vow—it is the first time I have been glad that the road here is a trifle steep. Had it been level, I'd not have suggested Peter look for you. Poor fellow, to ride out in that pouring rain. I'd not the least notion you would be walking. It was most fortuitous."

"That is a matter of opinion, surely," Jocelyn said with a barely restrained laugh. "Only you could see romance in a pouring rain and a bedraggled woman rescued by an irate man."

"Hero and heroine, please! If I am to re-create a Minerva Press novel, I wish to do it correctly. But I sense something more is bothering you. If you wish to confide, I am ready to listen."

"It is only Suzanne and her stares. She makes me so irritated with her pointed looks at my left hand and little barbs about forced weddings going astray. As though she could snatch Peter away from me at will."

"Do you not feel complimented that any woman as gorgeous as Suzanne is jealous of you?" Lora queried.

Much struck with this angle, Jocelyn nodded. "I had not considered that aspect. Well, I can cheer up, for I must be formidable, indeed!" She laughed and walked to the hall with Lora, taking her leave when Lora returned to the terrace while Jocelyn went to her room.

Pausing by her door, she was shocked to see Peter leaving the Valletort bedroom. Surely he had looked there before? "Psst!"

Peter looked her way, then crossed to her side. "Double-checking, my dear. I know the necklace must be around here, but I'll be jiggered if I can think where it might be. Is Suzanne still down on the terrace making eyes at Henri in order to irritate Uncle Maxim?"

"How well you put that. Indeed, she is there, ignoring your splendid catch and intent upon the still-piqued Henri. As I told Lora, the Valletort's are a race apart, scarcely mere mortals."

"Except for Adrian. He's a splendid friend, and I would wager an equally splendid husband. Have you thought what sort of wedding hat you will order? And your gown? My sister dithered for weeks selecting hers. I trust you can manage your decision in a single morning. I am an impatient lover, my dear Jocelyn."

Feeling her cheeks warm with that gleam in his eyes, not to mention the words he spoke, Jocelyn hastily replied, "I want taffeta in a soft white. It will not take me long to decide should the mantua-maker bring the correct fabrics along. My taste in styles is simple."

"And a hat with white roses on it," he added, reaching out to touch her cheek. "I shall go in Monday to buy a wedding band."

His knowing smile made her flustered. "Suzanne will be leaving then, I should think. I trust you, even if Suzanne thinks you are about to decamp with someone else."

"Namely her, I suppose?"

"Lora said she appeared extremely envious of the necklace when she viewed it last week during a costume fitting. Lora still suspects Suzanne."

Peter frowned. "I must consider that."

"Oh, do not do anything rash, I beg you."

"The most dangerous thing I ever did was ride out in the rain to rescue Lora's cousin."

Jocelyn didn't trust that gleam in his eyes. Hearing steps approaching on the stairs, she looked down that way, then whisked herself into her sitting room once Peter realized they were no longer alone.

The fluting sound of Suzanne's voice could be clearly heard through the crack in Jocelyn's slightly ajar door. She was flirting outrageously with Peter. Well, it would do her no good. Jocelyn gently shut the door, then crossed to her bedroom. She needed to arm herself for the evening.

Peter eyed the lush beauty who teased him with flashing eyes and seductive hints in her voice. Suzanne Fornier was a decided menace—perhaps in more ways than one?

"You have your costume planned for tomorrow's ball?"

"Oh, indeed, I have. At first I thought to present myself as one of our ancestors. Then when I saw Lora's splendid costume, I knew that would not do. So, I shall go as Cleopatra. There is such a rage for things Egyptian, you know. And such a costume requires little fabric." She batted her dark eyes at him with more than a little innuendo in her voice.

Peter didn't succumb to her allure. He asked, "You saw the fabled necklace, then? I understand it is quite remarkable."

"True, it is. Uncle Maxim is furious that Adrian has the care of it. I should like it were Uncle to take possession of it," she stated frankly. "I would be able to wear it, then, and those jewels are so delicious." She gave a provocative shrug of her shoulders, sending one sleeve down a slender arm.

Peter wondered why it was the dratted girl seemed to have trouble keeping her clothes where they should be.

"You would that your uncle *take* the necklace? In my book that constitutes stealing."

She shrugged as though stealing was of no importance. "He is the eldest and ought to have it by rights. I cannot see why Adrian was so favored. He has the money, the jewels, and the castle—everything. It simply is not fair."

"Suzanne, there are a good many things in this life that are not fair," Peter admonished.

"You are determined to wed the insipid Lady Jocelyn?" Suzanne said, stepping so close to Peter that she touched him, her breasts brushing against his coat most provocatively.

"Lady Jocelyn is anything but insipid. And this is not a hasty plunge into marriage," Peter said, backing away a step.

"Oh, yes, she rejected you five years ago if gossip is to be believed. I cannot fathom how a gentleman such as you would tolerate such manners in a woman." Suzanne abandoned her cozening ways to lash out in spiteful words. "You are a fool if you think she has pined for you all those years. What about her relationship with Simon Oliver? Most engaged women give themselves to their beloved before he goes off to war. Are you wedding damaged goods?"

Peter ignored her wild charges. "But then, you do not have to understand what attracts me to the lovely and charming Lady Jocelyn." Peter gave Suzanne a cold look, then beat a speedy retreat to his bedroom before he strangled the chit.

In his room he paced about, the poison Suzanne had dropped into his ears unwillingly lurking in his mind. He would swear that Jocelyn had not been that close to Simon. She had indicated as such. Did he believe her? She said she trusted him. Did he trust her? Then he realized that in his heart it didn't matter one way or the other. She would be his forever, and that was what mattered.

Yet the memory of her unrestrained response to his kisses remained in his mind to haunt him.

He turned his attention to Suzanne's revelation regarding the necklace. She wished Uncle Maxim to steal the necklace. How odd that she should mention stealing, as though it was a notion she herself had toyed with. As Jocelyn has said—it was a maddening mull. When it was over, he would marry Jocelyn and all this would be as a dream. And, he decided, he might curb his games from now on. Not all games were worth the struggle.

But, he also decided, he would return to Suzanne's room to have a second look. Perhaps she had been concealing that necklace while they concentrated on Henri and Pierre?

When he went down to the saloon, he looked for Jocelyn. Locating her, he wound his way through the clusters of guests until he reached her side.

"You did not wait for me," he said quietly.

"You must have dawdled. Did you have to shave? My brother always must or else look as though he has a shadowed face."

"I had an encounter with a particular person we discussed before I left you," he said obliquely.

Jocelyn immediately understood what he meant and nodded, with a discreet glance at where Suzanne flirted with Henri.

"You were correct about her envy of the gems. She even went so far as to say she wished her uncle would steal the jewelry so she might be the one to wear it. It seems that branch of the family feels hard done by, from what Maxim and Suzanne have said."

"Pierre as well," Jocelyn reminded him.

"Maybe we should give up," Peter muttered, with a frustrated expression in his eyes.

"This evening, then tomorrow we hand it to Adrian as we agreed."

Saxby appeared in the doorway, and the group surged in his direction, the day having given all a hearty appetite.

"Later on I intend to have a second go at one of the rooms. Cover for me if needs be, will you?" Peter murmured as he ushered her into the dining room.

"But of course. You need only to ask," Jocelyn replied as she sat uneasily on her chair.

The meal proved to be as delicious as all others had been. Jocelyn ate with relish, secure for the moment that Peter seemed to trust her as she trusted him.

Leaving the men to their port, Jocelyn joined the other women in the walk to the saloon. She expected Suzanne to sit down at the grand pianoforte and was surprised when she sauntered over to sit by Jocelyn.

"When do you marry Lord Leigh?" She leaned forward, offering an impressive view of her assets. Jocelyn couldn't think why Suzanne would want to behave in such a manner with another woman, unless it was to make her aware of some deficiency on the other's part. Since Jocelyn felt quite adequate on that score, she merely returned the query with a very bland, "I have the dress to order as well as my hat. Peter said something about a week, but I truly have no actual idea."

"If you marry him," Suzanne replied with spite.

"Do you know, I am rather tired of your little barbs, my dear. Why do you not find a nest and tend a few eggs?"

"How dare you?" Suzanne whispered.

"You would be surprised at what I dare. You play the pianoforte so well, would you favor us with a selection?"

Suzanne gave Jocelyn a disbelieving look, then rose, stalking to the piano in seeming high dudgeon. The girl spent far too much time seething, in Jocelyn's opinion. Too much emotion must be wearing on one's nerves.

The men soon joined the ladies, who it must be admitted, found their absence a trial. Deadly boring, Miss Murray called it. She immediately challenged Mr. Tremayne to a game of billiards.

Jocelyn thought it a clever move on her part. She could flirt all she pleased there. Miss Osmond and Mr. Fordyce joined them within minutes, prompted by Mrs. Osmond.

Peter strolled across the room to sit by Jocelyn. "I should like to go upstairs in a few minutes. Is there some manner of errand you might wish me to do?"

Jocelyn was about to say she needed nothing when she realized he wanted to leave with a good excuse.

"I had thought to wander out on the terrace before it rains again. I would like a shawl, if you would not mind, Lord Leigh," she requested with her polite manners.

He made a show of assuring her he did not mind in the least, and he would immediately go fetch one. "Wait for me in the hall to the terrace," he admonished before he left.

Which means I must stand about while he snoops, Jocelyn thought, but not with rancor. This was their last chance to solve the mystery. She'd not had time to relate Suzanne's latest little gibe, then decided it was scarcely worth the retelling. Jocelyn did not want Peter to feel pressured. It was enough that she experienced qualms.

Peter made his way along the hall toward Suzanne's room without a sound. He paused outside her room, listening. The servants were all at dinner; he had made certain of that. There ought to be no one here.

He silently turned the knob, then slipped inside. Twilight permitted some light into the room so he could prowl at will. Not bothering with anything else, he went straight to the wardrobe. Opening the door, he immediately spotted the blue box.

Could there be two of them? No, not possible. Quickly removing the box, he held his breath while he raised the cover. Inside he saw what he had hoped to find the first time—the necklace minus the stones that had been removed. Had Henri or Pierre taken those stones to show Suzanne as promise of what she would get if she went with him? Had they been a bribe?

Hastily closing the lid, Peter went to leave, strained to hear any sound, then opened the door. Sticking his head around the corner, he could perceive no one in the hall, nor could he hear any footsteps on the stairs.

It took but moments to quietly dart down the carpeted hall to his room. Once inside, he took the box to his desk to double-check the contents of the box. In the glow of his Argand lamp, he could detect tiny scratches where the stones had been removed. A good jeweler could repair that damage. This was definitely the real thing—the necklace that had been stolen!

He took the blue box with its valuable contents and walked to Jocelyn's sitting room. It did not take long to locate a shawl from her bureau. The scent of lily of the valley lingered in her things. It was a lovely fragrance, like Jocelyn.

Draping the shawl over the box to disguise it, he went down the stairs, hoping to find her waiting in the hall as promised. She might have thought him jesting so as to offer a cover for the time it took him. This was true, but he also wanted to show her what he had discovered.

As he neared the bottom of the stairs, he could see her. She wandered about the hall, gazing at pictures she must have seen a number of times. A radiant smile greeted him when she heard him cross the entry to join her.

Peter wished he did not have to tend to the matter of the necklace. A lovely welcoming like that deserved dalliance on the terrace. Her lips were certainly made for kissing. Suddenly he was jealous of Simon, who must have touched them more than once during their brief engagement. No one should know Jocelyn but himself, he vowed.

"The box?" she guessed when she saw the awkward shape covered by her shawl.

"Come—to the library."

Jocelyn obediently followed with no more than a puzzled frown on her face.

They entered the room with almost furtive care. Peter looked about. When assured they were alone, he locked the door.

"Now you are really in the suds," Jocelyn reminded. "*Not proper according to Society, my dear,*" she declared in her most snobbish accent, sounding a bit like Lady Thynne.

"I do not wish us to be disturbed. Come. See what I have here."

"Not the necklace? Truly?" Jocelyn followed closely behind him to the desk where he placed the box down and lifted off the cover.

"Ah," she declared with satisfaction. "Congratulations! You did it. How pleased Lora will be. Adrian as well. Where did you find it?"

"In the bottom of Suzanne's wardrobe as before. Only this time the insides were more rewarding."

"She needs to be punished for such a thing. But . . . how do we go about persuading Suzanne to confess? I should like to know her exact motive."

"Jealousy, I expect." Peter studied the beautiful piece of jewelry. "Seems a pity that such a small item should cause such dissension in a family."

"Shall I return to ask Adrian to join you here? You can scarcely take that box with you to the saloon."

"Tell him to bring Suzanne with him. I want to see her face when he confronts her with the necklace."

"I should like that as well." Jocelyn unlocked the door, then walked quickly to the saloon. Once there, she ignored the summoning nod from Mrs. Murray and sought Adrian. He stood with Lora and Mr. Whyte discussing the fishing contest.

"Excuse me, Peter wishes to see you a moment," she said to Adrian in an undertone. "In the library."

Adrian gave her a searching look, then without offering more than a hasty apology left the room.

Mr. Whyte, now that his host had gone, excused himself to join Lord Thynne and Mr. Corsham for further debate of the various techniques and materials used that day.

Lora gazed after the departing guest with relief, then turned to Jocelyn. "I think you have news?"

"Peter found the necklace. The gems can be replaced, and you will be able to wear it tomorrow and not have caused a scandal!"

Although the words could scarcely be heard, Lora listened with care. "Thank heavens. Where?"

Jocelyn looked to where Suzanne sat at the pianoforte flirting with her cousin Pierre. Henri stood just behind her, wearing a tight expression. He leaned over her shoulder, ostensibly to turn a page, but must have said something, for she froze.

"Pierre? Or do you mean Henri as you suspected," Lora inquired. When Jocelyn shook her head, Lora's gaze returned to the trio and she gasped. "Suzanne? Well, well."

At this point a footman made his way to the pianoforte with a silver tray in hand. Jocelyn bet she knew what was in the folded note on the tray.

"Adrian will wish to speak with her in the library. Peter awaited him when he left us. There are a few minute scratches, but nothing serious. And we were right, those were the only jewels to be removed."

"So . . . it is over."

"Let us hope so. I wonder what will happen next?"

In the library Peter and Adrian awaited the arrival of the young woman suspected of stealing the necklace.

"It is as Lora feared. Suzanne saw the necklace and coveted it. Witness that she was the one crawling about by the archery target, not one of the men. I would rather it had been Pierre or Henri. I dislike ordering a woman from the house."

Peter nodded but without sympathy. He would not have the slightest difficulty in ordering Suzanne Fornier to leave here. She had been nothing but trouble.

The door opened, and Suzanne slipped inside. When she saw both Adrian and Peter, she frowned. "I thought Lord Leigh wished to see me." She hesitantly stepped toward the desk where Adrian and Peter waited. Peter had crossed his arms before him and looked rather like a solemn judge. Adrian wore a forbidding expression.

"Actually both of us want to show you something. I should like to know what you have to say to this, Suzanne. It was found in the bottom of your wardrobe."

"The necklace! And the ruby I found and lost! I have no knowledge of what it was doing in my wardrobe. I swear I did not take it. Even had I wished to own it, I am not a thief!"

"And I suppose this necklace simply walked into your room and placed itself in your wardrobe?" Peter said, his voice laced with sarcasm.

Suzanne looked frightened for once. "I swear I did not put it there." She backed toward the door, only to find Jocelyn and Lora entering the room to cut off her escape.

"I am innocent, I tell you. I have no knowledge of any theft. I did not take the ruby from the necklace!"

"Where did you obtain it?" Jocelyn asked, after a glance at Peter.

"Uncle Maxim gave it to me, telling me he had found it." Suzanne turned her large, soulful brown eyes on Peter, then Adrian, as though to win them to her point of view.

"You believed him?" Lora demanded.

"I cannot recall anyone ever just 'finding' a ruby like a pebble or something," Jocelyn declared. "Surely you must have thought it odd?"

"Men often give me things," Suzanne replied with a snap.

"A lady does not receive valuable gifts from a gentleman," Lora reminded.

"But this was Uncle!" Suzanne argued.

Jocelyn exchanged a look with Peter. He in turn looked at Adrian.

"She is your cousin, and this is your necklace, old man. Jocelyn and I by rights have no place in this situation. The lost has been found, a trifle worse for wear, but nonetheless restored. Come," he said to Jocelyn extending a hand, "let us leave them now. It is a family matter after all."

"Thank you for everything, Peter, Jocelyn," Adrian said with fervent gratitude.

Nodding in return, Peter and Jocelyn left the library.

"What will he do?" Jocelyn begged to know.

"I cannot imagine. I know this; I'd not exchange places with him." Peter gave Jocelyn a worried look, then walked her to the terrace and took the stroll he had promised himself earlier. He needed to be restored, too, and who better to do it than the beautiful Jocelyn?

Chapter Sixteen

Jocelyn was most relieved to hear no comment on her disappearance with Peter the evening before when she came down for her morning meal. The breakfast conversation centered on the ball that evening and who was going to wear what. Suzanne failed to appear, and Jocelyn wondered if she had already left. To discover what had been decided, she sought Lora following her meal.

Lora glanced about them, then drew Jocelyn off to one side, where they were not likely to be overheard. "Adrian decided to permit Suzanne to remain until after the ball. He feared it would cause unwelcome comment if she left this morning. We wished to avoid scandal, if you recall?"

"So Suzanne remains in her room this morning—supposedly to prepare her costume?"

"The necklace is safe. Adrian sent to Derby for a jeweler to reset the stones. By this evening no one will know a thing has been amiss."

"You are truly remarkable, dear cousin. All these guests, arranging for the baptism of baby Charles, and the missing necklace to cope with this past week would put most women to bed with a megrim."

"Not you, I'd wager. Our family is made of strong character."

"Umm. Backbone, mother always called it," Jocelyn agreed. She left her cousin then so she might see to the wants of her other guests.

Upon leaving the breakfast room, Jocelyn bumped into Peter. "Sorry," she apologized, breathless with her proximity to him and the emotions he always stirred within her.

"You color up so delightfully, my dear. It almost makes me believe Simon did not touch you." Peter spoke casually, but there was an intentness that Jocelyn missed.

"Simon was exceedingly proper, I'll have you know," Jocelyn said defensively. "He did not believe a gentleman should take improper liberties—even with his fiancée."

"He did kiss your hand, I trust?" Peter asked with deceptive meekness.

"When it was proper to do so," Jocelyn responded, wondering why she had not been frustrated at Simon's lack of loving attention to her. Her brother had assured her that Simon's respect was most proper. Indeed, dear brother Christopher had seemed rather relieved that Simon rarely put in an appearance and had not lavished romantic attentions on Jocelyn.

Had she been paying the slightest attention to Peter, she would have observed the pleased expression that settled on his handsome face. "Of course," he said smoothly, "the proper gentleman would not insult his future wife by kissing her with passion or embracing her in secluded corners."

"If you are implying he was a bloodless pattern-card of respectability . . . I daresay you have the right of it," Jocelyn said with surprise. She began to walk to the terrace, joined by Peter. Outside by the pot of petunias, she paused to face him. "I confess I believed it was a deficiency on my part."

"May I humbly offer I find you deficient in no way, dear Jocelyn," Peter avowed.

She chuckled. "Dear Peter, you have never been humble in your life. Even without a fortune to bless your name, you had more self-assurance than any man I ever met. That and your overpowering er, warmth was what frightened me."

"But it does no more? Perhaps it is as well we waited these five years? You will appreciate me all the more."

Jocelyn fixed an admonishing look on him, then reluctantly turned to greet Uncle Maxim. She would welcome a time when she could talk with Peter without interruption.

"I hear my niece is confined to her room. Do you know why?" he demanded.

"I fear you will have to ask Adrian, Mr. Valletort," Jocelyn said with a sideways glance at Peter.

"Are you prepared for the ball this evening, sir?" Peter inquired courteously.

"Hmpf. Silly things, balls. I have changed my mind. Believe I shall go as an early knight. Henri and Pierre will as well."

. "You should encourage Suzanne to come to the ball as a medieval queen," Jocelyn said.

"Thought about it for a time. Chit will do as she pleases, though." He sniffed, helped himself to a pinch of snuff after delving into one of his capacious pockets.

When he had wandered off toward the lake, Jocelyn observed, "How odd it is that he continues to affect the old-fashioned coat style. He seems so *au courant* otherwise."

"Have you had a final fitting of your costume? Dickman insists I must try mine on so he can make any last-moment alterations."

"He must have spoken with Mercy. She reminded me of the same thing this morning. I suppose I had best be done with it, or it will be time for nuncheon." Jocelyn turned toward the house, surprised when Peter fell into step beside her.

"I had best do the same. Our servants seem to have established excellent communication."

"Mercy sings Dickman's praises daily. He is a valet much to be admired, I gather."

"We have been together a long time. As with your Mercy, it fosters a familiarity of sorts."

It spoke well of Peter that he had kept his valet for such a long period of time. Some men were forever changing valets, not to mention other staff.

She found her elegant costume was spread out on the bed when she entered the bedroom. Near the dressing table Mercy fussed over the hat, adjusting the soft peach bow that rested on the crown.

"I was hoping you would come, milady. Best slip that gown on so I can see if it needs changing. You have not been eating well of late."

"I have had a great deal on my mind, Mercy," Jocelyn reminded.

The gown fitted extremely well, Jocelyn thought.

"Mercy, please go to the landing on the stairs and check that painting for me. I would have the hat at the proper angle as well as this apron just so."

"With pleasure, ma'am," the abigail responded promptly. She returned within minutes, a puzzled expression on her face and a folded slip of paper in her hand. "I met a footman coming up with a message for you."

Jocelyn waited until Mercy had adjusted the apron and tilted the hat to a becoming angle before slitting the wafer that sealed the missive.

"Lord Leigh wishes to see me in the library. How odd. I saw him but a short time ago, and he said nothing about wanting to see me then."

"That jeweler from Derby has been here to repair the necklace, milady. Perhaps there is a need to try on a wedding ring?"

Hope soared within Jocelyn. It wasn't that she distrusted Peter Leigh. She wanted to show that detestable Suzanne that Peter did intend to wed, not dally.

Rising with alacrity, Jocelyn said, "I'll not bother to change. It would be rather romantic to try on my wedding band while wearing this gorgeous costume. It would be a time to remember for always."

"Your wedding day will be the day to treasure, my lady."

Jocelyn left the small bench where she had perched while Mercy fussed with the hat. "Nevertheless, I shall go at once." She winked at her maid and sped from the room with the impatience of a love-struck maiden.

She skimmed along the hall and down the stairs, thinking her feet scarce seemed to touch the ground.

When she entered the library, she found it empty. Frowning, she wondered if she had misread the message. She pulled it from the apron pocket—thinking that pockets were very handy things—when Peter opened the door.

"Did you wish to see me about something, Jocelyn?" he questioned.

"But you sent for me." She held out the paper for him to see. "It said to come to the library immediately, so I didn't bother to change from my costume. Neither did you, I see."

"The message a footman brought me said much the same. What do you suppose is going on here?"

"To settle your curiosity, ponder no more," Uncle Maxim said quietly, one hand in his large coat pocket as he advanced upon them.

Jocelyn felt uneasy. There was an odd note in his voice that disturbed her.

From behind her another voice added, "Do not think of calling on Adrian. He has been closeted with his steward and is likely to remain there for some time," Pierre said, a rather nasty pistol in his hand pointed at Peter.

She turned to look again at Maxim to see his hand was now out of his pocket and holding a similar pistol.

"You were confused, no doubt, suspecting first Uncle, then Pierre, and lastly me," Henri said as he rose from a wingback chair to confront the costumed pair who stood in astounded silence.

"All three of you stole the necklace? Why?" Jocelyn demanded, although she thought she knew.

"Money, for the most part. Maxim hated the notion Adrian had the jewelry and not our part of the family. Our branch is older in spite of the title going to Adrian. Pierre had his own reasons." He looked to his cousin.

"I wish to marry, and the money would be welcome. Suzanne is expensive."

Henri laughed. "You are a fool if you think she will wed you. She has promised me!"

"Silence, you fools. *Nothing* will happen unless we recapture the necklace that someone took from Suzanne's room."

"What a novel way of looking at things," Peter drawled. "You stole the necklace, then take umbrage when it is restored to its rightful owner."

"But Adrian is not the rightful owner," Uncle Maxim insisted, a look of fury on his face. "I should be the one who has the gems, not Adrian."

"Nevertheless, it has descended to him. You do not have the right to take it merely because you feel wronged," Jocelyn pointed out.

Uncle Maxim waved his pistol with careless regard for the hair-trigger Peter knew that model possessed. He pulled Jocelyn behind him. "I do not see why you summoned us here. I take it you *did* send those missives?"

"Indeed, we did. Adrian is strangely uncooperative about giving us the necklace. You must know where it is."

"Did you harm Adrian?" Jocelyn demanded.

"Such touching concern. Henri, bind her hands. I'll not have her doing something we all will regret."

Jocelyn couldn't imagine what that might be. She was forced to suffer Henri's hands touching her far more than was necessary to tie her hands behind her back. He also took a length of cambric to cover her mouth. "Can't have you alerting the staff, my dear Jocelyn."

Her muffled reply brought unkind laughter.

"I believe the jeweler has the necklace now, gentlemen," Peter said, his arms crossed before him as he surveyed the three opponents.

"I fear you are incorrect, Lord Leigh. The man left not long ago, and I feel certain you know where the necklace is being stored for use this evening."

Jocelyn listened, her heart sinking. What would he do to Peter now? She watched Pierre come closer to Peter, wondering what he would do.

"If you do not have a key, we can use our own methods to obtain it. Where is it?" Maxim demanded.

Henri jerked Jocelyn against him. He pressed the pistol against her side. She cried out, frustrated by the gag over her mouth. But Peter heard the sound and took note of the change of positions.

"It would be a shame to put a hole in the lovely costume loaned you by Adrian. Would you not agree, Jocelyn?" Henri said in a silky voice.

She nodded vigorously, then winced as Henri dragged her farther away from Peter. Evidently he didn't trust Peter in his present mood.

"You, my lord, have thwarted us at every turn," Pierre growled, looking anything but the proper gentleman now.

"And you, my lady Jocelyn, had the nerve to spurn the suits my nephews sought to establish. Had you cooperated, we might have let the necklace be. For that alone, you deserve to be punished."

"She did only as I requested," Peter stated. "Jocelyn and I have a long-standing agreement. She never would have married either of you."

"Most noble of you, my lord," Henri sneered.

"Thank you," Peter said, with a mocking bow to Henri.

"Well, give us the necklace," Maxim demanded.

"Jocelyn and I retired from the scene once the necklace was returned to Adrian. Neither of us have the slightest idea where it is now, particularly after it has been repaired by the jeweler." Peter stood defiant and looked quite splendid in his challenge, like the painting in the hall come to life.

"Where were the loose gems kept, once found?" Pierre queried.

"I cannot tell you," Peter replied, wondering if Adrian had transferred the necklace elsewhere once the repairs had been done. "I know that they were previously in this room, but Adrian is understandably close about the jewels. I can see why, with the three of you wanting to steal them. Why did you pry those few gems out?" he wanted to know.

Uncle Maxim paid no heed to the last query. He frowned, as though wondering what to do next.

"If they were here before, they are likely still here. As far as Suzanne knows, there is no locked safe in Lora's room," he said at last. "Search!" he demanded of Pierre. Maxim kept his gun trained on Peter while Pierre began a methodical examination of the room.

As fastidious as Pierre was, it did not surprise Jocelyn that he was meticulous in his hunt. He carefully removed paintings to study the wall, looked beneath the Turkish carpet for a drop vault, moved chairs, pulled out books from shelves to inspect both the books and to hunt for secret storage.

Minutes ticked past. Someone tried the door, then must have left, for all was silent once more. Jocelyn looked to Peter. He looked tense and ready for action, but what he might do with a pistol trained on him was more than Jocelyn could imagine. With three men willing to do harm, it was near impossible for one man to act.

At last Pierre reached the elegant desk in the center of the room. It was the first place Jocelyn would have looked, but Pierre commented, "An obvious place, too obvious, I suppose. But I cannot leave a stone unturned."

Peter moved slightly, the satin coat of his costume rustling as he shifted. He wished he had the sword that supposedly went with this costume. It must have been dashed handy to have a weapon on hand at all times. He looked to Jocelyn. How brave she was. She stood proud and tall even if Henri had pulled her against him in a most unseemly way—not to mention the pistol against her ribs.

"Is there a key for this drawer? I can see no reason why it shouldn't open."

"I have no idea," Peter said, his words terse, face set. He would offer no assistance, regardless of the threat to him. He did not think they would harm Jocelyn. Surely that gun at her side would not be used?

Pierre slipped a knife from one of his pockets and began prying at the drawer to no avail. It refused to budge a fraction. He knelt to inspect the underside of the desk center. "There is a lock here, but impossible to open without a key."

"Do not bother to ask me where it is," Peter quickly inserted, taking note that Uncle Maxim looked to be losing patience. "I am but a friend of Adrian's. He would not confide such a thing to me."

"Yet you knew of the missing necklace," Henri reminded.

"Lora confided in Lady Jocelyn. She knew me well enough to confide in me. Jocelyn has had little to do with this."

"She found you in the storage room," Henri reminded.

"So that was you, was it?" Peter queried.

"Can you not force that drawer open?" Uncle Maxim demanded, ignoring the words between Henri and Peter.

The sound of a thin knife scraping against the brass plate of the keyhole could be heard in the silence of the room. Finally there was a satisfied grunt, and Pierre rose to slide the drawer open.

Peter strained to see what was in the drawer.

"Papers! Nothing but papers!" Pierre muttered, his frustration most evident.

Peter breathed a sigh of relief. "Well, since they are not here and neither Lady Jocelyn nor I have the slightest idea where they might be, I would be obliged if you would let us go now. Teatime, you know."

"You and your damn manners," Uncle Maxim snarled. "We shall take care of you. Cannot have you telling on us, can we? We shall have to wait until this evening. Don't like it but have no choice. Lora will wear the gems. We can take them from her at some convenient time during the ball. Should have thought of that earlier."

"Certainly seems much easier to me," Peter commented. He suspected Adrian would have his most burly servants around to stand watch during the ball for just such an attempt.

"But what to do with you until after the ball?" Maxim murmured.

"May I suggest the little house on the island?" Henri said with a snicker. "In those precious costumes belonging to Adrian, they will be well and truly trapped. Both of them are too proper to strip and swim for shore. I doubt if Lady Jocelyn can even swim. Ha, ha, I am rather clever, am I not, Uncle?"

"Excellent suggestion, Henri. We shall go out that side French door to the terrace. This end is somewhat screened by the ivy and that statue of Hermes. We will seem an amiable group. Henri, untie Lady Jocelyn's gag and her arms. She will say nothing to disturb the tranquillity of our little group, I feel sure. Do recall three guns will be trained on you at all times."

"How could we forget?" Jocelyn demanded once her mouth was free. She gave Uncle Maxim a haughty stare worthy of Lady Thynne at her most impressive.

Evidently it intimidated him a wee bit, for he stayed away from her. The quintet left the library as planned. They strolled down to the lake, then over to the boathouse.

Here, Pierre and Maxim prodded Jocelyn and Peter into a boat that had been left at the ready, oars in the locks. Jocelyn and Peter sat close together on the rear seat while Pierre tackled the oars, and Uncle Maxim sat in the bow with his gun still aimed at the pair in the rear.

Henri looked at the little boat and declared, "I shall remain behind to fend off questions should they arise. I'd not wish to sink the boat. It would not do to spoil Lady Jocelyn's fine costume." Again, he gave that nasty laugh that Jocelyn found so disquieting.

The four set out across the lake, looking for all the world like a group bent on a pleasant late morning treat.

Peter placed a comforting arm around Jocelyn. "We shall persevere, never fear," he murmured. The sound of the oars splashing in the water covered his words.

Jocelyn nodded. "We must. I have a wedding to plan."

"Indeed. Late next week, unless we can hurry that mantua-maker along."

Jocelyn chuckled, as he had meant her to. "You are an impatient man, my lord."

"Only in some things, my love," he murmured in reply.

It was awkward to exit the boat when they reached the dock. It hadn't bothered Jocelyn to step up, thus exposing her calves and ankles, when she had been here with Peter. It was different with Pierre and Maxim staring at her. The old gown was full, and while a lot to manage, she found it did not reveal as much of her legs as she feared.

Pierre prodded them across the grassy expanse of the island to the cottage door. "I fancy you are well acquainted with this place, having spent an interlude here in the past. It ought to be downright cozy!" He sneered at Jocelyn, and Peter longed to plant him a facer.

The cambric that had been used to tie her hands was now reused. Peter was also tied, both hands and feet.

"There, that ought to keep you quiet for a time." Pierre stepped back after pushing Jocelyn and Peter to the floor, further complicating their ability to disengage from their bonds.

There was a key in the door, and Pierre took it out, locked the door, then left with Maxim at his side.

Peter waited for a time before beginning to work on the bindings. "Those chaps are not experts at this," he said as he freed his hands, then his feet. He released Jocelyn within minutes and both stretched their cramped limbs.

Jocelyn crossed to the window to see the little boat growing smaller as it sailed to the far shore.

"We are marooned," Jocelyn said, very aware of Peter standing at her side.

"We shall wait for a time—then I can swim to the shore and fetch a boat for us once the area is clear. Pierre was wrong. I have no qualms about removing my clothes. After all, Jocelyn, we are to be married within days."

She drew in a deep breath at this thought. "What a pity that everyone seems to be lingering on the terrace. There is no way you might swim across without being seen."

"Have I told you how fetching you look in that costume?"

"Oh, dear, the costumes!" Jocelyn cried in dismay, looking down at the beautiful gown she wore. "If we wear them all afternoon, they will soon be crumpled and soiled. This place has not been cleaned in a very long time," she observed, looking about her at the dusty interior.

Peter removed his elegant satin coat to hang it on a peg near the door. He then removed the beautiful waistcoat that had large brass buttons all down the front of it. It also went on a peg.

Jocelyn took one look at that muscular form clad in nothing more than a fine cambric shirt and the tight-fitting satin breeches, and found it difficult to swallow.

"You could remove that hat and perhaps the apron. It looks to be fragile." He reached out to remove the hat, placing it on a chair that didn't look terribly dusty.

Jocelyn fumbled with the ties of the delicate apron; of patterned white muslin, its age had made it weak.

"Allow me, I'd not have it torn." Peter deftly undid the ties, then draped the length of white over the hat. He studied her, then said, "I would wager you wear a petticoat and shift quite as modest as the gown. Am I right? It helps to have sisters, you know. There are few secrets kept within a family."

Jocelyn blushed but nodded. At his gesture, she began to undo the lacing of the gown. He did not allow the sack-back gown to fall to the floor. He caught it, helping her to step out of it before hanging it from the last of the pegs.

"There, now, you look estimably modest, my dear. I have seen evening gowns less proper than what you wear."

That might be, Jocelyn thought, but she felt terribly exposed. The straps of her shift were but ribands edged with lace, and the petticoat hugged her waist tightly, leaving little to any imagination Peter might have. She was relieved to note he looked out of the window.

"What do you see?"

"Henri and the others still on the terrace. I suppose they are behaving as though they have not seen us, nor threatened our lives."

"Do you think they really would have shot us?"

"I should like to think not, but Maxim does not seem quite right in his mind. Did you notice? Almost mad."

"True," she answered. "But could anyone be so crazy as to attempt to steal such a priceless piece of jewelry and think to get away with it?" She wrapped her arms about her, feeling chilled in spite of the mild day. That she also felt awkward with her future husband was uppermost in her mind. She suspected few women had such an intimacy with their husband-to-be prior to marriage. Her mother had always admonished Jocelyn not to appear in her petticoat outside her room—even if it was just her brother around.

"I think you are a trifle nervous, my dear," Peter said when he turned from the view of the castle.

"I confess I do not go about in my petticoat and shift as a rule."

"Pity. You look very fetching in it." He smiled gently at her, and Jocelyn felt her fears melt. This was the man she had loved for years, and he would be her husband as soon as possible. It was but a step into his arms, and Jocelyn willingly chanced the risk. Peter might be the most dangerous man she had ever met; he was also a gentleman. She had nothing to fear from him.

He wooed her with tantalizing kisses and a disarming exploration of the skin above the neck of her shift. It was not long before they both were in a state of passion that begged completion.

Peter took a step away from her, breathing deeply to quell his ardor. He would not take his wife-to-be in this dirty little cottage. He wanted the finest linen sheets on a soft, comfortable bed for their union.

"Come, before we go too far." He held out his hand to her. "There must be a way out of this place without breaking a window." He attempted to open the windows to no avail. They were stuck tight with age and a certain amount of paint. He stared at the last one he tried to force with evident frustration.

"I had a pin with that hat—to keep it on, you see." Jocelyn removed the slender pin and offered it to Peter. He took the pin and worked at the door lock. It took patience and a good many tries before he knew success. "Voila!" he exclaimed upon opening the only door to the tiny cottage.

Breathing deeply of the fresh, cooling air, Jocelyn took note of the sun's position. "It is drawing late. It must be long past nuncheon. They should be wondering where we are," Jocelyn said with a frown.

"Since we are both missing, they may jump to the conclusion we have taken a ride to be alone."

"Oh. I'd not thought of that."

"Come, we shall absorb what sun there is until it grows dark. You shall tell me everything about yourself while growing up, and then I shall do the same. That will keep us safely occupied until it is time to leave."

By unspoken consent, they kept a discreet and necessary distance while they talked about childhood and growing up. Jocelyn wondered if this was not a wonderful thing that ought to be required before every marriage. Her respect and love for Peter grew even deeper as she listened to him talk of his past.

At last he deemed it safe to swim from the island. "I shall return as quickly as possible, my love. Do not be afraid while I'm gone. Nothing can harm you here."

He left, and once she saw him far out in the lake, she strolled down to the little dock where she discovered the satin breeches and cambric shirt he had worn along with the shoes and hose.

"Heavens!" she exclaimed. "He will freeze with nothing on." She ran to the other side of the island to see that he had managed to reach the boathouse. She certainly hoped he would find something to cover his nakedness. The idea that the Misses Osmond and Murray might be exposed to a bare male sent Jocelyn into giggles.

He returned sooner than she expected, rowing swiftly across the water. She waited for him to don his garments, then turned to greet him when he rounded the corner of the cottage.

"Hurry. I did not see anyone around, but we do not want to dally here." He removed their costumes from the house, handing her the gown, apron, and hat while he pulled on the shirt with impatience. Flipping the coats over his arm, he drew her to the dock. They were into the boat and off before she had a chance to ask him more.

Jocelyn took care of both costumes until they reached the other shore. Peter assisted her from the rowboat, then into her gown. He donned on his waistcoat and coat, then almost pulled her up the slope to the castle. "As soon as Lora comes down in her costume, she is in danger, or rather the necklace is ripe for plucking."

They crept in by the library door, then went up to their respective rooms. Mercy fussed over Jocelyn, who wanted nothing more than to find something to eat.

She hurried down to the main floor to find Peter awaiting her. "Dinner is even now beginning. We may have missed the soup, but we ought to be able to dine well."

Jocelyn allowed him the privilege of making excuses and thought him quite clever. She observed Henri and Pierre appeared grim while Uncle Maxim wore a murderous expression.

She glanced sideways at Peter, taking delight in his returned gaze of warm regard. She need have no fears now—of anything, least of all him.

As soon as the guests left the table for the saloon, Peter quickly told Adrian what happened. He, in turn, looked quite horrified.

"I shall see them at once in the library." He conferred with his butler, then joined Jocelyn and Peter in the library to await the trio.

"I wish to see those scoundrels receive their proper censure," Jocelyn said fiercely to Adrian as they crossed to take a position behind the formidable desk.

"Indeed," he replied grimly, then busied himself while Peter captured Jocelyn's gaze with a melting smile.

She reluctantly tore her attention from her love when the doorknob rattled. The oak door slowly opened.

Pierre entered first, closely followed by Henri, with Uncle Maxim bringing up the rear in obviously reluctant fashion. If they were surprised to see Jocelyn and Peter in the room, they gave no indication.

Assuming an arrogant stance, Pierre challenged Adrian with a cold look. "I suppose these two have been bending your ear?"

"Why should you think such a thing?" Adrian wondered, successfully hiding his anger.

Pierre looked momentarily confused. Henri gave Jocelyn a narrow look, then queried, "Why do you wish to see us . . . away from the others?"

The door opened, and Lora poked her head around the corner. Even in the soft candlelight, the fabulous jewels glowed with myriad colors. Adrian nodded, beckoning her inside. "Come in, my dear. My cousins are about to explain a few things to us—like why they have betrayed our hospitality, not to mention our relationship."

Uncle Maxim glowered. Henri crossed his arms and pouted. Pierre sniffed. "I cannot see there is anything to explain, dear cousin."

"You did not steal the necklace? And when Lord Leigh found and returned it to me, you did not plan to steal it again? And from the countess's neck, no less?" Anger crept into his voice, and Jocelyn decided that regardless of his quiet demeanor, she'd not wish to cross him.

"Bah," Uncle Maxim retorted, stepping forward, "she is not suited to the role of countess. A nobody! That necklace by rights should be mine." With a glance at Pierre and Henri, he amended, "That is *ours*!"

"The law would disagree with you on that point, as do I. How fortunate I am to have a true friend, and a relative who is equally loyal." Adrian gestured to where Peter and Jocelyn stood close together in silent observation.

"You really ought to learn how to tie a knot," Peter taunted. "It was child's play to escape our bindings."

"We are not accustomed—" Uncle Maxim began, only to be interrupted by Henri, who swaggered forward a couple of steps.

"As long as Lora is here with the necklace, why do we not relieve her of it now and save our bother later?" He placed his right hand on the sword that was part of his costume, looking ready to slash his way from the room.

Jocelyn and Lora gasped at his effrontery. Peter moved to stand next to Adrian, who smoothly brought his pistol out from where he had concealed it, having had a fair idea of what his desperate cousins might try.

Pierre took a step toward the door to find his way blocked by a stalwart footman who had silently slipped into the room. Henri turned to the doors leading to the terrace only to discover three footmen standing guard there.

"Foiled, I believe," Adrian said in a chilling voice. He gestured with his pistol. "Stand still while my most capable friend ties you in a way that will assure you will not easily be free." He crossed to take the pretty sword from its case, thus depriving Henri of a weapon. While Adrian stood guard, Peter took the ropes brought by the footman and dealt with the cousins, taking care to separate them well apart and not allowing them much comfort.

The four burliest footmen Jocelyn had ever seen were delegated to watch over the well-trussed thieves until after the ball. She and Lora thankfully left ahead of Adrian and Peter, intent upon reaching the ballroom.

Adrian turned to Peter. "I intend to arrange their transportation to a penal colony immediately. I have endured quite enough from this trio. Such relatives!"

When the guests entered the ballroom, a few inquired after the absent relatives, but none seemed to miss them except for Mrs. Murray. She had enjoyed a delightful flirtation with Maxim Valletort and was sad when Adrian gravely informed her Maxim had taken ill.

The Valletort necklace was admired by all, even a subdued Suzanne. Once she learned what had transpired, she declared in a quiet aside to Adrian, "I shall travel to the Continent, for there must be wealthy men who will know nothing of my so-disgraced family." He nodded; obviously pleased she had offered a solution to her future.

At last Peter and Jocelyn escaped to enjoy a dance. The musicians began a waltz, and Jocelyn stepped forward to be lightly embraced in Peter's arms. What a lovely dance, the waltz. It afforded such splendid opportunities!

"Only a few days more, my love," he murmured to her while

they circled the room, his look searing hers with its intensity. She suspected her cheeks bloomed with color at his expression. Never had she thought that those silvery-blue eyes could hold such an expression of love. It was a wonder she didn't go up in flames; there was so much warmth in those unusual eyes. When his gaze settled on her mouth, she glanced at the French door that led to the terrace and possible privacy offered there.

Seeming to read her mind, Peter whirled her to the door, then onto the terrace. There, he immediately sought a secluded corner where none could easily see them.

"Oh, Peter, I can scarce wait," she confessed. "Five years has been a frightfully long time. I know now that I have loved you forever. That wretched brother of mine has a great deal to answer for when next I see him," Jocelyn said while nestling closer in Peter's arms. How good it felt to be in the embrace of the one she loved so dearly.

Not the least backward to claim kisses from his bride-to-be, Peter took advantage of the golden opportunity to assure his sweetheart of his ardent love and admiration. Then, hand in hand, they strolled along the terrace with the gentle light from the ballroom casting romantic shadows and the scent of roses enhancing the moment.

"You will like our home, I believe," Peter said after a time, when they paused to gaze out into the soft darkness. "I give you carte blanche to do as you please with the interior—and the gardens as well, should you wish." He paused a few moments, then added, "And your money shall be your own, to spend as you want. I'll have no man say that I married you for your dowry."

Pleased he proved so generous at a time when most men could scarce wait to take over what was rightfully theirs, Jocelyn beamed a contented smile at him. "Then, be prepared for changes. I will delight in decorating. I have never had a place on which to practice my taste, and it will be a double pleasure because the home will be ours." She boldly leaned against him, sighing with delight that at long last she would know true happiness with the man she loved, had loved for a long time. "Although, I would consult with you if you do not mind. I suspect I shall find any number of excuses to be with you, my love."

Peter slipped one arm about her and gave a satisfied sigh as well. "I had almost given up hope of ever knowing you as my wife. Your persistent refusal of all suitors was the one factor that offered me optimism. How fortunate that we have Adrian and Lora as connections. I was growing quite desperate, dearest." He tightened his hold on Jocelyn, causing her to feel most cherished.

"It has occurred to me that I have a gown that would be most suitable for a wedding," Jocelyn said thoughtfully. "And why not roses in my hair instead of a hat?" That she dared to be so immodest said a great deal for her trust in and love for Peter. A proper lady should not admit wishing to set forward the day of her wedding, no matter what she might feel.

"That sounds delightful, particularly the roses in your glorious hair. Have I ever told you how much I admire your tresses, my love? I shall adore letting its silken length cascade through my hands."

He gently caressed her shoulder as he spoke, bringing an ache to her heart. How blessed she was to have this man. The intimacy of his tone and the very thought of letting her hair down for him made Jocelyn tremble.

"I fancy we shall shock a great number of people," she noted after a time. "There will likely be a deal of gossip. But I shan't repine one moment. I have never given much heed to the gossips, and I will not begin now."

"I promise you will never regret our marriage, my love. With your permission, I shall fetch the wedding band and a parson as soon as the special license arrives." His tone told her that he felt just as impatient as she did.

Jocelyn's heart swelled with joy, and she replied fervently, "I do. I do give you my permission, that we may marry as soon as may be."

Her declaration was sealed with a tender kiss, and they continued their sauntering stroll, saying little but in perfect accord.